PRAISE FOR T

# Don't Make a Sound

"A heart-stopping read. Ragan's compelling blend of strained family ties and small-town secrets will keep you racing to the end!"

—Lisa Gardner, *New York Times* bestselling author of
*When You See Me*

"An exciting start to a new series with a feisty and unforgettable heroine in Sawyer Brooks. Just when you think you've figured out the dark secrets of River Rock, T.R. Ragan hits you with another sucker punch."

—Lisa Gray, bestselling author of *Thin Air*

"Fans of Lizzy Gardner, Faith McMann, and Jessie Cole are in for a real treat with T.R. Ragan's *Don't Make a Sound*, the start of a brand-new series that features tenacious crime reporter Sawyer Brooks, whose own past could be her biggest story yet. Ragan once more delivers on her trademark action, pacing, and twists."

—Loreth Anne White, bestselling author of *In the Dark*

"T.R. Ragan takes the revenge thriller to the next level in the gritty and chillingly realistic *Don't Make a Sound*. Ragan masterfully crafts one unexpected twist after another until the shocking finale."

—Steven Konkoly, bestselling author of *The Rescue*

"T.R. Ragan delivers in her new thrilling series. *Don't Make a Sound* introduces crime reporter Sawyer Brooks, a complex and compelling heroine determined to stop a killer as murders in her past and present collide."

—Melinda Leigh, #1 *Wall Street Journal* bestselling author

# Her Last Day

"Intricately plotted . . . The tense plot builds to a startling and satisfying resolution."

—*Publishers Weekly* (starred review)

"Ragan's newest novel is exciting and intriguing from the very beginning . . . Readers will race to finish the book, wanting to know the outcome and see justice served."

—*RT Book Reviews*

"Readers will obsess over T.R. Ragan's new tenacious heroine. I can't wait for the next in the series!"

—Kendra Elliot, author of the *Wall Street Journal* bestsellers *Spiraled* and *Targeted*

"With action-packed twists and turns and a pace that doesn't let up until the thrilling conclusion, *Her Last Day* is a brilliant start to a gripping new series from T.R. Ragan."

—Robert Bryndza, #1 international bestselling author of *The Girl in the Ice*

# OUT
# OF HER
# MIND

# OUT OF HER MIND

A
**SAWYER BROOKS**
THRILLER

# T.R. RAGAN

**THOMAS & MERCER**

Published by Thomas & Mercer, Seattle

www.apub.com

Amazon, the Amazon logo, and Thomas & Mercer are trademarks of Amazon.com, Inc., or its affiliates.

ISBN-13: 9781542093903
ISBN-10: 1542093902

Cover design by Damon Freeman

Printed in the United States of America

*To my readers.*
*Every single one of you.*

# CHAPTER ONE

The moment she spotted the little girl, her blood pumped faster through her veins. Even from a distance, she could see similarities to Molly. Fair skinned with a small, upturned nose. The blonde curls framing the girl's face reflected the last bit of daylight as the sun began its descent. Judging by height, she guessed the child to be nine or ten. She was perfect.

And she was alone.

Glancing in the rearview mirror, she turned the key in the ignition and merged onto the street. It was 6:00 p.m. on Sunday. Summertime. Dinnertime for many.

People might be surprised to know how many kids played alone at the park after school and on weekends. Never in a million years would she have dared let Molly play anywhere other than within the safety of their backyard. Even then, she always made sure to keep a vigilant eye on the child.

Kids disappeared all the time in front of their homes, at bus stops, and right off noisy streets bustling with people.

It didn't matter how many times it happened. Most people didn't take in their surroundings and pay attention. She'd done her homework, and there were reportedly 115 stranger abduction cases in the United States every year. Most victims were never found.

People tended to be complacent. They let kids walk alone, to and from school, without batting an eye. The notion boggled the mind.

Two blocks ahead, she pulled to the curb, the tire rubbing against the concrete before she stopped and turned off the engine. She'd rehearsed so often that it took little thought to get her plan rolling. In two seconds, she'd slipped her left arm, already covered in a fake plaster cast, into the sling hanging from her neck. She grabbed the syringe from the middle console, then climbed out and walked with an exaggerated limp to the back of her SUV, where she opened the compartment. Before setting out for the day, she had folded the rear seats to give herself plenty of room for crutches—just in case the sling didn't work—boxes, and little girls.

Out of the corner of her eye she saw the girl watching her.

*Perfect.*

She used her right arm to reach for a couple of boxes and pretended to accidentally drop them, setting her plan in motion just as someone called out the name "Krissy."

Frozen in place, she prayed the little girl wasn't Krissy.

The second time the woman, who was quickly approaching, called the girl's name, the child stepped out of the shadow of the trees. "I'm over here, Mom."

Motionless, she released a long sigh.

"What are you doing?" the mother asked the girl, her voice shrill. "You gave me and your father a scare."

"You said I could go to the park," the girl answered.

"I told you to be back in forty-five minutes. It's been an hour and a half since you left the house."

Krissy's head bowed. "Sorry."

"Tell that to your father. He's on his way to Beth's house to see if you went there without asking permission. Come on," the mother said with a huff. "We'll call him in the car."

"I need to help that lady first." The girl left her mom's side and came running over to help. She picked up both boxes and handed them over, one at a time.

A sparkle in the girl's pretty blue eyes caused a lump to catch in her throat. "Thank you."

Krissy's smile revealed a row of small, flawless teeth before she ran back to her mother.

She watched the woman usher Krissy away. It took everything she had not to drop to her knees in despair. The girl was perfect in every way.

An idea struck her. She would follow them home and see where Krissy lived. She tossed the boxes inside and shut the compartment door before making her way back to the driver's seat.

Through the rearview mirror she watched mom and daughter climb into a white minivan and pull away. She counted to five before merging onto the street, careful to stay a good distance behind them. A right on Oak Street and a left on Hickory brought them to a blue, two-story home with white trim. The newest house on the block. Her frustration mounted at the thought of returning tomorrow and the next day and the day after that. What would be the point? The mother's worry had been clear. For the next few weeks Krissy's parents would undoubtedly hover over her, not allowing her out of their sight.

*I can't wait that long,* she thought as she drove past.

It had taken months to work up the courage to begin yet another search for the perfect child to fill the gaping hole in her heart after losing Molly.

It was time for her daughter to come home, where she belonged.

As she approached a stop sign, ready to head home for dinner and try again tomorrow, her heart jumped to her throat when she spotted another young girl, maybe a year or two older than Krissy.

The girl was sitting on the bottom step outside a brick building, her nose buried in a book on her lap. One thick braid fell over a slender shoulder. The girl lifted her chin. Their eyes met.

Her heart nearly stopped. She was the one. The girl's small shoulders slumped forward again, and she went back to reading.

*Stay calm. Breathe. Stick with the plan.*

She clicked off the radio and stopped at the stop sign, counted to three, then made a left and pulled to the side of the road. Only a few feet away from the brick building where the little girl was sitting, she shut off the engine and repeated everything she'd practiced: Cast in sling. Syringe in place. Get out of the car. Open the trunk. Drop the boxes. Grimace and groan.

It wasn't until she bent over that she took note of the apartment building to her left. *Not good.* Her heart beat faster.

Struggling to pick up the box, she gasped when a small hand shot out and grabbed the package for her.

She hadn't seen or heard the girl approach. But here she was, book put away, backpack strapped over her shoulders, helping a stranger.

"Oh, my," she said, feigning surprise. "I didn't see you there. Thank you so much."

The girl placed the box inside the back of her car, then eyed the crutches and asked, "Do you need help carrying these someplace?"

A car drove by.

She swallowed. "You, my dear, are an angel. If you could help me take these to that brick building over there, that would be lovely."

The girl's eyes widened. "Are these packages for Mr. Brennan?"

Her eyes were green, not blue. Her hair was dirty blonde. Not bright yellow like Molly's, or even Krissy's, but still shiny and pretty. She realized the child was waiting for her to answer the question. "Um— why yes, they are! Do you know Mr. Brennan?"

"He's my music teacher."

"Such a small world." *You're taking too long,* she inwardly scolded. *Get things rolling. People could be watching.* She looked toward the apartment building across the street. With its aged concrete and peeling paint it looked as if it might have been abandoned. "I have one more box," she told the girl, "but it's heavier than these." She pointed into the compartment where she'd folded the rear seats and had left a box as far away as possible for just this purpose. It was too far to reach without climbing inside.

The girl hesitated just the slightest before using her right knee to propel herself upward and inside.

Adrenaline pumping, she grabbed the syringe and jabbed the needle into the girl's thigh. It helped that the child was wearing a summer dress.

"Ouch!"

She pulled the needle out, dropped it inside her sling, and pretended to swat at an insect as the girl rubbed her leg.

"I think it was a wasp!"

The girl shook her head and pointed to her sling. "You did something."

"Me? No." The girl should be unconscious soon. Inwardly, she counted to five.

The girl's eyelids appeared heavy as she rubbed her thigh. She began to scoot her way out of the car, leaving the box behind.

What was happening? Why was the child still awake? She needed to stop her. "What about the box?" she asked.

The girl looked confused. She opened her mouth, ready to say something, when her body collapsed and her eyes closed.

*Finally!*

She leaned inside, tossed a light-blue blanket over the girl, then shut the compartment door.

Another car drove past. She could see its reflection in the window. She didn't dare look toward the street. *Nothing to see here,* she thought as she opened the door and climbed in.

Only then did she dare take a breath. Once the engine started, relief seeped into her bones. She turned the radio on before merging onto the street, humming along to the sound of "Take the A Train" by Duke Ellington.

Life was good.

Her daughter was finally coming home.

# CHAPTER TWO

Sawyer Brooks, crime reporter for the *Sacramento Independent*, was the first one sitting at the conference room table, waiting for everyone else to arrive. Her boss, Sean Palmer, insisted on regular editorial meetings to make sure his team always met their deadlines and had enough content.

At 7:55 a.m., Cindy arrived. She was the editorial assistant, but everyone called her the Cheerleader. Every group needed one. She'd been working with Palmer for fourteen years. If someone on the team did a standout job, she was the one who made sure they knew they were appreciated. Not everyone in their small group thought she was sincere—just a robot hired to encourage the troops. Whatever. As far as Sawyer was concerned, Cindy's gratitude was refreshing.

David Lutz showed up a minute later. He was tall with a thick head of blond hair. He liked to wear suits, which made no sense. This wasn't the '80s. Nobody wore suits anymore. Even worse, he wore ties with his suits. Like Sawyer, David was a workaholic. Unlike Sawyer, he got handed most of the sensational stories— the breaking news and headliners. He'd been at the job longer, but she had a feeling it was the suit working in his favor.

Next to enter the room was Lexi Holmes. Forty-one, Lexi had dark hair, dark eyes, and a dark aura. A woman of few words in the editorial meetings, but she knew her shit when it came to reporting. She also knew the beat. She was resourceful and naturally inquisitive.

Despite all the talent sitting at the table, Sawyer liked to think she had something the others didn't have—endurance. Give her a story, any story, and she'd do whatever it took to cover it. Sleep was overrated.

It was five minutes past eight when Palmer joined them, which was unusual since he was never late. The only reporter missing was Donovan.

Palmer sat down at the head of the table and stroked his beard—Cindy's daily cue to get the show on the road.

One thing Sawyer had noticed since her switch from human interest stories to crime reporting a month ago was that there didn't seem to be a whole lot of real crime worth writing about. The *Sacramento Independent* was the sixth-largest newspaper in California, but so far she'd covered mostly drug arrests and assaults. Questioning people about their neighbor getting caught with a gram of meth was getting old quick. Since there wasn't enough room in the paper to report every minor crime, she prioritized by naming only those who harmed others. That included men who hit their wives, got DUIs, or texted while driving—anything that endangered another.

After Cindy finished listing the stories assigned to each reporter, David tossed out three ideas for news stories along with proposed length and deadline. His record, he was fond of saying, was six stories in a single day. Impressive, but old news.

Taking advantage of the lull, Sawyer raised a finger and said, "I'd like to do a story on the guy who uses dating apps to scam his victims out of their life savings."

"That's mine," David told her.

Sawyer looked from Cindy to Palmer, thinking maybe someone would help her out here since David hadn't included the scammer story when he read off his list of ideas.

*No help there.* Sawyer let it go and moved on to the number two idea on her list. "What about the man who lived with his wife's corpse for—"

"That story is taken," Cindy interrupted.

Lexi looked bored.

"Okay," Sawyer said. "Why don't I wait until everyone else is finished?"

"Good idea," David said.

*Asshole.*

By the time they were done tossing out concepts for stories that were either accepted or rejected by Palmer, Sawyer was left to cover a story about the man who had robbed a local bank and was caught afterward boasting about it on social media. A big yawn.

David stood and buttoned his suit jacket.

"Before any of you go," Palmer said, "you should know that Donovan was offered a job in New York City and will not be returning to the *Sacramento Independent.*"

"He will be missed," Cindy said without any emotion.

"What about the leads he was working on?" David asked.

Palmer lifted a hand. "The Brad Vicente follow-up will go to Sawyer. Cindy will take care of the rest."

Nobody protested. Not a surprise since none of them wanted to deal with Brad Vicente, the rapist whose dick was cut off by a group of vigilantes. From everything she'd read about the guy, he deserved what he'd gotten. A month ago, the media had eaten the guy whole. But recently the trolls had come forward and were doing a good job causing discord by posting inflammatory messages about the group of women taking the law into their own hands.

Palmer's cell beeped. He picked up the call.

David was gone in a flash, followed by Cindy and Lexi.

Palmer ended the call and then slid his cell back into an old-school holster attached to his waistband. "Come on," he said. "Grab your things and let's go!"

Startled, Sawyer looked at Palmer as she gathered her things. "Me?"

"Yes. You. Come on!"

She'd been working with Palmer for a month now, but this was the first time he'd invited her—make that demanded—that she go somewhere with him. It took her a second to realize he was serious. She came to her feet and slipped the strap of her bag over her shoulder. She had to jog across the carpeted hallway to catch up to him. "What's going on?"

"Bones."

"Bones?"

"A skeleton believed to have belonged to a child was found."

"Where?"

"Land Park. East Sac, across the lake from the amphitheater."

"Should I grab my camera?"

"No need. Geezer is already on the scene."

He pushed through the double doors leading out of the building and continued on at a clipped pace to his blue Jeep Wrangler Sport parked in the front row. The vehicle had two doors, a soft top, and was covered with dried mud. Palmer didn't strike her as the four-wheeling type of guy.

Once they were on the road, Palmer said, "Don't let them push you around."

"Who?"

"David . . . Cindy . . . they're testing you. Every time you throw out a story idea, someone takes it as their own, and you allow it to happen."

"I'm the rookie on the team," she said. "It seems disrespectful to question their authority."

He shook his head. "They have no power. I'm the boss."

"You didn't jump in and say anything, so I assumed I was the low guy on the totem pole and that was how things worked in the editorial meetings."

"Never assume."

During the editorial meeting, she'd thought she was being polite by stepping aside, but all she was doing was teaching her coworkers that she could be pushed around.

As silence settled around them, she attempted to keep her gaze straight ahead, but a one-by-one-inch picture of a little girl taped to the console caught her attention.

Palmer glanced her way. "My granddaughter. She'll be turning thirteen soon."

"Do you see her often?"

Gaze on the road ahead, he said, "No."

"She looks nine or ten in the photo."

"Nine. I haven't seen her since that picture was taken."

"How come?" The question was out of her mouth before she realized she might be overstepping.

"My son and I don't get along." The chuckle that followed was low and throaty. "Actually, that's an understatement. When I saw him, he made it clear that it would be the last time."

Sawyer said nothing.

"My son said most of the problems he wrestles with are because I never opened up to him about my own struggles in life. He said I've always expected too much from him and that I'm a judgmental son of a bitch."

She smirked. "I can't imagine why he would think that about you."

"Touché," he said with a chuckle. "Enough about me. How are you doing, Sawyer? That's what I want to know."

"I'm fine."

"You lost both your parents in one fell swoop. That can't be easy."

"One fell swoop" was putting it mildly, Sawyer thought. Against both her older sisters' better judgment, one month ago, Sawyer had returned to her hometown of River Rock for her grandmother's funeral, only to discover that her father was a pedophile and her mom was his protector, willing to do anything, including kill, to keep their secret safe. When Sawyer had confronted her dad, he'd admitted to his wrongdoings and even offered to turn himself over to authorities. But blind rage at the notion of giving up all they had worked so hard for prompted Sawyer's mom to swing a fireplace poker at her father's head, killing him.

She would have killed Sawyer too, if her sisters hadn't shown up. It was Sawyer's sister Aria who had been forced to shoot their mother in self-defense.

In the end, her parents' deaths had given Sawyer a sense of relief, but she kept that little tidbit to herself. "I imagine most people who lose a loving parent grieve for all the happy memories they shared," she told Palmer. "But I grieve for what my sisters and I never had."

He nodded. "Makes sense. My mom died when I was five. Cancer. I also spent more than a few years grieving for what I never had."

Although Palmer was known for being gruff and blunt, he seemed unusually melancholy this morning. Being that she was a curious cat, she couldn't help but wonder about his personal life. Was he happily married? Did he have more than the one son? Did he like to cook? Random questions rolled through her mind.

"What is it you want to know?" he asked.

"Me?"

"Is there anyone else in the car?"

His question had caught her off guard, but it shouldn't have. One of the things she'd always known about Palmer was that he was abnormally intuitive. "I like to know about the people I work with," she said. "That's all."

He made a left on Twelfth Street. "We're here." He found a parking spot, shut off the engine, climbed out, then stuck his head back in the car and said, "I'm divorced. Boy and a girl. Daughter lives in Los Angeles. In my spare time I like to crochet."

"Really?"

He was looking right at her, his eyes like lasers. "I don't crochet," he said with a shake of his head. "I'm just fucking with you. Are you coming or not?"

Sawyer felt a pang of sympathy for his son. Again, she was left to grab her things and chase after him.

She jogged across the pavement, slid between two cars parked close together, then hopped over a cement curb, following Palmer off the well-traveled sidewalk and up a grassy hill. At the top of the hill, past picnic benches and barbecue pits, she could see yellow crime tape encircling an area beneath a grove of trees. Walking at a good clip, she and Palmer approached Detective Perez.

Judging by the look Perez shot her way, he hadn't forgotten her. A month ago she had taken advantage of a security guard who'd left his post, and she'd walked into a crime scene, where she took pictures. Never mind that she'd helped solve a young woman's murder. Perez was like a crow. He remembered a face and held a grudge.

Palmer turned his back to Perez and said, "Why don't you check out the area, see what you can find out?"

*Fine.* She headed off to the opposite side where yellow crime scene tape had been strategically tied around the trunk of three trees, making a triangular area for investigators to work. Two technicians were kneeling and gathering evidence from within a three-foot-wide hole. Mounds of dirt, a shovel, and work gloves lay near a mostly dead tree, five feet in length, with odd-shaped leaves dangling from thin, gangly branches.

The tree was out of place among the oaks, redwoods, and even a few palm trees that dotted the neatly mowed green grass throughout the park.

With gloved hands, a technician photographed and then bagged a piece of fabric weathered by tragedy and time. The plastic bag was sealed and put inside a storage bin.

"It was a little girl," a young man standing outside the perimeter told her.

Sawyer looked at him. His long, molasses-colored hair was pulled back in a ponytail. She guessed him to be in his forties. Tall and lanky with bony arms and pointy elbows, he wore a T-shirt and jeans streaked with mud and grass.

"How do you know?" Sawyer asked.

"I was the one who found her."

"That hole looks pretty deep. How did you find her?"

"I'm a groundskeeper. One of my jobs is to replace trees hit hard by drought and winter storms. I've been meaning to replace this particular tree for a while now." He looked around. "There's a lot to do around here, so I didn't get to it until today."

She nodded. "Makes sense. How do you know the bones belong to a girl, though?"

He shrugged. "The clothes mostly. Looked to me like the shirt had little red hearts on it, and there were pink shoes. Leather must take a while to decay."

"I wonder how old she was?"

"Hard to tell since she was in a fetal position and there wasn't much left except for bones. If I had to guess, judging by the size of the skull, I'd say she was somewhere between seven and ten years of age."

She narrowed her eyes. "Watch a lot of *CSI*?"

He shook his head. "Nah. I have nieces, though. Three of them." He used a forearm to wipe a sheen of sweat from his forehead. "Before the police asked me to move out of the way, I heard one of the forensic team speculate that the girl was buried four to five years ago at the same time the tree was planted. Whatever she was wrapped in had helped preserve what little bit there is left of hair and skin."

"Interesting."

"Yeah, that's what I thought. Without a coffin, I guess it doesn't take as long for a skeleton to decompose."

"Any idea how old that tree was?"

He shook his head.

"Does Parks and Recreation keep track of when trees are planted?"

He scratched his chin. "No idea."

"Hey, Billy!" someone called. "The boss said it's time to get back to work."

"Gotta go," Billy told Sawyer.

After he left, Sawyer made notes on her cell of everything he'd told her.

She looked around, spotted Geezer taking a smoke break and flirting with the news reporter from Channel 10. Perez was talking to a police officer. Palmer was nowhere to be seen.

A quick search on her phone revealed names and ages of young girls who had gone missing in the area in the past four to ten years. Besides a string of possible runaways, she found a slideshow of missing children, boys and girls. Nineteen photos in all. Nine females, aged seven to twelve. She saved the link. When she got back to the office, she planned to do some digging and make a few inquiries.

A breeze sent a chill crawling up the back of her neck as she envisioned someone carrying a young child up the hill from the parking lot.

She turned back to view the scene of the crime. How could someone possibly carry a body, let alone a tree and a shovel, such a long way without being seen? The question niggled as she walked past the yellow tape in the direction Billy had gone after he was called off to work.

More trees dotted the grassy land that stretched on acre after acre. Across the way, the grass looked greener, the trees younger, but between where she stood and the greener areas was a long stretch of dirt and gravel where nothing grew. The gravelly path stretched on for at least fifty feet before disappearing beneath new growth.

Billy had returned for his gloves, and before he could get away, she pointed at the small strip of gravel and asked, "Any idea what happened here?"

"It's part of an old back road that the staff used to get to the building where we keep our equipment." He scratched the back of his neck. "Three or four years ago, they paved an easier route on the other side of the park and let this unpaved road grow over."

"Before the new one was constructed, could anyone get access to this?" she asked.

He pointed down the way at some unknown marker. "There used to be a chain about a mile down and a sign letting the public know that it was a private road, but yeah, sure, anyone could easily unlatch the chain and use the road if they wanted to."

"Thanks again," she said before he trudged off.

Assuming the tree was planted at the same time the bones were buried, Sawyer wondered how difficult it might be for someone to drag a young girl's body that she estimated to be between fifty and sixty pounds from the gravel road to the crime scene. She looked from the patch of gravel back to where she could see technicians still working the grounds. Between the body and the tree, it would take someone at least two trips to carry it all from point A to point B. But it was much more doable from the gravel road. Unlike the parking lot below where Palmer had left his car, there were no cameras or light fixtures in the vicinity where she now stood. *Yes.* Whoever buried the girl most likely drove up this road under the cloak of darkness and worked unseen.

As she walked back toward the crime scene, more questions arose. Why bury the girl here in the first place? Why take the time to plant a tree? Behind the yellow tape she saw a small stuffed animal that had been bagged, labeled, and placed in a bin. It could be a bear, but with its matted faux fur and missing nose and eyes, it was hard to tell.

A bell went off inside her head. She had her answer: This was no slash-and-dash killer. Someone had cared about the girl and wanted her to be put to rest in a happy place.

A killer with a heart?

Sawyer thought about her parents.

*No.* Killers didn't have hearts. They had no souls either.

With her gaze fixated on the young girl's bones laid out on a black tarp, Sawyer vowed to do all she could to help find this little girl's killer, so she could get the justice she deserved.

But first, Sawyer needed a name.

# CHAPTER THREE

Harper Pohler got situated at a table in the Sacramento Public Library and opened her laptop. She hadn't checked in with The Crew in weeks, but it was time. D-Day was approaching fast.

The Crew consisted of five women who had been abused at some point in their lives. They used nicknames: Psycho, Cleo, Lily, and Bug. Harper was known in the group as Malice.

Her insides turned, agitated, like too many clothes stuffed inside a washing machine, and not because she was close to three months pregnant, but because her association with The Crew reminded her that she—Malice, *not* Harper—was a murderer. The distinction was an important one. Harper was a wife and mother of two. She was a good person, a compassionate being. Malice, on the other hand, couldn't sit still for too long. She only saw black and white. She had a thirst for revenge. And as of a month ago, she was a killer.

Harper drew in a breath as she straightened in her chair.

Some might call The Crew "survivors," but that didn't make much sense to Harper since all five women had met out of their desire for vengeance. If being a survivor meant being alive, then, *Yay, cool.* But to her way of thinking, a true survivor was someone who found a way to move forward and live a whole and satisfying life, free from night terrors and symptoms of PTSD.

Although The Crew had known one another for a while now, they had not begun to dish out their punishments until recently. Their plan had been to scare their tormentors in some way, let the assholes know they were being watched and they would pay for what they had done. The Crew wanted their abusers to know humiliation and experience what it was like to feel trapped and have no control.

That was their goal.

But so far, things hadn't worked out as planned.

Lily's abuser, Brad Vicente, their first target of revenge, had made the mistake of pissing off Psycho, a woman who had chosen her nickname for a reason. They all agreed that Brad was a dick. When he refused to shut his mouth, Psycho cut off said appendage, and now Brad was a dickless dick. Surgeons had been unable to reattach his penis. Poor Brad.

Once Brad was taken care of, The Crew had moved on to the next abuser on their list: Otto Radley. Again things didn't turn out quite as planned. After Otto was released from prison, The Crew used Cleo as bait and abducted the brawny man. Like taking candy from a baby. At least it started out well. Unfortunately Otto freed himself from his bindings and was about to attack Psycho when Malice shot him dead.

A third abuser, Dennis Brooks, Malice's rapist father, and Joyce Brooks, her mother, were now dead.

In a short time, three out of five of The Crew members had experienced a reckoning of sorts. Not bad for a band of fucked-up misfits with absolutely no skills whatsoever.

Did Harper feel bad about her parents' deaths?

Not exactly.

After hearing about the deaths of her parents, a neighbor had brought Harper a pie—"comfort food," the woman had explained. Harper had said nothing, merely kept her gaze fixated on the hardwood floor beneath her feet. Taking her silence as grief, the neighbor had left. But sorrow wasn't the emotion Harper had been experiencing at the time. She'd been struggling not to smile. Harper's dad was dead, and he would never be a threat to her younger sisters, Aria and Sawyer, or to her daughter, Ella.

*Amen.*

The screen lit up. From the looks of things, Malice had missed one lengthy conversation. She said hello and then quickly skimmed through the earlier text, which was mostly about Brad Vicente. The rapist was in jail, trying to get enough people to sign a petition so he could appeal his sentence. His story was trending on social media. Thousands of people were taking sides. Team Vicente had 60 percent of the commenters, and Team Black Wigs had 40 percent, down 25 percent from the week of his arrest.

Lily was not happy about Brad having a voice after causing so many young women to suffer. They had videos as proof, but Brad Vicente had managed to convince his followers that someone had used high-tech equipment to put his image in the disgusting films on all those social media outlets. "Anyone can download deepfake software and create phony videos," he was fond of saying.

Malice caught up in time to join the other members in their conversation about D-Day.

It was Bug's turn for revenge.

Twenty-seven, five foot two with dreadlocks and dark eyes, Bug was feisty and highly intelligent. Ten years ago she'd been a cheerleader for the varsity football team when she was tricked into following the quarterback across the playing field and into a wooded area so thick with trees even the moonlight failed to shed any light on what was awaiting her.

Held down by a defensive linebacker, Bug was raped by the quarterback and a wide receiver. She was strong. They were stronger. She couldn't kick. Her screams were muffled.

Afterward, bruised and bleeding, she told her parents, and together they filed a report with the police. School authorities were alerted. The case went to court, but the rapists were from affluent households. Big money bought big lawyers, and in the end they were allowed to walk free. No slap on the hand. No lectures. *Boys will be boys.*

LILY: What's the plan for this weekend? Are we still on?

BUG: Yes. All three of my boys will be attending. Unfortunately the defensive linebacker is bringing his wife along. Not worried. I'll figure it out.

CLEO: How do you know your boys will be there?

BUG: I've been "friends" on Facebook with 90 percent of the football team for years. I use an alias. I know when my boys are on vacation or if they are enjoying adult beverages downtown. I know if they're married with children or if they're dating. I know as much about them, if not more, than Mark Zuckerberg.

It was probably true, Malice thought. Bug had talked about her job as a white hat hacker, a computer specialist who broke into protected systems and networks to test their security.

PSYCHO: How do you intend to get these guys away from everyone else?

BUG: I plan to trick them, just like they tricked me ten years ago. I already know their names, addresses, and cell phone numbers. On the night of the reunion, I'm going to send the defensive linebacker and his two rapist friends a text using a cell number belonging to one of their good buddies who can't attend because he'll be out of town. The text will ask my boys to meet at a specific area where The Crew will be waiting.

PSYCHO: More details, please. Transportation?

BUG: I have a van I got off Craigslist in Los Angeles over a year ago, weeks after we formed our group. License plates are registered to a sex offender in the area. Once my boys are tied up and ready to go, we drive to the cabin in Auburn.

CLEO: I received an email this morning. Looks like the cabin in Auburn is a no-go.

BUG: You told me the cabin was a sure thing.

CLEO: I'm sorry.

Malice instantly thought of the construction site where her husband had been working when the builder ran out of money and couldn't complete the project. She'd heard the project would be stalled for another two years at least.

MALICE: There's an abandoned subdivision in North Sacramento. Before phase one barely got started, the builder went bankrupt. Five houses were framed. Three others have everything except flooring and appliances. I was with my husband when he picked up his equipment, which was stored in the basement of one of the model homes. There was a steel security door, but you would need a padlock.

BUG: Is the subdivision fenced?

MALICE: Not all of it. To the left side of the construction site is chain-link fencing. If you walk or drive along the fence line, you'll come across an opening that will take you to what would have been the backyard of one of the homes.

BUG: If you have an address, I'll take a look tomorrow morning before work.

Malice gave her directions.

PSYCHO: Okay. Let's assume you'll take your boys to the abandoned house. The reunion is Saturday. How long do you plan to keep them tied up for?

BUG: I don't know. Two or three days at least.

CLEO: What's the plan?

BUG: I want to humiliate them. Scare them. Make them feel trapped. I want every one of them to know what it's like to have no control over what happens. I thought about making them sign a letter of apology, but I'm not sure what good it would do.

CLEO: Too risky. A letter like that would reveal your identity.

LILY: How so?

CLEO: I think he would easily guess who was behind this scheme.

BUG: Not true. When I took QB, WR, and DL to court, other women came forward. Two of the women agreed to get on the stand. Others came to me privately and told me QB had raped them too, but they wanted to remain anonymous.

PSYCHO: I vote no to the letter idea, but yes to everything else. Make them sweat.

CLEO: I think we should only take QB. We have trouble handling one man, let alone three. These guys all have jobs, which means they have bosses and coworkers who will want to know where they are. Not to mention family. All three men attend a reunion and fail to return home by morning. That's going to bring the FBI right to your door, possibly my door.

LILY: I agree with Cleo. Even without family and friends, cars driving in and out of an abandoned subdivision will call attention to us. Somebody will take notice and call the police.

MALICE: There are no homes surrounding the abandoned subdivision. Nothing but dry grass and oak trees, so that won't be a problem.

BUG: Just help me get these men to the destination, and I'll do the rest.

CLEO: I still don't understand why you can't just focus on QB.

BUG: It's not only QB's face I see in my nightmares. QB and WR may have raped me, but it was DL who held me down. I can still hear his laughter.

Malice's mind was made up. If Bug had her mind set on holding three men captive for several days, even a week or two, then so be it. Malice had helped form The Crew for a reason. Too many offenders, like her father, got away with this abuse. It was up to them to send a message.

MALICE: I'm in. After the targets have been secured, I can help during the day while my kids are at school.

PSYCHO: I can do whatever you need me to do.

LILY: I'm in.

CLEO: I'll be there Saturday night, but I'll leave the rest to Bug.

BUG: Thank you.

After Bug told everyone where and what time to meet, they signed off.

Harper sat quietly for a moment. She thought about her husband and children, including the child growing inside her womb. She had made a promise to The Crew to do all she could to hold certain sexual predators accountable. These men, every one of them, deserved what they had coming.

And yet all she really wanted was to find a way out before it was too late.

# CHAPTER FOUR

Surprised her daughter had almost outgrown her shiny new red Mary Janes, she put a little more muscle into getting the shoe over the arch of Molly's foot.

"That hurts. Stop! Please! I want to go home."

"Don't be silly, Molly. You *are* home."

"My name is Riley."

"No, dear. It's Molly. And from now on I'd like you to address me as Mom."

"I will never call you that!"

The shoe finally slid fully onto Molly's foot. *Thank goodness.* "There. That's better." Leaning close to her daughter, she brushed a loving hand over her pale, soft cheek. Every time she looked at Molly, her heart swelled. It was difficult to pull her gaze away. And yet the longer she stared, the more concerned she became. After all she'd done to make the girl comfortable and at home, Molly seemed unreasonably obstinate. A moment of goodwill washed over her, prompting her to say, "You're obviously having a difficult time adjusting to your new bedroom after being gone for so long. So I have an idea. My . . . Someone very dear to me used to call me Bubbles." She leaned over the bed and patted Molly's leg. "From here on out you may call me Bubbles."

No response.

Molly's stubbornness showed in the stiffness of her shoulders and arms. Bubbles sighed. "I have to go to work, but there's plenty of food and drinks in the cooler."

"You're leaving?"

"I'm sorry. I must."

"Are you going to unlock the chain from around my foot before you go?"

"If you're a good girl, the chains will come off very soon."

Molly broke down in a flood of uncontrollable sobs.

"Now, now. We've talked about this. Enough is enough. No more crying."

"What about school? I was supposed to start fifth grade."

Bubbles snorted. "When you do go back to school, you'll be starting fourth grade, not fifth."

Molly wiped her eyes. "Can I start today?"

It made her proud to see how eager her daughter was to soak up knowledge. "Of course we can. As soon as I return home, we'll get started."

"What do you mean?"

"You're going to be homeschooled." She pointed toward the stack of books next to the cooler. "I left you everything you need—books, assignment sheets, and pencils—so you'll be all set! After an early dinner, we'll get to work."

Bubbles admired Molly's adorable yellow dress with the big bow at the waist. It was a little big, but her daughter would grow into it soon enough. She swept the flyaway hair out of Molly's face. The girl growled, and she yanked her hand back. "Maybe I should give you another dose of medicine before I leave."

"No," Molly pleaded. "I'll be good. I promise."

She stared at the girl for a long moment, trying to decide.

Her eyes widened. She'd almost forgotten the most important part. Rushing across the bedroom to the nightstand, she opened the top drawer and found the mini instant camera that had arrived yesterday. The batteries and film had been installed, everything ready to go. Her old Polaroid had stopped working a long time ago. The price of film was outrageous, but *everything* was overpriced these days. Walking back to the foot of the bed, she held the camera up so she could see Molly through the lens. "Say cheese."

Molly looked away.

She was already running late. Irritation flowed like lava through Bubbles's body, sparking electrical currents in her brain that flickered and glowed. "I said, 'Say cheese.'"

Molly didn't move.

Her body stiff, Bubbles walked forward and set the camera on the bedside table. She then went to the ground on all fours and reached under the bed until she found what she was looking for. Chains rattled.

"What are you doing?" Molly asked, her voice rising.

On her knees, her chest level with the mattress, Bubbles grabbed hold of Molly's wrist and clamped the metal cuff tight.

"Please don't," Molly begged. "I'll smile. I'll say 'cheese.' I promise."

"Too late," Bubbles said as she made her way to the other side of the bed. Again she reached under the bed. Chain in her grasp, she reached for Molly's left wrist, but Molly pulled away defiantly.

Bubbles pounced, grabbed the girl's arm again, and yanked it toward the cuff attached to the end of the chain. Click. Her vision clouded as she marched to the nightstand at the other side of the room and opened and closed drawers until she found a long-sleeve cotton shirt. With the cloth grasped in both hands, she ripped the shirt in two as she returned to Molly's side.

"Please don't hurt me," Molly begged.

It was almost as if the child was no longer in the room. With single-mindedness Bubbles wound the cloth through the wooden slats of the headboard and around Molly's forehead tightly so Molly had no choice but to look straight ahead.

Satisfied, she went in search of a red permanent marker and used it to draw a big red smile on the girl's face.

*Perfect.*

Breathless, she grabbed hold of the camera, positioned herself at the foot of the bed once again, and peered through the lens at her daughter. "That's better," she said before snapping the picture. "You're a scrappy one, aren't you?" She waved the picture through the air and waited for it to develop. "Look at that smile," she said when it was done. "I'm going to cherish this picture forever."

# CHAPTER FIVE

That same day, back in her cubicle at work, Sawyer clicked on the link she'd found earlier and searched for children who had gone missing over the past five to seven years. Many of them had since been found and were now accounted for. The Polly Klaas Foundation website had a master list of missing children in the state of California. She also checked out information on the National Center for Missing & Exploited Children. Statistics revealed that less than 1 percent of abductions were nonfamily abductions.

In under an hour Sawyer had the names of three young girls missing from the Sacramento metropolitan area.

Cora O'Neal, Alexa Moore, and Carly Butler.

Cora O'Neal had disappeared five years ago near David A. Simpson Park in Elk Grove as she'd walked home from school.

Sawyer opened the bottom drawer of her desk, found a map of the Sacramento metropolitan area, which included seven counties, and made a red *X* where Cora had disappeared.

It amazed her that tens of thousands of children went missing every year and yet so few got national coverage. When it came to active investigations, sometimes law enforcement was reluctant to get the media involved. In other cases, if there was any hint of the child being taken by a family member, the media often didn't cover the story. Age, race, and gender bias also played a part as to how much attention a case received. Evidence showed that missing white children received more media attention than black children due to socioeconomic status. Resources of wealthy parents and neighborhoods were shown to improve the chance of recovery. Overall, despite the studies and theories, there was no evidence that law enforcement efforts varied by race or gender. As a whole, children who went missing received more attention than adults because they were vulnerable. Most adults who were reported missing disappeared because they wanted to.

In the case of Cora O'Neal, Sawyer noticed, her disappearance had received national attention because a family member advocate had made all the difference. But sadly, Cora had yet to be found.

Sawyer's research often took her down several rabbit holes, which could be time-consuming. But more often than not, the information she pulled together from different sources allowed her to collect and organize it in a way no one else had before. And that was one of the things she liked best about investigating. All these different paths, in her opinion, made it possible for her to see what others might miss if their focus was too narrow.

In this case, her exploration eventually brought her to an article about runaways. It had been written five years ago by a reporter who used to work at the *Sacramento Independent*. The article discussed how missing children were often mislabeled as runaways. And how crime, neglect, and abuse were so prevalent in most communities. The reporter's story focused on Danielle Woods, an eleven-year-old girl who was last seen getting off a school bus in Arden-Arcade, nine miles away. Because she'd run away once before, her case received no attention at all from authorities. Relatives believed she was one of the forgotten children, also known as "thrown-away children," because she'd suffered neglect and abuse at the hands of her mother and was told repeatedly to leave home and never return.

Sawyer wondered if Danielle Woods's parents simply hadn't reported their daughter missing because of the abuse she'd suffered at their hands. Could they be responsible for her disappearance?

Or maybe Danielle had been lured away by someone she'd met online?

She could have gotten lost or injured or taken by a family member trying to help her.

Bottom line, the missing children problem was far more complex than headlines suggested. Midway through the story, there was a mention of a young girl who'd narrowly escaped being abducted. No name was included. This tidbit intrigued Sawyer, but further research revealed no additional information. The byline read MITCH DEMATTEI, REPORTER. He had left Sacramento to work for a paper in San Francisco, but she didn't have an address or telephone number. LinkedIn, however, provided her with an email.

She sent DeMattei a message, letting him know she was researching missing children in the area and was interested in talking to him about his article on runaways. Then she resumed her search on Alexa Moore. It took some time, scouring through articles where Alexa's name popped up, but ultimately led nowhere. It wasn't until she typed in "Mary Jo Moore," a relative of Alexa Moore's, that she learned the ten-year-old was kidnapped by her father, which then led to a one-year court battle between Alexa's parents. The judge granted full custody to the mother. Alexa was now in high school and doing well.

Sawyer crossed Alexa Moore's name off her list and then did a search for Carly Butler. On her eleventh birthday, Carly had disappeared on her way home from school.

An email from Mitch DeMattei popped up on Sawyer's computer screen. She opened it and saw that he'd provided her with a telephone number, telling her to call anytime. She picked up her cell and tapped in his number.

Mitch DeMattei answered on the first ring. He had a lively, friendly voice.

"This is Sawyer Brooks with the *Sacramento Independent*," she said before thanking him for taking her call.

"Not a problem. What can I help you with?"

"In your article on runaways you mention a near abduction that occurred almost five years ago in the Sacramento area, but I don't see a name, and I couldn't find anything else on the internet about it."

"The girl's name is Paige Owens. The reason you can't find anything is because Paige's mom, Rene Owens, refuses to talk to the media or anyone else about what happened."

"Why?"

"Because the ordeal absolutely petrified her. She was convinced that the woman who had tried to abduct her daughter as she walked to the bus stop was still out there, watching and waiting to steal her daughter away at any given moment."

"A *woman* tried to abduct the little girl?"

"Unusual, but it happens," he said.

A chill raced up Sawyer's spine. The thought of this woman failing to kidnap a child and then stalking the family was beyond horrifying. "Did Rene Owens have reason to believe she was being watched?" Sawyer asked. "I mean, did she see someone parked outside? Was she being followed?"

"Rene Owens talked to me on one occasion, a week after the near abduction. She told me she saw a woman in a white SUV following her on multiple occasions. As if that wasn't bad enough, she said she was adding garbage to the waste container outside when she spotted the same white SUV parked down the street. There was a woman in the driver's seat, and she took off without bothering to turn on the headlights. When Mrs. Owens opened the waste container, she found her beloved cat of many years dead on top of the heap. She said it was a warning. Days later, Rene Owens got a court order to have the police report sealed, and she stopped talking to the media."

"Do you have an address for the Owens family?" Sawyer asked.

"Mr. and Mrs. Owens divorced within a year of the incident, but they live in Carmichael. Rene Owens and her daughter were still in the house after the divorce. Pertinent information has been blacked out of the report, but the name and address should be there."

"Thank you for your help. If you can spare another minute, I did have a few more questions for you."

"No problem."

"I was wondering about Danielle Woods, the runaway teen you focused on in your story. What do you think happened to her?"

There was a pause before he said, "From everything I gathered, and I'm not saying eleven-year-olds don't run away, because they do, I don't believe Danielle ever should have been labeled as a runaway."

"She's not listed at all in the NCMEC's database."

"Parents need to insist that their child's name, date of birth, and description be logged in to the National Crime Information Center. In Danielle's case, nobody seemed to care."

"So if Danielle didn't run away, what do you think happened to her?"

"You tell me. I spent hours talking to family, friends, and teachers. Danielle may have been neglected at home, but those closest to her all said the same thing—that Danielle had no intention of running away."

"Did they say why they believed that to be true?"

"Because the first time she ran off, she spent the night in a cold, dark alleyway, and that was enough to convince her she'd rather take her chances at home."

Sawyer added Danielle's name to her list and then thanked him for his help. Before the call ended, though, he asked her about Sean Palmer and whether he was still working at the paper.

"He's still here," Sawyer said.

Mitch DeMattei laughed. "I shouldn't be surprised, but I am."

"Why is that?"

"All he used to talk about was retiring and spending more time with his family. But I sort of guessed it would never happen. Journalism is in his blood. Nobody can breathe life into a story like Palmer."

"Agreed."

She thanked him again, and after they said goodbye, Sawyer thought about what Palmer had said the other day about his relationship with his son. It wasn't easy, learning to balance family with work. She knew that firsthand since she couldn't recall the last time she'd done something that wasn't work-related. After vowing to exercise or do yoga in the near future, she pushed the thought aside and went back to work, tracking missing children.

Sawyer stared at the three names: Cora O'Neal, Carly Butler, and now Danielle Woods. She jotted Paige Owens's name at the bottom of the list and then logged in to the *Sacramento Independent*'s website and searched the archives for Rene Owens. The file, including the police report, popped up. She wrote the address next to Paige Owens's name and was about to print the report when her phone buzzed. A text from Palmer read: A twelve-year-old girl has been missing since yesterday. Come to my office.

Sawyer's heart skipped a beat. A twelve-year-old girl missing? The timing was bizarre. She grabbed pen and paper and headed that way.

Through Palmer's open door she saw his feet propped on the corner of his desk and his arms crossed tightly over his chest as he stared at the TV mounted on the wall in the corner. "Shut the door," he said.

She did as he asked, then took a seat in one of the two chairs in front of his desk and watched along with him. The anchor on Channel 10 was talking about a twelve-year-old girl named Riley Addison, who had gone missing Sunday night.

The picture switched to a local reporter talking to a music teacher who had given Riley piano lessons on the day she disappeared. The man said after they were done, just as she'd done every Sunday for the past year, Riley went outside and took a seat on the front stoop to wait for her mother.

The interview concluded, and a commercial came on. Palmer picked up the remote and clicked the television off. He dropped his feet to the floor. "Earlier it was reported that the girl's mother was on her way to pick up her daughter when another car ran a red light and hit her vehicle. Her car swerved, then rolled down an embankment. She's at Sutter General Hospital."

Every part of Sawyer tingled at the thought of another girl being snatched off the streets in and around Sacramento. "Did you get the mother's name?"

"Vicki Addison."

"Want me to drive to the hospital and see what I can find out?"

"It's worth a shot."

"Have you heard anything more about the bones found earlier today?" she asked.

Palmer shook his head. "It'll be a while before we know more."

Sawyer placed her notepad on Palmer's desk and slid it closer to him.

He read through the names, then looked at her. "What is this?"

"I've only scratched the surface and already found two girls between the ages of ten and twelve who went missing in the past five years. There could also be a third female, Danielle Woods. She's currently listed as a runaway, but I talked to Mitch DeMattei—he says hello, by the way—and he doesn't believe Danielle ran away from home." She shrugged. "So I added her to my list. The name I highlighted," she said, pointing at her notes, "is a fourth female who was nearly abducted, but who managed to escape unharmed. She's sixteen now."

He rubbed the back of his neck. "All in Sacramento?"

"No. Carmichael, Elk Grove, and Sacramento." After a short pause, Sawyer said, "Riley Addison needs to be added to the list."

When Palmer failed to respond, Sawyer placed her hands, palms down, on his desk and leaned closer. "We could have an epidemic of kidnappings on our hands."

"If there were that many young girls taken within a few short years, not only would media be all over it, citizens would be waving their pitchforks in front of the capitol."

"Sadly, I don't believe that's true. Thousands of people go missing every year, many of those are children. The majority of missing children are either taken by a relative or they're runaways. And then you have children who are considered 'thrown-aways' because they were told by their parents or guardians to leave the house." Sawyer sighed. "Only two of those girls are listed in the national database. Nobody knows much about the girl who got away because her mother won't talk about what happened. If all four of those girls were, in fact, abducted by a stranger, nobody would be the wiser."

"What are you proposing?"

"Let me dig deeper," Sawyer said. "Let me see if there are other girls aged nine to twelve who have gone missing in Sacramento and bordering cities in the past five to seven years."

"And then?"

"And then I need to find out if they were ever found and if they are dead or alive. Once that has been established, I will talk to family members and learn all I can about these girls." She gestured toward the TV screen, referring to the report they had just listened to. "I would like to make a list of character traits to try to learn their likes and dislikes. Did they take piano lessons or swim lessons? What were they doing when they went missing?"

"You're looking for some sort of connection between these missing girls?" Palmer asked.

"Yes, although I'm not insinuating that the same person took all of them. I'm just curious to know if *particular* girls are being taken. If so, I think our readers would be interested to know more."

Palmer tugged lightly on his beard as he talked. "Riley Addison, the newest missing girl, is close to my granddaughter's age."

Thinking he might say more about his granddaughter, Sawyer was surprised when he pushed her list back toward her and said, "You have a lot on your plate already."

She picked up the notepad and wiggled it. "Nothing I can't handle. I'll be writing an update on the vigilante group the media is calling the Black Wigs, and I have a few other stories that won't take much time." When their gazes met, she said, "I can do this."

"You know the drill," Palmer said. "We can only do so much."

"What if I do most of the research on my own time?" she asked.

"Isn't that what you do already?"

"A little girl is missing," she reminded him. "It's not too late for her. Give me a week to find out what I can. That's all I'm asking."

"I'm feeling déjà vu coming on."

He was referring to her time spent in River Rock last month when a young girl was found murdered and Sawyer had asked for more time to investigate. "I won't disappoint you."

"Famous last words. Go ahead. Dig a little deeper. See what you can learn."

"Thank you." She left his office before he changed his mind. As she walked back to her desk, she caught sight of Derek Coleman at the end of the hallway, making his way toward the exit. Derek was a thirty-five-year-old widower and, before her promotion, her former boss. She and Derek had been seeing each other for the past month. She'd called him yesterday to talk about the managing editor's retirement and never heard back. Rushing to his side, she caught up to him as he was exiting the building. "Hey, did you get my message?"

He kept walking. Not one word.

"Where are you off to?" she asked.

Outside, before stepping off the curb toward the parking lot, he stopped and turned to face her. "What do you want, Sawyer?"

Gobsmacked, she frowned. He wasn't a moody person. In fact, he was the nicest guy she'd ever met, and she couldn't remember one single time that he'd been rude to her. "Are you mad at me?"

"No."

*Bullshit.* He couldn't even look her in the eyes. "Everything about you right now says you're annoyed with me."

He exhaled. "When was the last time we talked? In person, face-to-face?"

She squinted into the sun as she thought about that. "Two days ago at my apartment?"

"Five days," he said. "It's been five days."

His attitude made her feel off-balance, like a spinning top, teetering right before it fell on its side. She tried to recall how she'd spent the past week, but the pressure was too much. Her mind was a blank. "It can't possibly have been that long. I called you yesterday and left a message." She cringed as she recalled the message she'd left him about the managing editor's retirement. She hadn't asked Derek anything personal, like when she might see him again. Nothing about what he was up to. No *How are you? I miss you. Call me back.*

His eyes softened. "I like you, Sawyer. I like you a lot, but it's clear you're just not that into me. A month ago, when I asked you out, I had no idea you were living with someone and had just broken up."

"I explained all that. My relationship with Chad was complicated. Chad and I never should have been together. It was—"

"None of that matters," Derek said, stopping her from going on. "I never should have asked you out once you told me. I simply plowed forward and pushed myself into your life. It was too soon. It was a mistake."

When Sawyer had rushed after Derek and followed him outside, this was the last thing she'd expected. Was he breaking up with her? "So you think I'm not into you because five days passed before I called to see what you've been up to?"

"That's part of it."

"The other part is you believe I might still be dealing with my breakup?"

"Yes. Between your recent breakup and your parents' deaths and all you've been through, I think you need some time to yourself. So I've decided to back away and give you space."

Her insides twisted into knots. She didn't know what to say.

"There's more," he said.

She kept her eyes on his, searching for answers. "I'm listening."

"Remember when I first called you after you returned home to River Rock and you read off a list of issues you're dealing with?"

She nodded.

"At the time I joked around with you, but the truth is I have a few problems of my own."

She waited for him to elaborate, which he did.

"I had been mourning my dead wife for so long I didn't recognize the signs at first. I knew you were a hard worker and that you were smart, but suddenly I was noticing other things about you. The way you rubbed your brows when you were deep in thought." He sighed. "Your mouth, the tiny dimple in your cheek when you smile, the freckle below your left ear. For the first time in years, I thought maybe, just maybe, it was time for me to move forward." His brows lifted. "Get the picture?"

"Yes," she said. "I think so. There's a 'but' in here somewhere, right?"

He nodded. "*But* then I realized I was the one calling you, texting you, and stopping by your apartment to say hi. It wasn't until I spent a day at my parents' house that I realized you hadn't called or texted. I'm not proud of it. I've never been the kind of guy to keep track of these things, but being new to the dating game after all these years, I couldn't help but notice you hadn't reached out. So it was then I decided to wait and see when you would call me."

Frustrated with herself, Sawyer rubbed her forehead. Why hadn't she called him? She didn't have a good answer for not doing so. Was she sabotaging the relationship on purpose? She'd always had a difficult time letting people in. Maybe he was right, and she'd been shutting Derek out of her life without even realizing it.

He laid his hands flat on his chest. "I have a good, healthy ego," he said, "so I knew I could handle whatever happened. But after five days passed with no word from you, it wasn't difficult to see that this relationship between the two of us was one-sided."

Before she could spit out any intelligent thoughts or opinions on the matter, he gently placed his hands on her shoulders and said, "I don't want you to feel badly about any of this. You didn't do anything wrong. We're both adults. I want the best for you, Sawyer. I really do." He glanced at his watch. "I need to go. Take care."

He turned and walked away.

*Take care?* She stood as stiff as a fence post and simply watched the back of him grow smaller as he moved farther and farther away.

Her feet felt as if they were glued to the asphalt. Why wasn't she running after him? Was it true? Was she not that into him?

Inwardly she shouted at herself to say something, do something, stop him from leaving. He had it all wrong. She liked him . . . a lot. He wasn't like any guy she'd ever met, let alone dated before. He was normal—if there was such a thing. He was nice too. And funny. It sounded cliché, but it was true that nobody had ever made her laugh as much as Derek had.

But she merely stood there, paralyzed by anxiety and fear, even though there was no dangerous threat.

This wasn't the first time her anxiety had kept her from moving forward. Her therapist had called it emotional paralysis when she'd located her sisters and was unable to talk to them. Her internal fear of trying to think logically and rationally while dealing with her anxiety, which at the moment felt like a brick pressing against her chest, was too much.

So she simply turned around, walked into the building, and went back to work.

# CHAPTER SIX

After hearing the front door click shut and the sound of the car's engine as the vehicle drove away, Riley cried out, screaming and begging for Mom and Dad to find her.

Exhausted, she leaned back onto the pillows behind her. The odds of anyone finding her were slim. She'd learned that from her parents. Her dad was a prison guard, and her mom was a psychologist. They knew firsthand that the world wasn't right. They dealt with "crazy" every day. They had spent countless hours teaching Riley and her older brother how to avoid situations like the one she was in now. She rubbed her wrists, thankful the woman had given her the freedom to move both arms before she left.

If her dad were here now, he would cry with happiness to see her alive. And then he would shake his head and ask her how in the world she had allowed herself to be abducted by a lady with a cast and a sling. Dad had talked about Ted Bundy on many occasions. Riley knew about the women who had disappeared off the streets of Seattle in the '70s. Bundy would lure them to his car by wearing a cast or by using crutches. He would then purposely drop something, and his kindhearted victims would get a crowbar to the head for their efforts. She had been warned.

*It doesn't pay to be nice.*

That's what her dad would say when he lectured her about never talking to strangers. And yet he was one of the friendliest people she knew.

The woman had put on a show for Riley, limping and grimacing in pain, and Riley had fallen for the act. Not once had Ted Bundy entered her mind. Not even for a hot second. She simply climbed into the back of the SUV to get the box, just like the crazy lady asked her to, and now she was paying the price for her stupidity. How dumb could she have been? That would be the first question her brother would ask her if she was lucky enough to ever see him again.

*Don't think like that. You're smart and clever.*

That's what Mom had been telling her since the day she was born. She needed to stay focused and think of a way out of here.

The room smelled old, musty, like it hadn't been used in a while. Riley rubbed her thigh where the crazy lady had poked her with the needle. At least she hadn't bonked Riley over the head with a crowbar. She looked around the room, taking it all in. To her right was a square oak table with lots of scratches and discoloration. Across the room was the nightstand with five drawers where the woman kept all her goodies: instant camera and film, markers, and who knew what else.

There was one window in the room. It looked as if it had been tinted like the ones in her brother's car. Gauzy white curtains hung over each side. On the wood floor was a red, blue, and yellow oval braided rug. There were also two closed doors.

Hoping one of the doors might lead to a bathroom, she slid off the mattress, surprised by the heaviness of the chain around her ankle when it hit the floor. She looked at the red shoes and thought about clicking her heels together, but this wasn't Dorothy's make-believe world. This was real life. A lump formed in her throat.

*Don't cry, Riley!*

The chain rattled and pinched her skin as she yanked the shoes from her feet and tossed them across the room. The relief was instantaneous.

On wobbly legs she shuffled her feet across the room so she didn't have to lift the chain with every other step. Her stomach gurgled. She was starved. The first door she tried to open was locked. The other door opened into a bathroom. She used the toilet, then washed her hands before taking the time to look around. The cabinet was filled with toilet paper and soap. Most of the drawers were empty except for the top one that was filled with colorful rubber bands and a toothbrush and toothpaste.

Her reflection in the mirror above the sink caught her attention. She leaned closer, her stomach resting against the tiled countertop. The red-marker smile made her look like a bad imitation of the Joker. Using soap and water, she scrubbed at the marker until it was nearly gone. Her skin tingled from her efforts.

She stared at her reflection. *What now? What am I going to do?*

Crying for Mom and Dad wouldn't help. Crying was for sissies, and she was all cried out anyway. She needed to find a way to escape. She needed to think. Plunking down on the cold tile floor, she examined the metal cuff around her ankle. There was a keyhole. That gave her hope. She'd watched Dad pick a lock one time when they were stuck outside the house without a key. She pushed herself to her feet again and went through the bathroom drawers and cupboards once more, reaching way in the back, making sure she hadn't missed anything the first time. The toothbrush was too big to be of any use. She needed a hairpin or a paper clip.

That gave her an idea.

Dragging the chain along with her, she exited the bathroom and made her way to the stack of books and school supplies that the crazy lady had left for her. Inside a small plastic bin she found a ruler, an eraser, and a sharpened pencil. She shoved the pointed end of the pencil into the keyhole and fiddled around, trying to get a feel for the locking mechanism. The lead tip snapped off.

*Crap.*

After looking through the stack of books, she opened the cooler. There were two water bottles, a plastic spoon and a yogurt, an egg salad sandwich, potato chips, and a cookie. She gobbled down the sandwich first.

It didn't taste too bad.

She opened the chips and brought the bag with her, munching as she explored the rest of the room. The chain kept her from reaching the dresser. The window was closer. If she stretched her arm out she could brush the tips of her fingers against the windowpane. The glass had definitely been tinted. She yanked the curtain to one side where she saw part of the tinting had flaked away.

She could see the neighbor's backyard. There was a swing set and toys littered about. How old were the kids? she wondered. Had they already started school, or was there a chance they would come out to play and she could somehow get their attention?

If they did show up, how would she do that?

She could throw something at the window. But what? She looked around. The cooler might be heavy enough to crash right through the window, and then she could clink the chains against the floor. It was early, though. If the kids next door had school, they might not come out to play until later. She thought about tossing the cooler at the window right this minute, but what if no one was home? What then? The woman might move her to another room without windows. Patience is what she needed if she planned to escape.

Her gaze followed the chain around her ankle. It disappeared under the bed. She went that way, got down on all fours, and crawled under the bed, where she could see a metal pole where four chains connected. The other three chains were in neat little piles. One for each leg and arm.

She pulled on the chain attached to her ankle, hoping it would break free.

Nothing happened.

As she lay beneath the bed in the semidark, faceup, feeling defeated, she noticed a tiny hole in the mattress. She pushed her finger inside, wriggled it around until she was poked by a metal coil.

If she could somehow break one of the coils loose, she might be able to use the wire to pick the lock around her ankle. She managed to tear the fabric enough to get her thumb and forefinger inside the mattress. The wire was thick and difficult to bend, but she knew she had to keep trying. She kept at it, bending the wire to the left and then to the right until her finger and thumb throbbed where she could feel an indentation in her skin. *"Patience,"* her mother's voice whispered. *"Patience always wins the day."*

# CHAPTER SEVEN

Sawyer parked at the back of the hospital's lot. As she walked toward the entrance, she noticed several media vans double-parked out front. Reporters and cameramen were huddled outside the emergency room.

The hospital's doors slid open automatically as she approached. A silver-haired woman sitting at the front desk told Sawyer she was only allowed to give patient information to family members. Sawyer walked away and headed through the lobby, looking around at the people waiting to get help. She stopped when she overheard two women talking about Vicki Addison.

Family members?

"Vicki is doing better," the woman wearing a yellow dress said. "Her condition has gone from serious to fair."

"Thank God." The other woman had to be six feet tall. She glanced Sawyer's way, prompting Sawyer to pull out her phone and pretend to make a call as she eavesdropped.

"What exactly did they tell you?" the taller woman asked.

"They said her vital signs are stable and she's conscious, but she won't be able to have visitors for a while."

"You would think they would allow her own sister in to see her."

Sawyer put her phone away, then approached the two women and held up her lanyard. "Hi, my name is Sawyer Brooks, and I'm with the *Sacramento Independent*."

Both women stared at her, but neither said a word.

"Mind if I ask you a couple of quick questions?"

"Go ahead," Vicki Addison's sister said.

Sawyer found a pen and notebook. "Your name is?"

"Sara Croche."

"Are you and Riley close?"

"Yes. Of course. She's my only niece."

"When was the last time you saw Riley?"

"Um, last week when I stopped by my sister's house to bring her some persimmons."

"Can you tell me a little bit about Riley?"

Silence.

"Does she have any hobbies, likes or dislikes, things like that?"

"She's a straight-A student. Talented too. She plays the piano and the flute. She loves to read and help her parents in the garden." Sara Croche's smile was tinged with sadness. "I don't think there's anything that girl can't do."

"So she's happy?"

"Of course."

"Never talked about running away?"

The woman frowned.

"Does she have a boyfriend?" Sawyer asked.

"She's only twelve! Of course not."

"I'm sorry. I'm simply trying to—"

The taller woman grabbed Sara's arm and pulled her away, muttering something about reporters all being heartless.

Sawyer exhaled. Asking for detailed information was part of her job. If she was going to write about Riley Addison, she needed to know as much about her as possible. But Sawyer realized too late that she'd come on too strong, too fast.

Back inside the used black Toyota Camry Sawyer had found on Craigslist after her Honda Civic died, she looked up the telephone number for Patrick Addison, Riley's father, and made the call. After three rings, a robotic voice said to leave a message after the beep. Sawyer stated her name, letting Patrick Addison know she worked for the *Sacramento Independent* and she wanted to help. She left her number and told him to call anytime. She then looked through her file for Paige Owens's address, the girl who had escaped her abductor, and plugged the information into the navigation system. The Owens lived seven miles away, off La Riviera Drive in Carmichael.

On the way Sawyer found herself thinking about Derek. Despite what he'd said, she missed him. Everything about him: his voice, his jokes, the way his eyes lit up when he looked at her.

She was definitely into him.

Some people overanalyzed their relationships. She tended to do the opposite. But she thought of Derek all the time. For instance, last week she'd seen what looked like a drug deal going down right outside her apartment, and her first thought had been to call Derek. But she hadn't. A few days ago she'd heard a gunshot that turned out to be a car backfiring, and again she'd thought of Derek. And what about the time she saw an elderly couple holding hands and wondered what Derek was up to? She thought about Derek constantly, and yet she hadn't called him. Why?

Her hands tightened around the steering wheel. She knew exactly what her problem was. Ever since returning home from River Rock a month ago, she'd been apprehensive, constantly worried that something bad would happen. She'd always known Mom and Dad were selfish and neglectful. But nothing had prepared her for the shock of discovering that they were monsters.

Sawyer couldn't think about her parents without feeling numb inside. It wasn't surprising that her anxiety had ramped up a notch after she returned home to Sacramento. Everything freaked her out these days. Whenever her heart raced, she found herself wanting to call Derek. But if she did that, she would appear needy. She liked to think she was independent and didn't need anyone else, and maybe that was partially true. Maybe she could live her entire life all alone. But was that what she wanted?

She drove up to the front of the Owens's house on La Riviera, pulled out her cell phone, and left Derek a text: I need to talk to you. Please call me back.

Pushing thoughts of Derek away, she reached for the manila file on the passenger seat where she'd put her notes and a copy of the police report Rene Owens had filled out five years ago. Most of the report had been blotted out using a black marker, rendering it useless.

Sawyer stepped out of the car and made her way toward the house. If not for the colorful blooms lining the walkway, the box-shaped house would have looked like a clone of every house on the street—one story with four small windows and a single-car garage.

Sawyer knocked and waited.

"Who is it?" asked a female voice from the other side of the door.

"Sawyer Brooks with the *Sacramento Independent*. I was hoping I could talk to Paige Owens."

"What about?"

The door opened a couple of inches, enough for Sawyer to see the woman's thick dark hair interweaved with wiry gray strands. Her lips were pressed into a straight line. "Are you Rene Owens?" Sawyer asked.

"I am."

"I was hoping I could talk to you and Paige about her near abduction five years ago."

The woman's eyes narrowed. "Every time another little girl goes missing, you people come knocking on my door. We have nothing to say to you. Leave us alone."

Sawyer caught a glimpse of a young girl in the background. The dark eyes framed by thick lashes and the heart-shaped face told her it was Paige. She'd hardly changed from the picture Sawyer had seen online from five years ago. "I wouldn't have come if it wasn't important," Sawyer said.

Rene Owens snorted. "Ratings and personal glory is all you people want."

Sawyer didn't back down. Although it might be a stretch to think this newest abduction was related to what happened to Paige Owens, Sawyer wanted to know more about every girl on her list and see where it led, if anywhere. "As you might have seen on the news, a young girl named Riley Addison went missing," Sawyer said. "Maybe someone saw something and yet they're afraid to come forward. Your bravery in talking to me could help authorities find her."

"Mom," the girl said. "Let her in. We should help if we can."

"I'm sorry," the woman told Sawyer. "We can't help you."

Sawyer placed a hand on the door to stop Rene from shutting it so she could hand her a business card through the gap. "Take my card, please. If you change your mind, please call me anytime."

The woman took the card and promptly closed the door in Sawyer's face. More than one lock clicked into place.

Sawyer exhaled. Rene Owens knew she was one of the lucky ones. Her daughter was home, safe and sound, and Rene planned to keep it that way. As Sawyer walked back to the curb where her car was parked, she scanned the neighborhood. Paige had been eleven when she was walking to the bus stop. Exactly what happened after that wasn't yet clear.

Her phone vibrated as she slid into her car. There was a text from an unknown number: This is Paige Owens. Meet me at Starbucks on Rosewood Avenue in fifteen minutes.

A jolt of excitement shot through her. Eager for the chance to talk to Paige, Sawyer looked toward the house and saw Paige's mother through the front window, most likely waiting for her to drive off, so that's what she did. When she was far enough away, she pulled over

50

and looked up the Starbucks address and logged it into her navigation system.

Twenty minutes later, Paige walked into the coffee shop where Sawyer had been waiting.

"Sorry it took so long," Paige said as she plopped onto the seat across from Sawyer. "I had to wait until Mom calmed down."

"Not a problem," Sawyer said. "Thanks for meeting with me. Can I get you anything?"

"No. I don't have a lot of time. My mom is a good person," Paige said, not wasting any time. "She wants to help, but she's scared."

"What is she afraid of?"

Paige's shoulders dipped. "White vans with tinted windows, shadows . . . the dark. Everything, I guess. Mostly she's afraid of the woman who tried to take me."

"Most of the police report has been blacked out. How old would you guess the woman to have been at that time?"

"Gosh, about forty, at least," Paige said. "The police were skeptical of the person being a woman."

"Why?"

Paige shrugged. "I just remember my parents getting angry when the police asked me over and over if I was sure there wasn't someone else in the car. At one point I started crying because I could tell they didn't believe me."

Earlier Sawyer had read about profiling criminals, including child abductors, who tended to be single men and social outcasts.

"Mom thinks that the woman who tried to take me has been watching us all these years."

Sawyer's skin prickled. "Does she have reason to believe that's true?" Sawyer asked. "I mean, has she seen someone?"

Paige's eyes narrowed. Her gaze fixated on Sawyer's backpack. "You're not recording this, are you?"

"That would be illegal unless I asked you for permission. But the answer is no. I'm not recording our conversation." Sawyer opened her backpack and showed her in hopes of gaining the girl's trust.

Paige peeked inside, then nodded.

Sawyer sipped her coffee. "Do you think the woman who tried to take you that day is watching you?"

"Sometimes."

The girl was fidgeting, clearly uncomfortable. Sawyer waited.

"In the beginning," Paige explained, "right after the incident, we would find dead birds and rodents on the pathway to our house. Dad thought it was pranksters, but it scared Mom, and she was convinced the driver of every white SUV was the woman who tried to take me."

"Did you ever see her again?"

"I saw a similar car parked outside the house a few times, but the vehicle never stuck around long enough for me to get a look at the driver."

"That would be unsettling. Has your mom always been easily frightened?" Sawyer asked.

"Not until after I was almost taken. She changed after that. My parents started fighting all the time because Mom wouldn't let me out of her sight. They ended up getting divorced." She swallowed. "*Everything* changed after that day."

"Do you still remember what happened?"

Paige's eyes watered. "I don't think I'll ever forget. But it's weird because after it happened I thought I remembered every little detail. Like what I ate for breakfast and Mom saying I should get going so I wouldn't miss the bus." Paige fiddled with the button on her shirtsleeve. "I was excited about a history test because I knew I would ace it." Paige met Sawyer's gaze. "I even remember what the woman was wearing. I mean, I can still see it in my head."

"Mind if I take notes?"

"Go ahead."

Sawyer found pen and paper in her bag. "What was she wearing?"

"Those plastic shoes. Crocs! Red, with holes in them. And a jean skirt, white top, and a red button-down sweater with little ladybugs. The weird part is that I didn't remember the red sweater until months after it happened."

Sawyer lifted a brow. "It just popped into your head suddenly?"

Paige shifted in her seat. "Yes. I was sitting in the cafeteria, eating lunch with a group of people, when my best friend joined us. She was wearing jeans and a red sweater. Hers didn't have ladybugs or any design at all, but all of a sudden, I saw the woman standing on the side of the road with her arm in a sling. The red sweater stood out. Every button. Every ladybug."

"Did you tell anyone?"

"No way. By that time I knew my mom would freak out if I brought up anything about that day."

"It sounds like repressed memories."

"That's exactly what the psychiatrist said."

"So you did tell someone?"

Paige swatted at a fly. "Just a psychiatrist I saw on and off after it happened. My parents couldn't afford it, so I stopped going."

Sawyer couldn't help but worry about the girl. The divorce. Her mother always hovering and frightened. That couldn't be good for Paige. "So this person—"

"Psychiatrist."

"So this psychiatrist thought you might be experiencing repressed memories?"

"Yes. She said the brain sometimes hides things to keep the bad memories away, and that's why, little by little, new details like the sweater could sneak up on me over the years. And she was right."

Sawyer had a million questions, but she didn't want to overwhelm the girl. "Do you mind telling me from the beginning what happened that day?"

Paige looked at the clock on the wall. "I'll have to talk fast."

Sawyer nodded. Waited.

"It was early in the morning. My bus arrived at 8:05, so it had to be around 7:55 a.m. Like I said, I was excited about taking the test, eager to get to school. My bus stop is only two and a half blocks from my house. When I saw the woman with a sling on her arm, she was standing at the back of a big white car—"

"Do you know what kind of car? Ford? GMC?"

"No, but I saw two number sevens and the letter $L$ on the license plate. It was parked next to the sidewalk, and the woman stood at the back. Right as I passed by, she moaned as if she were in pain. That's when a package dropped to the ground. I was close enough to the bus stop to see a group of kids still waiting, so I decided to help the woman."

Sawyer nodded as she took notes.

"Because I had my eyes on the bus stop, I didn't really get a good look at the woman's face in that moment. I just walked right over to where she stood and then bent down to pick up the package. And that's when I saw it."

"Saw what?"

"Something in her hand—the one in the sling. It was a syringe with a needle that doctors use to give shots, and she was about to poke me in the arm with it, so I twisted around and swatted it away. But that made me lose my balance, and I fell to the ground. I tried to crawl away, but she grabbed hold of my ankle and held tight, so I used my other foot to kick her."

"And then you ran?"

"I was on the ground and felt trapped, which is why I scrambled underneath her SUV. With my backpack strapped to my back it was a tight squeeze. When I looked back at her, she was reaching for me. 'Stop!' she said. 'Come back here!' She called me by someone else's name, Holly or Molly. I'm not sure which. I hurried out the other side as fast as possible. Once I was on my feet again, I ran, and I never looked back."

"Where did you go?"

"I know it sounds stupid, but I went to the bus stop. It was closer than home."

"Not stupid at all."

"A couple of parents were standing there with the other kids. I was crying by then. I had scrapes on my face and hands. By the time I took one of the parents to the spot where it had happened, the woman with the needle was already gone."

"I know you and your parents went to the police and filled out a report."

"That's right," Paige said. "Mom didn't like the way we were treated. She thought the police didn't do enough. It got worse a few days later when one of Mom's good friends asked her if maybe I made up the story to get attention." Paige exhaled. "I wish I'd never said anything to anyone."

"But you're talking to me now."

Paige perked up a little, her expression quickly changing from sad to determined. "Because it *did* happen," she said. "And I want to help find the girl who disappeared the other day." She grew quiet for a moment. "It's true what Mom said: every time a young girl goes missing, somebody knocks at our door. My mom tells them—reporters, detectives, whoever—to go away."

"Does that happen often?"

Another shrug. "Often enough," Paige said. "Even when a young girl disappears in another state, I spend weeks thinking about the missing girl, obsessing about where she is and what she's doing. I also see the woman's face as she shouts at me to come back, and I feel sick to my stomach at the thought of her taking me home with her. The woman who tried to grab me was crazy."

"Besides the obvious, why do you say that?"

"She had big, I mean *huge*, marble, glossy-brown eyes. The kind of scary eyes that look right through you and make it seem as if they know what you're thinking. She had a long, thin face with pointy cheekbones and chin. Her hair, a dull grayish-blonde, hadn't been combed, and her lips were pale and cracked."

"I thought you hadn't seen her face."

"After that girl was taken—"

"Riley Addison?"

"Yes. Riley Addison. I saw the news right before bed last night, and when I was trying to sleep, *bam!*"—Paige put her hands to both sides of her head and gestured outward as if there was an explosion—"when I was under her car, crawling away, I looked back, and there she was on hands and knees. Our gazes locked. That's when I saw her face and those big, scary eyes."

"That must have been frightening."

"I'm fine," she said unconvincingly as she pushed herself to her feet.

"You didn't tell your mom?"

"Nope. I should go now."

Sawyer stood too. "Thanks for your help, Paige. If you remember anything else, will you call me?"

"Sure. I have your number." Before she left, she turned back to Sawyer and said, "I do have a question for you."

"What is it?"

"I've been keeping track of girls who have gone missing in and around Sacramento. If I text the names to you, can you tell me if any of them were ever found?"

"Send me the names. I'll do what I can."

"Okay," Paige said before heading for the exit.

"Goodbye, Paige," Sawyer said.

Paige seemed much older than her age. Like Paige's mother probably did every chance she got, Sawyer kept her eyes on Paige as she climbed into her car, kept watching until she drove away.

As Sawyer gathered her things, she found herself once again looking at her notes:

Cora O'Neal: disappeared five years ago—Elk Grove

Carly Butler: disappeared three years ago—Sacramento

Paige Owens: near abduction five years ago—Carmichael, escaped

Danielle Woods: listed as a runaway four years ago—Sacramento

Riley Addison: disappeared one day ago—Sacramento

Cora and Carly had both received media attention, but neither had been found.

Paige Owens's mother had kept the media at bay. And Danielle Woods was thought to be a runaway. What if she wasn't a runaway? If Paige had disappeared five years ago, and Danielle Woods had been abducted, that would mean there could possibly have been five abductions in five years.

Could it be that young girls were being plucked right off the streets, never to be seen again, and nobody cared? The idea of it caused the fine hairs at the back of Sawyer's neck to stand on end.

Palmer was right. Where was the media uproar?

Was anyone searching for them? Could Riley Addison's case be connected to the others somehow?

And who the hell was the woman in the red sweater?

# CHAPTER EIGHT

The Crew sat inside the 2012 Ford Econoline that Bug had purchased the year before just for this occasion. They were parked at the farthest corner of the parking lot at Green Meadows High School. Everyone had on their black wigs. They would wait to put on their masks.

Psycho had volunteered to drive and was positioned behind the wheel, slumped back into the seat to stay hidden.

Malice occupied the passenger seat, and Bug and Lily were in the very back of the vehicle, hunched on the floor. The back seats had been removed to make room for the football players. Tasers would be used to subdue the men so that they could bind their arms and legs with heavy-duty zip ties. Their faces would be covered with burlap bags so they could breathe but couldn't see.

Having graduated from Green Meadows High, Bug had received an invite along with an itinerary of the night's events. Cocktails would be flowing freely from the moment a guest walked into the high school gym. Dinner was scheduled for 7:00 p.m. There would be dancing and plenty of room to mingle. Awards would be given throughout the night to the people who'd traveled the farthest, had the most kids, had the most unusual career, et cetera.

Psycho tapped her fingers against the steering wheel. "I thought Cleo said she would be here."

"Something came up," Bug replied. "She had to cancel."

Lily snorted. "What happened to 'all for one and one for all'?"

"It's probably for the best," Malice said. "There isn't enough room for everyone as it is."

"It's ten o'clock," Psycho said. "Time to send the first text."

"Are you sure it's going to look as if the text is from his friend?" Lily asked.

"Positive. All I needed was Tony Bryant's mobile number, address, and date of birth to get the carrier to 'port out' his number to my burner." Bug let out an audible breath. "Is everyone ready?"

They all answered in the affirmative.

Bug read the text: Surprise! I made it, after all. Remember what we used to do before class? I scored some quality shit. I'm in a van at the far end of the parking lot. Back doors are open.

"Okay," Bug said. "The text has been sent."

The next few minutes were spent in the quiet. Malice felt the beat of her heart pick up its pace.

"I hated high school," Lily blurted, nerves seemingly getting the best of her. "Mean girls and bullies," she went on. "Shitty teachers who didn't want to be there any more than the students did. I wouldn't go back and do it over for all the money in the world."

"Not me," Psycho said. "High school was everything. I was young and happy. I had friends and hope for the world. I would definitely go back in time and do it again, but I'd be ready for any piece of shit who ever tried to touch me," she said in a voice that sent shivers down Malice's spine. "I would carry a switchblade, and after college I would start a program to teach women how to defend themselves."

Malice smiled. She liked the idea. A year ago, when they formed The Crew, Malice wished she hadn't been so blinded by anger and bitterness. Because maybe then she would have suggested they form a group to coach and train young girls on how to protect themselves from predators. Give them a fighting chance.

Lily pointed at a shadow in the dark. "Look over there! Is that him?"

The back cargo doors were partially open.

Everyone wore black from head to toe. The van was parked where there were no cameras or streetlights. Whoever was approaching would not see them until it was too late.

"QB didn't text me back," Bug said. "Maybe he knows something is up."

Psycho's seat was pushed back as far as it would go. She put on her black cap and mask.

Malice kept her eye on the shadow coming their way. He passed by the last parking lot light with its high-intensity discharge, and for her that's when things got real.

Earlier Bug had turned off the switch near the ceiling, mounted behind the driver's door. She'd also removed the bulb from the rear light to keep the interior dark when the back doors opened.

Quietly, Malice slipped out of the van, leaving the passenger door partially open.

"Why is he stopping?" Lily asked.

There was a spark and then a small flame as the man lit a cigarette. A collective sigh of relief sounded inside the van.

Malice put on her mask and made sure her legs and feet were hidden behind the van's back tires as he continued toward them. If he walked up to the driver's window, the plan was for her to step toward the cargo doors and call his name to get him to come to the back.

She could hear his every footfall against the pavement. She swallowed as she willed herself to stay calm. Everything would be okay. The man was a rapist. Time didn't heal all wounds.

"Hey, Tony," he called. "Are you there?"

He was walking toward the back of the van.

So far, so good. QB thought his friend Tony had sent the text. He'd fallen for the ploy, just as Bug had fallen for his ten years ago.

He was close now. Malice could see the smoke from his cigarette rise into the night and disappear. She didn't move a muscle. She just waited. They all did.

"What the hell are you doing?" QB asked. He opened one side of the cargo doors, laughing now.

Lily lunged first. And then Bug.

Malice heard the buzz of the electrodes being fired as he was hit multiple times with a Taser. He cursed, grunted. His cigarette dropped to the pavement. They were on him fast, pulling him inside the van. No time was wasted. They all knew what to do. His ankles and wrists were zip-tied. Psycho leaned over the front seat, grabbed a fistful of his shirt, and helped pull him closer to the front. His legs were stiff and straight, his muscles contracting as his body seized.

"How many times was he tased?" Malice asked, worried that they might have gone too far.

"Don't worry," Bug said through gritted teeth as she worked. "He's fine."

Once he was bound, they rolled him to the front, pushed him against the back of the driver and passenger seat, and zip-tied him to the metal frame underneath so he would have no way of escaping. Bug fastened duct tape over his mouth to keep him quiet, then covered his face with a burlap bag.

"Okay," Bug said. "I'm sending another text."

Malice inhaled. Cleo had been right to worry about attempting to abduct three grown men at one time. Adrenaline pumped wildly through her veins. QB groaned and tried to jerk his hands free from the metal bars beneath the seats as they waited. His name was Myles Davenport, but calling him "QB" made him less human and the shit going down less real.

From behind the van Malice kept her gaze focused on the path QB had taken a few minutes before. The cargo door was still ajar. So was the passenger door. When the grunts and groans coming from QB got louder, she poked her head inside the van. "Someone needs to quiet him."

"He has tape over his mouth," Lily said. "There's not much else we can do."

Psycho pulled a handkerchief along with a small plastic bottle from her sweatshirt pocket. She doused the cloth with liquid, put the bottle away, then twisted her body around and clamped the cloth over the front of the burlap bag where QB's mouth and nose would be.

Silence followed.

"What did you do?" Lily asked.

Psycho shoved the handkerchief into her pocket. "Chloroform. You're welcome."

"Damn it!" Bug said, her gaze fixated on people coming their way.

Three human forms walked under the parking lot light.

Bug whistled through her teeth. "WR must have shown DL and his wife the text."

"We're fucked," Lily said.

"There's no way we can get all three of them at once," Psycho said. "Besides, the woman had nothing to do with any of this. QB is going to have to be enough for tonight." She started the engine.

Malice looked at Psycho. "What are you doing?"

"What does it look like? Get in!"

Malice jumped inside, shut the door, and buckled up.

"We're not leaving!" Bug shouted.

The van lurched backward. The cargo doors swung open.

Malice kept her gaze on the three people approaching. The two men broke apart, each taking a different route. What were they doing?

Bug cried out for Psycho to stop, while Lily struggled to pull the cargo doors closed.

Malice knew Psycho well enough to sense that she'd made up her mind. She was getting out of here.

Psycho pressed her foot hard on the gas pedal. Tires screeched. The van lurched forward and up and over a cement curb. The undercarriage squealed as it scraped against cement. She wrenched the wheel to the left, almost hit a parked car.

As she picked up speed, one of the men jumped in front of the van and held his hands up. Malice raised her arms to cover her face. Psycho slammed on the brakes, shoved the stick into Reverse, and backed up, tires smoking before they all felt a bump.

Wondering if they had hit another curb, Malice looked over her shoulder just as Lily shut the back doors before the van shot forward again and headed to the right, clipping the back of a Jeep before leaving the parking lot.

"You hit someone," Lily said, her voice shaking.

"It was a Jeep," Psycho said, leaning forward, eyes on the road ahead of her.

"No," Bug agreed. "It was a person. I saw him. I think it was DL."

"Shut the fuck up," Psycho said. "I didn't hit anyone."

"You fucking ran into the man because you don't know how to stick to a plan," Bug shouted, arms flailing. "You never stick to the plan. You just do whatever the fuck you want. As soon as you volunteered to drive, I knew it was a mistake."

"You're the one who had grandiose ideas of capturing the whole football team in one fell swoop," Psycho shot back. "An idiot move if ever there was one."

"Stop," Malice said, her stomach queasy, her mind jumbled. "Yelling at each other isn't going to help. We need to get to where we're going and then finish this."

"You're right," Lily said. "We all need to cool down, regroup. We'll figure this out."

Nothing was ever going to be okay, Malice thought as an uncomfortable quiet fell over them. She'd vowed to see this whole bloody mess to the end. And yet too often she found herself wondering if that were possible.

Justice would never be served. How could it be? So many rapists, like QB, had secure jobs and beautiful wives and happy children. Living the dream while their victims suffered, their lives forever disrupted.

Why couldn't she and the other crew members seek forgiveness and love for those who wronged them?

Malice closed her eyes and saw her father's image as he locked her bedroom door and then quickly undressed and lay down next to her. A sliver of moonlight sliced through the blinds, forever capturing the look of lust, love, and torment on his face the first time he'd touched her undeveloped body. "Shhh," he'd said. "Don't make a sound."

Her father was dead now, and she was glad for it. She would never forgive him. Not even in death.

The world was unjust, and those who used manipulation and violence to prey on others deserved to be punished.

# CHAPTER NINE

A knock on the door jolted Sawyer awake. She sprang from the couch and grabbed hold of her laptop before it hit the floor. The cat bolted for cover. It took her a second to gather her wits and get to the door, where she saw her sister Aria through the peephole.

"I'm so sorry," she said when she opened the door. She had told Aria she would go on a run with her this morning. "Give me a minute and I'll get ready."

"I already ran. It's ten thirty," Aria said, walking inside, peering around. "I've been calling all morning. Where's your phone?"

Sawyer shut the door, rubbed her eyes. "It's around here somewhere."

Aria used her cell phone to call her number. They both followed the buzzing sound into the bedroom. Her phone was underneath her backpack. Eight missed messages from Aria. No missed calls or texts from Derek.

Sawyer followed Aria back into the main room. The decorative pillow had a dent in it where her head had been, and the faux fur throw had sunk between the cushions.

Aria frowned. "Did you sleep on your couch?"

"I was working and must have conked out."

Aria picked up a pile of papers and notebooks from one side of the couch and took a seat. After flipping through a few pages, she asked Sawyer if she was working on the Riley Addison case.

Sawyer told Aria about the bones that were found, the missing girls, and her conversation with Paige Owens.

"Did the bones belong to one of the girls on your list?"

"We won't know until the lab reports come in." Sawyer went to the kitchen. Her apartment was small enough that she could still see and talk to her sister as she readied a pot of coffee.

"Would these missing persons be thought of as cold cases?" Aria asked.

"I don't know. I would assume that all missing children cases would be considered active investigations, but I need to talk to Detective Perez."

Aria continued to read Sawyer's notes. After a moment, she set the stack of papers to the side. "What if the same person who tried to kidnap Paige Owens also kidnapped some of these other girls?"

"I thought about that too. It's worth considering."

"Definitely," Aria said. "Think about it. Why would anyone go to all that trouble to try and abduct a child and then simply give up on the idea? I would think once the media stopped talking about the incident, the abductor would try again, don't you think?"

Sawyer exhaled. "I wish I knew, but it's all just speculation on our part."

"But if nobody ever speculates about these things, how do they ever find these missing children?" After a short pause, Aria said, "Let's pretend the same person is responsible. What if these girls are still alive?"

"Where would the abductor keep them?" Sawyer asked, playing along. "How would he or she feed them and care for them without anyone noticing?"

"Do you remember Michelle Knight, Amanda Berry, and Georgina DeJesus?" Aria asked, turning the computer screen so that Sawyer could see their images.

"I do," she said. "Those girls were kept restrained inside that man's house in Cleveland. I also remember hearing that limited resources were used in looking for Michelle Knight because everyone thought she'd run off."

"But Amanda Berry's name was everywhere back then," Aria said. "And still no witnesses. Nothing. It was as if all three young women had gone poof in the night."

Sawyer rubbed her chin, thinking, wondering. "No matter who abducted these kids, whether it's the same person or not, if the bones that were found recently belong to one of those names on my list, I'm betting they're all dead."

"Which could mean that Riley Addison is running out of time," Aria said.

It was true. Time wasn't on any of their sides. "I need to find her," Sawyer said.

As Aria was consumed by something on the computer, Sawyer thought about how it was so easy for people to get away with shit. Her older sister, Harper, was a good example, repeatedly raped by their father, night after night, while her sisters slept peacefully down the hallway.

And what about Aria and Sawyer? They had both been used by their uncle Theo as a sexual prize for rich men at his high-priced rape fantasy parties. And yet nobody had done anything to help. Not one person had stepped forward and said, "Stop. This is wrong."

And then there was Sawyer's best friend, Rebecca. What had happened to her kept Sawyer awake most nights. Rebecca had disappeared when Sawyer was fourteen. The police promised Rebecca's family that they were doing all they could. And yet all that time her friend was trapped in the crawl space beneath the floorboards in the house where Sawyer grew up. Sawyer often dreamed that she'd walked down the stairs to the basement, unlocked the small door leading into the crawl space, and saved Rebecca. If only she'd thought to look there, maybe Rebecca would still be alive today.

Aria's brows lifted. "Need some help?"

"Really? You have time?"

"Harper and Nate offered to pay me to take Ella to and from school every day and to help her with her homework, so I quit my part-time job at the coffee shop. I'll still be working odd hours at the SPCA, though." She rubbed her hands together. "I've got all day."

"Why can't Harper pick up Ella?"

"I don't know. I think her hormones are out of whack. She said she needs to get out more. She's made a few friends and even joined a yoga class for pregnant women."

"Harper has friends?"

"Yeah. I haven't met any of them yet, but I have to admit it's good to see her getting out of the house and doing something other than scrubbing toilets."

"Is she still going to therapy?"

"I don't think so. She's glad our parents are gone and has never felt so free."

"What about you?" Sawyer asked.

"What about me?"

It was Aria who had shot their mother in self-defense, leaving Sawyer to wonder if Aria was okay. Taking your own mother's life, Sawyer imagined, could leave a scar. "You know what I'm talking about."

Aria's chin came up a notch. "I don't feel an ounce of remorse for shooting Mom. I had no choice. Besides, I aimed for her leg, not her chest, but if I hadn't pressed the trigger, she would have shot one of us instead."

"I know. I didn't mean to upset you. I just thought maybe you were having a tough time dealing with it."

"I'm fine," Aria said. "I think you're the one who's struggling with everything that happened, and you don't even realize it. I have forgiven Mom and Dad and all the rest of those assholes. I try to concentrate on the present and appreciate the people I care about. I've learned from the past, but I've also let it go. It does no good to dwell."

Sawyer was still seeing a therapist. Maybe she wasn't going as often as she should, but she *was* doing her best. Dealing with all of life's demons, big and small, took time. Which is why she worried about Aria. Her sister was kindhearted and sensitive, not the type of person who could shoot her mother dead, even in self-defense, and then simply push it out of her mind.

Sawyer knew Aria better than most. She was holding back. But until Aria was ready to talk about it, Sawyer was the one who would need to let it go.

# Chapter Ten

Riley sat on a stool in the bathroom, watching Bubbles's reflection as the woman attempted to make a french braid. Riley's hair was still damp from the bath Bubbles had made her take. The woman had watched her the whole time and insisted on helping. She used a cloth to clean Riley's back and neck and armpits. Riley didn't like the woman touching her or looking at her. It was humiliating. Everything Bubbles did was creepy, including giving her a bath morning and night.

Riley had been forced to stand naked in the bathtub as it drained. Bubbles then dried her off and dressed her in a cotton nightgown with scratchy lace around the neck and wrists.

This was Bubbles's third attempt at weaving Riley's hair. Each time Bubbles started over, she gripped her hair tight and tugged hard with the brush.

Gritting her teeth, Riley did everything she could not to cry. If she whimpered, she'd get a swat on the arm with the back of the hairbrush. "No tears," Bubbles said both times it happened, pointing a stern finger her way.

All Riley had wanted to do since she'd been trapped in this place was cry. Telling her she couldn't shed a tear only made things worse. But in the time she'd been living with the woman, she'd learned there was no use arguing.

Bubbles was insane.

If Riley's mom met Bubbles, she would argue that "insane" wasn't an appropriate term to use. She'd say something about Bubbles having a mental disorder due to genetics. Whenever Mom spoke about one of her patients at the prison, she'd usually mention neurotransmitters and hormonal changes when it came to people like Bubbles. Dad would argue that environment most likely played a role in why Bubbles was the way she was, which made Riley suddenly curious. "Do you have a mom?" she asked.

Bubbles lifted her head. Their gazes met in the mirror above the sink. It was easier to look at Bubbles's reflection than to face her head-on. She wasn't sure why. But then Bubbles's eye twitched. "Why do you ask?"

Riley swallowed. "I just wondered if she fixed your hair when you were little."

"No. She had other things to do with her time."

"Like what?"

"You're a nosy girl, aren't you?"

"I'm sorry."

"No, don't be sorry. You asked, so I'm going to tell you. My mother was big, freak-show-circus big. So fat she couldn't fit in a chair or fly on a plane. And you want to know why she was so big?"

*Don't cry. Don't cry.* Riley shook her head.

Bubbles grabbed hold of Riley's arm and yanked her out of the bathroom and to the folding table she'd brought into the room earlier, where a plateful of food waited. She dragged Riley to the stool next to the table and pushed her shoulders down. "Take a bite," she said.

Riley picked up the fork.

"Not with the fork. With your hands."

"Why?"

"Because you asked me what my mother did with her time, and so I want to show you. Scoop up some of those mashed potatoes and gravy with your hand and put them in your mouth."

Riley's bottom lip trembled as she brought her hand to the plate.

"For fuck's sake. Like this." She grasped hold of Riley's hand, forced it through the middle of her dinner, scooping up a mixture of potatoes, peas, and pork, some of it falling off the side of the plate, and said, "Now open your mouth."

Riley cracked her lips apart, but it was difficult to do while she was crying. She couldn't help herself. She'd held back for too long, and the tears were streaming down the sides of her face as Bubbles started cramming food between Riley's lips, shoveling it in, her fingers pushing against Riley's front teeth, one scoop after another. Riley coughed, trying not to choke or vomit. She was suffocating. Food dripped in giant gobs down her chin and onto the nightgown. Riley grabbed the woman's wrist with her left hand and tried to stop her. She couldn't breathe.

"Drop your hand, or I'll tie both hands to the headboard and feed you on the bed."

Riley dropped her hand.

"Stop crying!"

Riley cried harder.

"You asked, so quit being a baby. This is what my mother did all day. She ate and ate and ate. Anything she could get her hands on. If I bothered her while she was eating, she tied me to a chair and made me watch. Just like this. She loved her food more than she loved me."

Seemingly exhausted and out of breath, Bubbles stopped. She left Riley sitting alone and went to the bathroom to wash herself off. Riley spit everything still in her mouth onto the plate, choking as she sucked in a giant breath of air, and then used the sleeve of the nightgown to wipe her mouth and chin. Her gaze was fixated on the open door where she could see the railings of the staircase. The cuff and chain Bubbles used to clamp around her ankle was in a pile near the bed.

*Run*, the voice in her head said. *Run!*

A heavy weight landed on her shoulders. Bubbles had returned.

"Thinking about making a run for it, huh?"

Riley shook her head.

Bubbles snorted. "Stand up."

Riley stood.

Bubbles grabbed the hem of the nightgown and pulled it up and over her head and tossed it aside. Grasping her arm again, she dragged Riley back into the bathroom where she used a washcloth to wipe the mess from her face and neck.

"Sit," she ordered, gesturing at the stool.

"What about clothes?"

"Modest, are you?" Bubbles sighed and then left the room long enough to grab a cotton nightgown from the dresser. This nightgown featured Tweety Bird and had pink, fluttery ruffles around the sleeves and hem. Riley wondered who it used to belong to.

Once she was seated, Bubbles said, "Go ahead and ask me anything you want to." She patted Riley on the arm, pretending to be suddenly friendly, but her fingernails gouged into Riley's skin, and it hurt.

Bubbles's face contorted. Her mouth twisted. Her eyes bulged. "Go ahead," she said louder than before. "Ask!"

Riley's stomach turned. More than anything, she wished she'd never tried talking to Bubbles. She'd only done so because she'd thought of her dad and how he'd once told her it was a person's environment that made them crazy. She also remembered a movie she'd seen about a woman who made friends with the man who kidnapped her. The victim in the movie was nice to her abductor. Even when he was mean. She promised the bad guy she would never tell anyone if he let her go. It took days for her to come up with a plan and convince him that letting her go was the right thing to do. And it worked. He drove her back to where he'd taken her and set her free. And she called the police the first chance she got.

Bubbles haphazardly undid the messy braid and then ran the bristles of the brush through Riley's tangled hair. "Ask me another question."

Riley said nothing.

A hard tug of her hair made Riley look at Bubbles's reflection in the mirror.

"Ask me another question, or we're going right back into that room and you're going to finish your dinner."

"Who is Molly?"

"You are!" Bubbles laughed, a quick burst that ended as abruptly as it began. Her hands shook as she reached into the basket of toiletries she'd brought into the room before Riley's bath and pulled out a pair of scissors. "Time to cut your hair."

Riley stiffened.

"You've been a very bad girl. Now hold still."

Frozen in place, Riley felt numb as she watched long wisps of hair fall to the ground. A strange rumbling stirred within. She'd thought if she hung on long enough, sooner or later Bubbles might leave the house without chaining her to the bed, or maybe even let Riley go. But that was never going to happen. Posture held straight and strong, she began to strategize how she would escape.

It might not happen today or tomorrow, but she would find a way out. And then she would make sure Bubbles spent the rest of her life in prison. When the time came to show the jury who was responsible for the atrocities she would have already described in detail, Riley envisioned pointing at the monster wearing the old, partially buttoned, overwashed red sweater. The one dotted with ladybugs, some of them hanging by a thread, some with their legs missing.

Because what else would Bubbles wear?

Bubbles had been wearing the sweater the day she'd told Riley to call her Bubbles. Every five minutes she would brush her hand lovingly over one of the ladybug appliques and then sigh as if the sweater was some sort of lifeline.

Bubbles yanked hard on her hair.

Riley looked at herself in the mirror. Her hair looked as if it had been cut by a three-year-old. It was all different lengths and angles. She didn't wince or tighten her lips. Never again would she give the woman the satisfaction of seeing her in pain.

Holding Riley's gaze, Bubbles made the last snip, chopping her bangs so that nothing remained but little stubbles of hair.

The quiet hovered between them. If this were a staring war, Riley would win.

With scissors in hand, Bubbles pointed out the door to the chain heaped on the floor by the bed. "Put the cuff back on your ankle."

Slowly, Riley came to her feet. The bedroom door was still wide open. If she ran, where would she go? The only thing she knew, because she'd seen the neighbor's backyard below, was that she was most likely on the top floor of a two-story house. What if she made a wrong turn, or found the entry door, but it was locked?

Bubbles was strong. The maniac had dragged or carried her dead-weight from the car to the bed. If she dared to attempt to escape without a plan, where would she go?

Her insides churned, her skin tingling.

It was as if the woman's eyes were boring a hole into the back of her neck. This was a test. She felt it in her bones. If she ran, Bubbles would lunge for her, and if she didn't lunge for her that would mean she had all her bases covered: doors triple-locked. Windows secure.

Not today, Riley thought as she walked toward the bed, plunked down on the hardwood floor, and wrapped the metal cuff around her ankle.

Once she finished, Bubbles checked to make sure the cuff was on securely and then helped her into bed. "After I clean the mess you made, I'm going to read you a story, just like old times." She tapped her finger to the end of Riley's nose.

It took everything she had not to bite the tip of Bubbles's finger right off.

# CHAPTER ELEVEN

It was Sunday afternoon when Bug decided to pay QB a visit. The original plan had been to spend the night in the unfinished house, but she had decided to let the man spend some time alone in his new cell. Let him wonder if anyone would ever return to check on him. Besides, he had everything he needed—food, water, and a pot to pee in.

Like all the members of The Crew, she wore a mask and wig at all times. The black mask was made of neoprene and covered her eyes and nose. It was breathable and easy to wear for long periods of time. The wigs they wore were good quality, made with thick black hair and styled in a blunt cut that ended two inches past the chin.

She walked down a set of wide stairs and then stopped in front of the cell where QB had been locked up. She set her duffel bag on the floor. At the moment, he appeared to be asleep, curled up in a ball in the far-right corner. "Good morning," she said happily.

He jerked upright, then jumped to his feet. "Let me out of here!"

"Not so fast. This is a representation of the cell you should have been locked up in long ago," Bug told him.

The "cell" was actually an unfinished wine cellar that the construction crew had used to lock up their equipment at night. It was rectangular in shape with three cement walls, the fourth wall made up of iron bars secured with a chain and a heavy-duty lock.

Hanging on the chain around her neck was the key.

Inside the cell was a case of water bottles, two metal buckets in which he could relieve himself, and plenty of toilet paper. There were also granola bars and a washrag.

Bug stared at QB, real name Myles Davenport. This was the first time since they had brought him here that she'd had a chance to get a good look at him. She'd spent the past ten years living in fear of this man. Always looking over her shoulder. Always ready for the worst. She carried Mace and a handheld alarm that could be engaged just by tossing it to the ground. Not a minute had gone by in all those years that she hadn't thought of him and wondered when he and his friends might return.

Myles Davenport looked less scary behind bars than in her nightmares, where she relived being crushed by the heaviness of his body, his sour breath warm against her face, his grunts and moans loud in her ear.

He wasn't even thirty, and yet his skin tone was uneven. Broken blood vessels and a receding hairline were already an issue. His lifestyle habits, including the extra hundred-plus pounds on his five-foot-ten frame, had not been kind to his face or body. And for this she was glad. It was the little things.

"Who are you?" he asked. "Why are you doing this to me?"

"*This,*" Bug said, arms spread wide as if she were on a game show, revealing what he'd won, "is all *your* doing." Taking a step closer, she said, "Sometimes bad things happen to bad people." Bug knew she wasn't the only woman he'd sexually assaulted. She often wondered how many women he'd harmed since he'd walked out of court a free man.

"Treating women like objects," she told him, "and forcing yourself on them is fucked up. Why do you rape women? Did your daddy abuse you when you were growing up?"

"I've never had sex with a woman who didn't want me."

"That's a lie. At least five women I know of fought and screamed and begged for you to stop. Some were paid off. Others were too afraid to come out of hiding. But you already know all this."

Bug had a degree in computer programming and had graduated with honors, but because of this asshole, she knew as much about the tragedy of rape and the effects on its victims as she did about software applications and coding. It made her sick to know that rape was becoming white noise in a chaotic world. One out of four women would be a victim of assault in their lifetime, and yet rape rarely made headlines.

"You've got the wrong man. Let me go." He rubbed his chest. "I need my heart medication."

"Being overweight causes high blood pressure, which causes strokes. You should—"

"What? You're a fucking doctor? Fuck you!"

His frustration made her smile. "You're not getting out of here until you admit to wrongdoing and apologize to all the women you've ever harmed." She pulled out her cell and readied the video app. Before tapping the button she said, "This can be over in a matter of minutes. All you have to do is say you're sorry and promise never to touch another woman without her permission." This was all part of her plan. Guys like QB didn't like to admit they'd made mistakes, especially to the woman who held the key to his freedom.

He fidgeted, his nostrils flaring. The poor guy was getting upset. *Perfect.* She hit the video button and then pointed a finger at him, letting him know now would be a good time to apologize.

His face reddened and his hands clenched and unclenched around the bars.

"Apologize," she said, keeping his image centered on the screen on her phone.

"Let me the hell out of here!"

"Rape is a disturbing crime," she said, ignoring his pleas. "Some victims of rape end up pregnant. How many of the women you raped had your baby? Do you know?"

The answer was one, but she wasn't sure he knew the answer to the question. And she didn't care if he did.

He picked up a bucket and tossed it her way. The metal clanged against the bars. Urine splashed his face and shirt, then rolled across the cement floor. "Let me the fuck out of here!"

Bug refused to cower. "Some rape victims are horribly injured during an attack," she went on. "Others contract whatever STDs their attacker has. Worse than all that is the emotional trauma that men like you cause their victims. They have nightmares and panic attacks. They no longer trust people and are often riddled with self-doubt. Their lives are forever changed, their innocence taken from them in the most physically devastating way possible."

"You are the dumbest bitch I've ever met. My father will—"

"You're almost thirty," she said, cutting him off midsentence. "Are you still living with Daddy?"

"Fuck you."

"No. Not me. Never."

For the first time since they locked him up, he was silent as he stared at her.

His body tensed. "It's you," he said, his face twisting into a familiar expression. "You're the scrawny little flat-chested cheerleader with the big ass." He brushed his hands over his face in a feeble attempt to clean himself up and went to the back of the cell, where he sat down, elbows resting on the top of his bent knees.

"Jesus. This is your fucking idea of payback?" He laughed. "Black wig and black mask." He shook his head. "You're part of the same group that cut off that guy's dick, aren't you?" He quieted, perhaps momentarily concerned that they might do the same to him. With the crazy amount of press the dickless wonder, Brad Vicente, had received, it didn't surprise her that Myles had heard of their group. And it made no difference to her since she wasn't worried about being identified.

She'd had a lot of time to think about QB and how she would give him a taste of his own medicine.

She also knew he would never walk out of here alive.

But that was her little secret. Until the time came to finish him off, she planned to fuck with the asshole every chance she got. She'd done her homework, and she knew absolutely everything there was to know about Myles Davenport. "Once I decide to let you go," she said almost gleefully, knowing it would never happen, "you'll never talk about what went on here. Not to anyone."

He wagged a finger at her. "That's where you're wrong, honeycakes. You obviously didn't learn a thing about who's in control. Even now I can see right through the false bravado. The fear in your eyes is downright palpable."

She stepped closer to his cage. "I know things about you, Myles." He was playing the game, trying to get the upper hand, but the sweat glistening across his forehead was a telltale sign that he was nervous. "I want you to think about all the things you've ever done wrong. Every. Little. Thing."

He squirmed. "You're out of your mind."

"If I were, I'd let my friends have a go at you. It wouldn't be pretty. You're lucky you got the nice one." She grinned. "I'm just teaching you a lesson so that when you're released, you'll think twice before you do shit you shouldn't be doing."

"You think cutting off my dick is going to stop me from telling the whole fucking world what I know about little Tracy Rutherford?"

She winced, mostly an act on her part, although she didn't like hearing her name on his lips. "I'm not going to cut off your dick. But I am going to keep you locked up until you can prove to me that you understand the difference between right and wrong."

He rubbed his hands together. "I can't wait to have a chat with your parents to tell them what you've been up to."

"My parents had me late in life. Mom passed away, and Dad is in a home. He doesn't remember me, and he certainly wouldn't remember you. But he loves visitors." She grabbed a water bottle from the box nearby, twisted the top, and drank. "It's *your* parents you'll need to watch out for once I send them the letter I wrote."

"They know who you are," he said. "They won't believe anything you tell them. They know how much you enjoyed our time together. They sat in that courtroom along with everyone else, remember?"

"I'll never forget it," she said, which was true. A part of her wanted to see his parents suffer as much as their son for what they and their lawyers had put her through, making her out to be a slut. "The difference is, Myles, that back then, your mother and father believed wholeheartedly in the goodness of their son."

He smiled, but she could tell his heart wasn't in it.

"What kind of person steals from his own family?"

His eyes narrowed.

"I'm surprised your coworkers haven't complained to your father about your excessive absences at work and the change in your lifestyle."

His jaw hardened, but he said nothing.

"I have multiple documents that show the lengths you've gone to, to try and cover up the money you continue to embezzle from your father's company. I don't know why no one else has called you out on it. There are so many signs: decreased collections, past-due invoices, difficulty paying expenses on time. Was it financial strain that caused you to steal from the family company? Or is it just a general sense of entitlement on your part?"

"I don't know what you're talking about."

"The unexplained changes in financial metrics are quite revealing," she said. "Unfortunately for you, I also have receipts showing every purchase you've made since you started working for your dad's company." She lifted a brow. "What do you think he'll say about the oceanfront home you bought in Florida? How about the closet full of expensive suits and Saint Laurent ostrich boots?"

"You're such a dumb bitch. Someone at the company has been feeding you crap. None of it's true."

Bug walked over to her bag and retrieved a couple of papers that she carried to the cell, slid through the bars, and left on the ground. Researching his finances had been something to do in her spare time. It wasn't until she hacked into the family business accounts that she saw red flags pop up after Myles was promoted to an executive position at the age of twenty-five. All she had to do was follow the money. Fake refunds from customers who didn't exist all led straight to Myles. He also paid fictitious employees and ghost suppliers.

Myles tried to play it cool, but curiosity must have gotten the best of him because he pushed himself up from the cement floor and made his way to the papers. He grew pale as he flipped through copies of receipts and signature pages, solid proof that he'd bought much more than clothes, cars, and a beach house.

"I know how much your parents pride themselves on their oldest son's honesty and good morals. For days I listened to them on the stand, talking you up. 'Myles this. Myles that.' Money is everything to people like them . . . and you."

"So you want a piece of the pie, is that right? How much?"

A smile played at the corners of her mouth. "I already told you what I want. Let me know when you're ready to grovel on video."

"I'm sorry," he said flatly. "Can I go now?"

"Nice try. I want a *real* apology." Bug grabbed the camping chair she'd lugged downstairs to this bleak, windowless room, opened it, and took a seat. "We have time," she said as she pulled off her wig and mask and got comfortable.

She rubbed her scalp. *Much better.*

She didn't have high expectations when it came to getting a genuine, heartfelt apology, but she hoped to see him beg for forgiveness, maybe even shed a tear or two. That could happen in three minutes or three days. She would then pump him full of opioids, wait until the sun went down, and drive him to Auburn near Quarry Trail, where the grave she'd dug awaited him. No one, including The Crew members, would ever know what she'd done.

Once Myles was taken care of, she would go home and put on a blonde wig and contacts that made her eyes a lovely shade of emerald. Everything she needed to travel abroad was ready to go. She might go to Brazil or Lyon, France, where it would be easy to get lost in the lively city. Once she was settled in, she would find a way to anonymously send proof of Myles's wrongdoings to his parents and to all those at the company who had power and influence. She would also send a summarized version to their company shareholders. And then for the first time in years, she would sleep deeply and soundly as the waves slapped gently against the sandy shores.

"I said I was sorry," he whined. "What more do you want?"

"I want it all, Myles." *Blood, sweat, and tears,* she thought but didn't say. "When you can tell me in your own words everything you've done wrong and convince me that you feel remorse and regret—that's when we'll be done here."

Complete bullshit, which was the best part. Bug knew the only remorse Myles Davenport would ever feel would be regret that he'd been caught and she was holding him accountable.

She wasn't a therapist. And even if she were, she had no interest in trying to find ways to tap into a conscience he didn't possess. She knew it was silly on her part, but she did, in fact, want a video, genuine or not, of him apologizing.

And then she wanted to bury him and forget he ever existed.

# CHAPTER TWELVE

It was late afternoon when Sawyer checked her cell to see if there were any missed calls or texts from Derek.

Nothing.

After using her iPhone to help research the missing girls, Aria had left to pick up sandwiches at a local deli and would be back in ten to fifteen minutes.

It upset Sawyer that Derek hadn't answered any of the multiple texts she'd sent or returned her call, though she had no right to be angry with him. This was all her fault. But it would be nice if he would at least give her a chance to tell him how she felt. She had been caught completely off guard when he'd told her they were finished. She'd needed time to process.

*To hell with it,* she decided as she hit "Call." She felt an empty numbness in the pit of her stomach as she listened to his voice mail. "Hey," she said after the beep. "It's me. Sawyer." She swallowed the lump that had formed in her throat. "I understand why you don't want to talk to me, but I want—need—to tell you that you're wrong about me, especially the part about my feelings for you. I like you, Derek. I like you a lot." She glanced heavenward before adding, "There were so many times I thought about calling you but didn't because I was worried I would come across as weak and needy, sort of like how I must sound right now. You're the first *normal* guy I've ever dated. Well, I do realize 'normal' is subjective, but what I mean by that is you're the first guy I've ever dated who dresses nicely and has an eight-to-five job. I didn't think I deserved to be with someone like you." She exhaled. "See? This is exactly why I've avoided calling. I sound pathetic. Unlike you, I don't possess a healthy, well-fed ego. My parents were monsters, and now—"

Voice mail cut her off. Call ended.

Sawyer redialed his number and waited for the beep so she could start off where she finished. "Part two," she said with a laugh that came out sounding like a bark. She cringed at the sound of her awkwardness. "Let's see . . . Where was I? Oh, that's right—my parents were monsters. Point being that I felt sort of bad about a guy like you getting mixed up with me. From what you've told me, you have a large family filled with even more normal people. I'm sure there must be a black sheep in there somewhere, but still." She paused, wishing she could erase this entire message and start over. "I guess I just want you to know that you were wrong about me. I *am* into you. I just didn't know how to show it. This isn't the first time I was a day late and a dollar short, but I wanted you to know—"

The call was cut off again. *Damn.* She called back and waited for the beep. "Hi. It's me again. Last message, I promise. I wanted you to know that I think you're special and that I care about you. That's all. If you ever want to talk, I'll be around."

Sawyer sat there for a moment, feeling a little better now that she'd gotten to have her say.

Her phone had vibrated while she was leaving Derek the message. Scrolling to the top of her messages, she saw that Paige Owens had sent her the list of names of missing girls she said she'd been collecting. One name stood out since it wasn't on Sawyer's list: Katy Steiner. Twelve years old when she disappeared three years ago.

Sawyer typed the name into the search engine on her laptop. Two links popped up on her screen. She clicked on the first one, confirming that Katy Steiner had been abducted near the school she attended in North Highlands, twelve miles outside Sacramento.

Sawyer added Katy Steiner's name to her growing list. Not counting Paige Owens, that made five missing girls in the past five years. All within a fifteen-mile radius.

Chills raced down her spine.

Sawyer continued her search for more information, but every article she found gave the basics. She put her laptop to the side and reached for the notebook that Aria had left on the couch.

On the first page in neat handwriting, Aria had written RILEY ADDISON. Beneath Riley's name was a lot of information crammed onto one page. Apparently Riley Addison's father knew the importance of media attention because according to Aria's notes, Riley's abduction was on every media outlet possible.

The more eyes on his daughter's picture, the better, Sawyer figured. Intense early media coverage meant that people would be looking out for Riley.

At the bottom of the page Aria had jotted down her sources, including the *Washington Post*, the *New York Times*, CNN, MSN, and dozens of other outlets.

The page after that read MARK BRENNAN—PIANO TEACHER.

Beneath his name Aria had noted that Riley was last seen outside Mark Brennan's home in Sacramento. She then continued on with information about the music teacher. Mark Brennan was forty-five years old and single. Never married. His parents still lived in North Highlands where Mark was born and raised—

The tiny hairs at her nape lifted.

Mark Brennan grew up in North Highlands?

Sawyer grabbed a pen and made an asterisk next to North Highlands. Then scribbled in the margins:

*Katy Steiner disappeared in North Highlands.*

Sawyer read through the rest of Aria's notes, stopping to use her iPhone to take a picture of Mark Brennan's address in Sacramento.

Aria was turning out to be a big help, and Sawyer was eager to get going. The minute Aria walked through the door, Sawyer jumped up from the couch and said, "Let's hurry and eat. I want to drive across town and see if we can talk to Mark Brennan."

"The piano teacher?"

Sawyer nodded as she grabbed the bag of food from her sister, found the grilled portabella and avocado sandwich on sourdough, and took it to the kitchen where she unwrapped it and took a bite.

"Hungry?" Aria asked.

"Starved."

"Why the hurry to talk to the music teacher?"

Between bites, Sawyer said, "I read your notes. He's from North Highlands. His parents still live there."

"So?"

Sawyer swallowed. "Three years ago, another girl, Katy Steiner, disappeared near the school she was attending in North Highlands." She took another bite, chewed, swallowed, then gulped down some water. "It's a stretch, I know. But it's something. If Mark Brennan is home, and if he doesn't mind talking to us, we need to find a way to mention Katy Steiner's name without being too obvious. See if he has any sort of reaction to her name."

"I did wonder why he wasn't already a suspect."

"I'm sure he is, but police can't make an arrest without reasonable grounds to prove that it is warranted."

"Interesting," Aria said. "Let's do this."

"Aren't you going to eat first?"

"I ate some tasty olives stuffed with sausage while I was waiting. I'll save my sandwich for later." She headed for the door, then turned back around and said, "If he's been abducting young girls, do you think Riley could be locked away in his house somewhere?"

"If he gives piano lessons to students at his home, I highly doubt it. Let's not get ahead of ourselves. We just want to ask him some questions, feel him out, see what he has to say."

"Okay," Aria said. "I'll play it cool."

Sawyer wrapped the other half of her sandwich, grabbed her purse, and followed Aria out the door.

When Mark Brennan opened the door, his friendly smile drew Sawyer's full attention. Five foot ten. Short hair with bangs that slid effortlessly to one side—a Mr. Rogers look-alike.

"What can I do for you gals?" he asked.

Sawyer thought maybe he was kidding. Nobody opened their door to a pair of strangers with a smile that wide and big and asked what they could do for you. "I'm Sawyer Brooks, and this is my intern, Aria. We work for the *Sacramento Independent*."

"Oh, I see." His eyelid twitched. "You want to talk to me about Riley?"

"That's right. We hate to bother you—"

"No bother at all. I hope media coverage will help in the search for Riley. Come in," he said, ushering them into his home before she could finish her spiel.

The inside of his house was semidark. The curtains were pulled shut so that only tiny slices of sunlight managed to squeeze through. The room he brought them to looked like a consignment store with furniture crammed in every available space. It was large enough to accommodate two pianos, an upright and a baby grand, and an eclectic assortment of other furniture.

Every bit of wall space was covered with artwork. Oil paintings, wood art, and framed photography. There were two coffee tables and an endless number of fabric-covered chairs, none of them matching.

Sawyer and Aria took a seat on a wood settee carved with a leaf pattern.

"How about some iced tea and a blueberry scone? They're fresh from the bakery."

"That would be amazing," Aria said before Sawyer could stop her.

After Mark Brennan left the room, Aria squeezed Sawyer's arm. "I just wanted to get him out of the room for a minute. Look at this place. What have you gotten us into? I feel like I'm inside some sort of weird art museum. What if he's dangerous? Nobody knows we're here. He's probably off to find his sharpest knife with a three-inch blade right now."

"Calm down. And lower your voice. We'll be fine."

"That's what all the victims of serial killers think before they're bopped over the head with a shovel."

"Quiet," Sawyer said with a nudge of her elbow. "He's coming back."

Mark Brennan set a silver tray on the rectangular wood table in front of them. On the tray were three glasses of iced tea and a plate piled with blueberry scones.

Sawyer smiled at him. "Thank you."

He took a seat in an upholstered red velvet chair across from them, then leaned forward and helped himself to a tall glass of iced tea. "It's hot out there. I keep the curtains closed in hopes of keeping the house cool."

"Good idea," Sawyer said as she pulled a notebook and pen from her purse. Not wanting to be rude, she reached for a glass of iced tea and ignored the little particles of what she hoped were fresh squeezed lemon as she took a swallow.

"Riley Addison has been taking lessons from me for about a year now," Mark Brennan said without prompting. "She's a smart young girl and a quick learner. I hope they find her soon." His eyes glistened. "Any news about Vicki?"

It took Sawyer a second to recall that Riley's mother's name was Vicki. It made sense that someone as outgoing as Mark Brennan would be on a first-name basis with his students and their guardians. "I went to the hospital," Sawyer told him, "and I heard that Mrs. Addison's condition had gone from critical to fair."

He nodded. "Good to hear. It's all so upsetting. Bad enough to be in such a tragic accident only to learn your daughter is missing." He shivered. "I had flowers sent to her room. I wish there was something more I could do to help." He exhaled. "I've been racking my brain, trying to recall every detail of the day Riley went missing, but overall it was just a regular day."

Sawyer watched him closely. He appeared genuinely upset.

"How often was Riley here at your house?" Aria asked, taking Sawyer by surprise since they hadn't discussed her asking any questions.

"Most of my students come once a week," he said as he set his glass on the tray. "That includes Riley."

Aria got to her feet and gestured from the baby grand to the upright. "Which piano do your students use?"

"Nobody is allowed to touch the upright," he said, concerned, as if he were afraid Aria might touch it. "It's an antique. I use the Steinway for lessons."

Standing by the baby grand, Aria picked up something and held it up for everyone to see. "Looks like someone left behind a sparkly hair clip."

Sawyer inwardly groaned.

"I have a box, 'Lost and Found,' filled with stuff my students have left behind." Again, he looked at Sawyer. "Would you like to take a look?"

"No. That's not necessary." Sawyer kept hoping Aria would look her way so she could give her sister the side-eye and let her know she would take over from here, but Aria was too busy flipping through a music book.

"What's the usual protocol for when a parent is late to pick up one of your students?" Aria asked next.

Mark Brennan didn't appear put off by Aria's random line of questioning. "It's different for everyone," he said. "There are no hard-set rules unless a parent specifies their preference. For instance, Izzy Benson's mom, Sheila, has always insisted that Izzy sit quietly inside until she arrives. A few of my students can drive, so they take off as soon as they finish their lesson."

"Are you married?" Aria asked.

"I'm sorry," Sawyer cut in. "This is my intern's first interview."

Aria screwed up her face. "What did I do wrong?"

Mark Brennan smiled. "No worries. I've never been married. No children either. My partner of many years passed away eighteen months ago. Music and my students are what keep me going."

"I'm sorry for your loss," Sawyer said.

Aria returned to her seat beside Sawyer.

"The healing process never ends," he said. "But I've learned that the pain is a reminder that I was lucky to have found love to begin with."

Goose bumps spread across Sawyer's arms. This man was still in mourning.

"Have you ever heard the name Katy Steiner?" Aria asked.

Sawyer cringed at her sister's timing. Aria's bluntness made her question whether it had been a good idea to bring her along.

"The name doesn't ring a bell," he said without hesitation.

"If you don't mind," Sawyer asked, hoping to change the subject and keep things moving along, "I'd love to know a little bit more about Riley."

Mark Brennan brightened. "I could go on and on."

"Please do," Sawyer said.

"Although Riley is nearly a teenager, something she often reminded me of, she looks much younger. She's petite. Fragile looking. As far as personalities go, she's very independent and motherly."

"How do you mean?" Sawyer asked.

"For example, Riley made it clear that she didn't like me living alone, even suggested I get myself a pet to keep me company. She said picking a dog from the shelter would be a good idea."

"I like her already," Aria said.

Mark Brennan nodded. "She's also given me advice about the way I dress and how I style my hair." He laughed. "She always asks me how I'm doing. She's one of a kind." He pulled a tissue from the box on a side table and dabbed at the corners of his eyes. For the next fifteen minutes, as promised, he went on and on until Sawyer felt as if she knew Riley Addison.

Mark Brennan was still smiling when he said goodbye and shut the door.

As they made their way down the brick steps, Sawyer stopped at the last step and breathed in an enticingly sweet scent of a gardenia shrub lining the front window of Mark Brennan's house.

Aria was two steps ahead of her, already stuffing her nose into a white bloom surrounded by waxy green leaves. "I've never seen such a perfect gardenia," Aria said. "Come here," she ordered, "and get a whiff."

Sawyer had forgotten about Aria's fondness for plants. She walked to her sister's side and breathed in the scent of one of many blooms. "I wonder if a gardenia bush would grow in the small square of dirt outside my kitchen window?"

"Not enough sunlight," Aria said before asking, "so what did you think about Mark Brennan?"

"We'll talk in the car." Sawyer headed that way, slipped behind the wheel, and started the engine. The moment she pulled away from the curb, Aria said, "I don't trust him. He was way too nice."

"I disagree. I think he genuinely cares about Riley."

"It was an act," Aria said matter-of-factly.

Sawyer shook her head. "His voice and breathing were steady the entire time. His stories about Riley were detailed, and he held just the right amount of eye contact while talking."

"Okay," Aria said. "So what now?"

"I want to stop by Carly Butler's house. She disappeared on her way home from school three years ago. The house where she was living at the time isn't far from here."

Aria frowned. "Two young girls disappear practically in Mark Brennan's backyard. I think he's up to no good. He only has thirty minutes with Riley every week, and he knows everything about her. Didn't that strike you as odd?"

Sawyer kept her eyes on the road. "He seemed sad and lonely. His house was cluttered but clean, no sign of anything weird going on, in my opinion."

"There was a clipboard for his students to sign in on a stack of music books. While you and Brennan were talking, I flipped through it and took pictures using my cell."

Sawyer perked up at once. "Did anyone sign in after Riley?"

"No," Aria said. "But the funny thing is, in the weeks and months prior, every once in a while, I saw the name 'Bob Upperman' signed in after Riley."

"But not every week?"

"No."

"Why," Sawyer asked, "would Mark Brennan have harmed the girl when he had no way of knowing that Riley's mom had been in an accident?" Before her sister could answer, Sawyer said, "It seems a bit crazy that nobody saw Riley come or go that day."

Aria put her phone away. "Mark Brennan was the last person to see Riley, the only person who could corroborate that she'd been waiting on the steps for her mother."

Silence hovered between them until Aria added, "If Bob Upperman saw Riley waiting on the steps, then at least we'll know that Mark Brennan was telling the truth."

"Yes," Sawyer agreed.

"But even if he did see Riley," Aria continued, "that wouldn't mean Mark Brennan didn't invite her back into the house after the guy left."

"Either way, we need to find Bob Upperman." Sawyer pulled to the curb at 1511 Juniper and shut off the engine. "We're here."

"I get that Mark Brennan came across as a nice guy," Aria said. "But what do you feel in your gut? Do you think the piano teacher knows what happened to Riley Addison?"

"I have no idea. As a crime reporter, I need to be objective and write what I see and hear and nothing else. No thoughts or opinions, hunches or guesses."

A solemn expression crossed Aria's face. "It's not your job to search for missing persons either, but you want to find Riley Addison, don't you?"

"More than anything," Sawyer admitted. "I want to know what's going on. Five young girls disappear in the span of five years, and nobody's talking about it?"

"That's because some of them disappeared outside Sacramento. And only two of them, one being Riley Addison, got much media attention," Aria said. "One escaped, and one is thought to have run away. I read that two thousand children go missing in the US every single day. One hundred and fifteen a year are stranger abductions. That's a lot of kids to search for."

"It is. That's why our main focus should be on Riley Addison. I can't stop thinking about her. If she's still alive, she's got to be terrified and wondering if anyone is looking for her."

"Thinking about what she might be going through won't help us find her. Come on," Aria said. "Let's see if anyone's home."

"I'll do the talking this time," Sawyer said as she reached for the door handle.

Aria was already outside, but she stuck her head back in the passenger side of the car. "Are you kidding me? I'm good at this shit."

"You're too blunt. If we get invited into the house, no cursing and no drilling anyone with questions."

"Sure," Aria said. "Whatever. Your loss."

It turned out to be both their losses when the person who answered the door told them the Butler family had moved away six months ago.

As they returned to the car, Sawyer again found herself questioning if it had been a good idea enlisting Aria's help. But the answer came quickly. It was a resounding yes. Aria could be blunt, bordering on unprofessional, but she was inquisitive and unafraid to ask questions, and besides, Sawyer needed all the help she could get.

# Chapter Thirteen

Bubbles was standing at the island in the center of the kitchen, preparing lunches for the week—chicken, rice, and vegetables—when the anchorman on a local station stated that an update on the Riley Addison case was coming up next.

All it had taken was a quick search through the girl's backpack for her to know Riley's name and home address. Even so, she'd been tracking media coverage on the girl since day one. Vicki Addison's car accident had made everything worse since it quickly became a sensational story. The media was all over it. Headlines read Mom Fights for Her Life While Police Search for Her Missing Daughter.

*Give me a break.* Vicki Addison was recovering nicely. She had a loving husband and son to go home to. They would be fine.

Leaving the plastic containers on the counter, she wiped her hands on her flowery apron as she walked into the family room and sat down on the plastic-covered couch.

She sat quietly through three commercials before the news anchor came back on the screen.

"Police are still searching for twelve-year-old Riley Addison, who is considered at risk because of her young age. She was last seen on the steps outside a home in West Sacramento, where she took piano lessons. No suspects have been named. Her mother, Vicki Addison, is at Sutter General Hospital after a car accident prevented her from picking up her daughter from her music lesson on time. She is in fair condition and could be released tomorrow. In other news, bones found near the lake at William Land Regional Park have been identified, but the name will not be released to the public until relatives have been notified."

Stunned by what the man said, Bubbles grabbed the remote and turned down the volume. Her head was spinning like the teacup ride at Disneyland—swinging to the left and then jolting to the right.

Bones were found?

How had she missed it? She read the news every day, took pride in being one of the few who still paid for the paper to be delivered to her doorstep.

Her heart thumped against her ribs.

She never thought they would find the girl. It was so long ago . . . How long . . . ? Four years? Five? How had they identified her?

*No. No. No.* This couldn't be happening.

Had she wrapped the girl with a plastic tarp or a blanket? She prayed it wasn't a blanket. What if they found a hair or something, and her DNA gave her away? She'd read about forensic genealogy. Her DNA wasn't in the system, but if her DNA matched with some long-lost relative on one of those popular genealogy sites, she would be screwed.

She shook her head, her thoughts returning to little Cora, Molly's first replacement. Such a sweet girl. Too bad Cora'd had no backbone. The girl wouldn't stop crying for her mother.

Bubbles had done everything possible to make Cora happy. But she just couldn't pull herself together. What a waste. If only the kid could have learned to shut her trap and turn off the waterworks. Luckily, it had all ended quickly. An accident, really. All it took was one little nudge, and the poor girl lost her balance and fell down the stairs.

A shock is what it was.

Seeing that beautiful child with her body twisted like a pretzel, her eyes wide open, staring right at her . . . That was an image she'd never forget.

She remembered scooping little Cora off the floor. For the next twenty-four hours, she'd held the small girl close to her chest and rocked her while she sang lullabies. But reality set in, along with a foul smell, forcing Bubbles to come up with a plan. She'd recently read about new trees being planted at Land Park. It was her favorite place to visit on a nice summer day. And most important, she knew Cora would love it there.

And so the next day she bought a shovel and a Japanese maple that was two feet tall, waited until well after midnight, and drove to the park. The dirt turned out to be soft, but digging a hole deep enough to fit Cora took longer than she'd thought it would. After the hole was ready to go, she'd rolled the suitcase from her car and said a prayer before plopping the little bundle right in.

It rained off and on for weeks after that, which worked in her favor since it made for few, if any, visitors. Every month for a year she visited the burial site. Once she felt confident the tree had taken root, the trips to the park stopped. All in all, the experience had been much too risky. If there was ever another accident, she'd decided she would have to find a better way to dispose of the body.

And that's exactly what she'd done.

The bones could be a game changer. In a bad way. A very bad way. Reopening an old missing person's case was never a good thing for someone like her. Investigators had identified Cora. What else did they know?

She thought of Paige Owens. The one who got away. *Lucky little duck,* she thought. After Paige ran off, Bubbles had been unable to let it go. She'd wanted the girl. She'd known she should lie low for a few months, but she hadn't been able to stay away. She'd spent hours before and after work watching the girl. But Mrs. Owens was always hovering, never leaving her daughter's side. Mrs. Owens was a weak, pathetic woman. Always glancing over her shoulder with short, jerky movements. Looking at her, you'd think she was the one who was nearly abducted instead of her daughter.

Bubbles began leaving the woman subtle messages. Instead of scribbling CLEAN ME on her dirty car, she'd written I SEE YOU and then DON'T SAY A WORD. And then she killed the stupid woman's cat. Mrs. Owens fell apart. She stopped brushing her hair, and her clothes were always rumpled. Dark circles appeared under her eyes. She was a wreck, divorced within the year.

But Paige wasn't like her mother. Paige was a force to be reckoned with. She was sixteen now. Bubbles hadn't known the girl had her license until she did her weekly drive-by and saw Paige hop in her mother's car and take off. Curious, Bubbles followed her all the way to Starbucks. She parked and watched Paige walk right into the coffee shop and take a seat across from a woman who looked familiar. A blink of an eye later, she recognized the woman as Sawyer Brooks. The youngest of three abused and neglected sisters. Both parents dead now.

Bubbles had followed the Sawyer Brooks story closely. The rookie investigative reporter had lucked out and not only solved the deaths of at least three girls in River Rock but also played an integral part in figuring out another murder right here in Sacramento. She was batting one hundred.

And that was a problem.

From everything she'd read about Sawyer Brooks, the young woman was slightly unstable and hanging on by a thread. Sometimes people needed a little push in the right direction to get them in line.

But, Bubbles quickly decided, first she needed to concentrate on what to do about the bones.

Ignoring the throbbing pain near her temple, she mulled it over. Something big and bold needed to occur. An event or a discovery that would redirect everyone's focus to someone other than Cora.

But what? Or who?

It came to her in a flash, like a bolt of lightning shot down by Zeus in a moment of anger.

On her feet, her insides thrumming, she began to pace. Blood. She needed blood—Molly's blood.

And she had everything she needed right here in her home.

It only took her a few minutes to gather a latex band to use as a tourniquet, a syringe, and a Band-Aid.

Standing quietly at the door to Molly's bedroom upstairs, Bubbles could see her daughter's chest rise and fall, her breathing shallow. A warm, velvety twinge swept through her, giving her a taste of the thing she craved most . . . love.

Molly just needed a little more time to adjust before Bubbles would be able to switch the metal cuff out for the collar. In the event Molly stepped out of bounds, the electrical signal ranged from a mild tickle to a painful shock. The modern collars were thinner and lighter, and the electrical shock was more of a stinging vibration. Once the collar was activated, Molly would be free to move about the house whenever Bubbles was home. If Molly tried to slip through a window or door, the shock treatment would keep her inside.

Molly was such a lovely girl. She looked ten and yet acted twenty. Stubborn at times, but also curious and highly intelligent. She had already zipped through her school assignments and had read *Animal Farm* and *To Kill a Mockingbird*, books meant for a more mature reader.

The floor creaked beneath her feet as she walked to Molly's side and set the items in her hand on the bedside table.

Molly stirred, but her eyes remained closed.

Bubbles crouched down on all fours and slid one of the chains out from beneath the bed. The chain rattled as she stood, pulling the chain along with her so that she could clamp a cuff around Molly's right wrist.

Molly snapped to attention. "What are you doing?" She used her other hand to try to free herself.

"Calm down. This will only take a minute." It was a bit of a struggle to get the cuff around the other wrist, but once that was done, the rest happened fairly quickly. Lights on, she wrapped the rubber tourniquet about four inches above Molly's vein, inserted the needle at a fifteen-degree angle, and cautioned Molly to hold still while the collection tube filled with blood.

"There," she said when the worst of it was done and she was covering the area with a Band-Aid. "All done." She put all her goodies away. "That wasn't too bad, was it?"

Trembling, Molly shook her head.

"You're a good girl, Molly. The two of us are a team." She couldn't stop smiling. "Everything I've been through happened for a reason. It all led to you and me being together . . . forever."

# Chapter Fourteen

Later that day, Sawyer and Aria returned to her apartment. Her cat, Raccoon, was curled up on the rug beneath the table shoved in the corner of the room. The cat spared Sawyer a glance and then yawned and went back to napping.

Sawyer grabbed her laptop and took a seat on the couch.

"What are you working on first?" Aria asked.

"I promised Palmer an update on the vigilante group that went after Brad Vicente. The media has dubbed the group the Black Wigs. I need to finish this write-up before I continue investigating the missing girl case."

Aria made her way into the kitchen and put a kettle of water on the stove. "I've been seeing Brad Vicente's name everywhere. Even from prison, he seems to be doing a good job of getting people to side with him. Not only was his story trending on social media last week," Aria said, "it was also on the front page of Reddit, which is a big deal."

Sawyer shook her head. "What are people saying?"

"That Brad Vicente is a victim of the #MeToo movement."

"You're kidding me?"

"Nope. Sad but true. Fifty percent of people questioned believe that the videos of Brad assaulting women in his bedroom are fake. They're jumping on the bandwagon and signing his petition for an appeal."

"If I had to pick a side," Sawyer said, "it wouldn't be Brad Vicente's, but as far as this story goes I need to remain unbiased."

Aria unwrapped her sandwich and took a bite.

"Come look at this," Sawyer said.

Aria walked that way. "What is it?"

"Apparently the Black Wigs are back in the news. Just last night a twenty-nine-year-old man, Myles Davenport, was at his ten-year reunion when, according to his friends, he received a text from a pal who said he had a surprise awaiting outside. When he didn't return, his friends went to investigate. As they approached a van, the vehicle took off, hitting one of them in the process. Witnesses are saying that the driver was wearing a wig. Somebody posted video footage taken from a cell phone on YouTube."

Together they watched the video.

Sawyer squinted, trying to make sense of what she was seeing. It was dark, but she could hear the screech of tires and see shadows as a van jerked to a stop, reversed, hit a person, and took off, clipping another vehicle on its way out of the parking lot.

"It's hard to see the driver," Sawyer said as she hit "Replay."

Aria frowned. "It's way too soon for anyone to assume that the same women who cut off Brad Vicente's dick are involved."

The kettle whistled, sending Aria rushing back to the kitchen.

Sawyer typed the name "Myles Davenport" into her laptop's search engine. "This is interesting. It looks like Myles was eighteen when he was accused of rape. There was a trial. Three women testified against him."

"Are you going to include Myles Davenport in your write-up?"

"I think so. Maybe I'll write two versions just in case Palmer isn't comfortable including Myles Davenport, since it will be a few days, I'm sure, before authorities have gathered evidence."

"After I eat, I'll do some more research on Carly Butler and see if we can figure out where her family moved to."

"I appreciate you helping me out," Sawyer said. She then pointed to her backpack. "There's a map of the Sacramento metropolitan area if you want to mark the regions where girls have disappeared. I already put an *X* for Cora."

"Okay. I'll do that."

By the time midnight rolled around, the couch, coffee table, and living room floor were covered with paper. The map took up most of the floor space. Aria had marked it with red dots representing all six girls they were concentrating on, which included Paige Owens.

"There's not really any connection between these girls," Sawyer said, "other than they're all white and most of them have light-colored hair."

"They all fall between the ages of ten and twelve," Aria said. "And if we add Mark Brennan into the equation, we can link Katy Steiner, Riley Addison, and Carly Butler into one group based on location. Riley disappeared after her lesson. Katy Steiner disappeared in North Highlands where his parents still live, and Carly Butler disappeared when her family was living just a few blocks away."

"Wait a minute," Sawyer said. "There is something else that connects almost all the girls."

Aria lifted a questioning brow.

"Bus stops and schools. Cora, Paige, Danielle, Carly, and Katy all disappeared at the bus stop or walking to or from school, right?"

"Everyone except Riley Addison," Aria said.

"Five out of six. We need a focus point, so I'd like to begin by concentrating on bus routes and the schools these girls attended."

"Including Riley Addison?" Aria asked.

"Definitely."

"I'll take schools," Aria said, "and you focus on bus routes."

"Okay."

"If it's okay with you," Aria said, "I'm going to stop by the Butler home tomorrow."

"Where did they move to?"

"West Sacramento. Only a few miles from the house they lived in when Carly disappeared."

"Sounds good. Let me know how it goes." Sawyer lifted a finger. "By the way, I couldn't find any information for Bob Upperman. What about you?"

"Nothing yet. I'll keep looking tomorrow. I'm exhausted." She reached for her backpack and slid the strap over her shoulder. "I'm beginning to understand why so many cases go unsolved."

"Why is that?"

"Are you kidding me? This is literally like trying to find a needle in a haystack. These girls, any one of them, could be absolutely anywhere." She raised her arm high above her head. "Riley could be in the apartment upstairs for all we know."

"Go get some sleep," Sawyer said, unwilling to lose hope when they were just getting started. "We'll get a fresh start in the morning."

# Chapter Fifteen

The chilly night air caught Bubbles by surprise since the arid heat had burned her lungs when she stepped outside to take out the garbage earlier today.

The black sweatshirt she had on was zipped up tight. She'd left her car a block away, parked on the other side of a field covered with tall, dry grass. The hardened tips of foxtails had attached to her socks and shoes and were already digging in, scraping against her skin.

The house was up ahead. Its occupant was fond of posting pictures of his daily life on Facebook and Instagram, making it easy for her to see what kind of car he drove, what he did for a living, who he hung out with, his past and current relationships. She'd used social media in the past to learn about young girls she was interested in getting to know. She recognized the brick stairs leading to the front entrance of the house from a picture he'd posted recently. Beneath the moonlight, the white blooms framing the front window drew her like a moth to fire.

Her gloved hands were stuffed into her pockets along with the tube of Molly's blood. Flicking off the rubber lid, she took a breath and then made a beeline for the gray Kia Optima LX, making quick work of smearing blood beneath the latch that opened the trunk.

Heart racing, she daubed more than a drop's worth on the driver's door handle and then wiped a bloody gloved finger across the back door.

Working fast, her eyes now fully adjusted to the dark, she dripped blood on the edge of the brick stairs where it wouldn't be too obvious since the police would know the blood hadn't been there before when they paid him a visit. But she wasn't overly worried; the police force and every detective in the area was overworked and underpaid. Most didn't have time for minute details.

Finally, she shook what was left inside the tube at the gardenia bush, brushing her gloved hand across the flowers as she made her way back to the sidewalk.

*Done. Easy peasy.*

A dog barked in the distance. Head held high, she walked along at an even pace. It was late and it was dark, and people had enough problems without resorting to staring out their windows. On the off chance someone suffering from insomnia did see her pass by, she would appear to be a mere shadow beneath a velvety black sky.

# Chapter Sixteen

Harper mindlessly scrolled through news headlines on her iPhone. It was all depressing. She'd been sitting inside the unfinished house within the abandoned construction site for hours. QB was locked up in the wine cellar below.

Being inside an unfamiliar house was uncomfortable enough—mentally more than physically—without having a stranger held captive below.

Every creak set her on edge.

She jumped when her phone buzzed. A text from Aria: The package has been delivered.

The corners of her mouth lifted. The package she referred to was Ella.

For someone who had been through so much, Aria came across as a well-adjusted human being. She was loving and caring, and oftentimes, Harper found herself treating Aria like one of her children. She'd been protecting and caring for Aria for so long it made sense she felt that way.

Harper loved Sawyer too, but Sawyer could be difficult. Smiling didn't come naturally, and, of course, there was the no-touching rule. Even after everything that had happened between them, Sawyer still held a grudge against Harper for not being able to save her. Harper had only just turned eighteen when she'd run away from home, taking Aria with her. Why couldn't Sawyer understand that she'd tried to take them both? She'd carried Sawyer to the car, and when Sawyer cried out and ran back to the house, she'd left Harper with no choice but to drive away without her.

She'd done her best, Harper told herself. But that was just another lie to make herself feel better, wasn't it? She could have done better. She could have returned to River Rock at some point and tried to talk to her little sister, but she'd been in survival mode, and the idea of going back to a place where so many bad things had happened had been out of the question.

The self-hate that lived within expanded. Most days she saw her self-hatred as another person who constantly looked over her shoulder, criticizing and pointing out flaws. Her inner critic could be exhausting and isolating. Instead of practicing forgiveness, though, she'd doubled down on dishonesty. Her husband, kids, and both sisters thought she was enrolled in school at California State University, Sacramento. The lies were stacking up, growing bigger and scarier, taking their toll, wearing her out emotionally.

A clanking sounded from below, reminding her that she wasn't alone.

Cleo was supposed to have been here with her today, but nobody had seen or heard from Cleo since their email conversation before the reunion.

Cleo was married and had two children. Maybe she had grown disenchanted by The Crew's desire for revenge. If Harper had made a guess when they'd first gotten together who might go AWOL, Cleo would have been her last choice. Cleo was fierce. All five foot five inches of her. Every time The Crew went after someone, Cleo was the first to volunteer to be used as bait. Nobody wanted to make these men pay for what they did more than Cleo.

Maybe she cared too much.

Maybe she'd hit a wall and decided she'd had enough.

Another loud bang brought Harper to her feet. Robotically she put on her wig and mask and then grabbed a sandwich from the cooler she'd brought and made her way downstairs.

Earlier, when she'd first arrived at the house and had gone downstairs to check on QB, the man had begged and pleaded for his release as she slid a McDonald's bag through the bars. When his cries for help didn't work, he'd switched tactics, yelling and screaming every obscenity in the book, calling her names she'd never heard before in her life, which was saying a lot.

The second her foot hit the landing, he caught sight of her. "Please," he said. "Your friend is wrong about me. She's got me all mixed up with someone else. I would never harm a flea."

"You're wasting your breath."

"Seriously. I can prove it."

She wasn't falling for his act. She thought about all the times her father had begged for her forgiveness only to physically assault her that same night. Visions of her father coming into her room still replayed in her mind. Sometimes her father's face would be distorted, which she preferred. She wondered if the images would ever go away.

Years ago Harper had met a woman in group therapy. She was seventy-five years old, had been in therapy most of her life, and was still trying to find a way to deal with the trauma her parents had caused. Almost everything reminded the woman of what her parents had done to her. The flick of a light being turned off was a major trigger. Barking dogs, loud footfalls, rustling paper, and water faucets being turned on were also triggers. Every little thing upset her because it reminded her of the suffering she'd endured. She would visibly begin to shake and shiver. The woman knew she would never forget what had happened to her, but she was desperate to find a way to forgive them in hopes she could then move forward and find peace.

*What a load of shit.*

Harper wanted peace, but not forgiveness. She didn't need to forgive, she just needed to forget. Her parents' deaths were a good start. Harper bent low and slid the sandwich between the bars.

"Bitch! I'm talking to you!"

QB's voice yanked her from the tangle of thoughts that had invaded her mind. But it was too late. She'd hardly straightened before his arm shot through the metal poles and hooked around her neck. Her head hit the bars. The pain was excruciating. She screamed, but no sound came out of her mouth.

She sucked air in through her nose and then the room fell silent.

No choking or coughing.

Nothing escaped her lips as her airway was cut off.

She grabbed his arm, dug her fingernails into his skin, but he had a good, strong hold. It was no use.

She was going to die. She would never find peace.

"What the fuck!"

Harper's body went slack as she imagined hearing another voice.

The bars rattled, and that's when she realized somebody was here. Through half-lidded eyes she saw Cleo. Her long black hair and the black mask covering the upper half of her face contrasted with the sharp white teeth that chomped into QB's arm, eliciting a painful cry. His arm loosened around Harper's throat, long enough to let air into her lungs.

*Thank God.*

Too weak to free herself from his grasp, Harper reached her arm up and over her shoulder through the bars and blindly clawed at his face, digging her fingers into his eyes. Another piercing cry emerged as he turned his head from left to right in an attempt to disengage her fingers.

Her lungs were on fire, but she could breathe.

Adrenaline soared as she burrowed her fingers deeper until finally he pushed her away so that he could free his arm of the teeth ripping into his skin and muscle.

Harper staggered away from the cell and dropped to the floor, gulping in air.

The cries coming from QB were deafening now. Cleo had ripped a chunk out of his arm. Blood dripped down her face and chin. She spit out a piece of him.

Bloodied and in pain, QB shouted incoherently.

Cleo came to where Harper had fallen and held out an arm to help her to her feet and up the stairs, where Cleo sat her down in the folding chair, removed her mask, and made her drink some water.

Harper's throat was on fire. If Cleo hadn't shown up, she would have died. She was sure of it. "You saved my life," Harper said, her voice hoarse.

Cleo used paper towels and water from a five-gallon jug to clean her own face. "We should kill the asshole and be done with him. What's the point of keeping him here, other than putting ourselves in jeopardy of being caught?"

Harper held the cool water bottle to her throat. There was something different about Cleo since she'd seen her last. She looked as if she hadn't slept in a week. "What's going on, Cleo?"

"Are you fucking kidding me?" Cleo's dark eyes narrowed. "I just bit a chunk out of that idiot's arm, and you're asking me what's going on?"

"Yeah, I am," Harper said, undeterred. "When The Crew was first formed, you were game for anything. As long as we went after the people who had destroyed our lives, you were the one who suggested we should each be in charge of how these predators would be dealt with. But you clearly don't agree with how Bug is handling all of this. You didn't show up on Saturday night, but you're here now. So what's your problem?"

"It's true. I was excited at first. The idea of finally taking action got me fired up." Cleo gulped down half a bottle of water, then looked toward the ceiling. "That feels like a lifetime ago."

It did feel that way, but Harper said nothing, in hopes that Cleo would go on.

"I'm angry," Cleo finally said. "Taking care of Brad Vicente was invigorating. Knowing what he'd done to Lily and having full control of what would happen to him felt right. And then came Otto Radley, a beast of a man who hadn't been out of jail for twenty-four hours before going on a hunt." She took a breath. "I thought burying him ten feet under would change everything. We were doing what we set out to do. One man is dickless, Otto Radley and your parents are dead, and yet I don't feel any different than I did before I joined The Crew." She met Harper's gaze. "Now that your parents are dead and buried, do you feel better? Did anything change for you?"

"I'm relieved that they're gone. But lately, more than anything else, I mostly feel numb."

Cleo unfolded another camping chair and took a seat across from Harper, their knees only inches apart as she leaned forward and said, "I thought things would change. But it's only gotten worse. I can't sleep. I can hardly eat. I don't see one face in my dreams, but six. Six fucking frat boys. Not one of them cared that I was tied to a bed. They just climbed up and fucked the shit out of me."

Cleo's eyes glistened. "They were young and foolish," Cleo said, every word dripping with sarcasm. "That's what my best friend told me recently. 'Let it go!' she said. Sadly, she's not the first person to give me that advice, and she won't be the last, but every single time someone tells me to *let it go*, I want to strangle them."

Harper recalled her husband saying something along those lines. He'd regretted saying anything, of course, after she proceeded to lay it all out for him and tell him every detail of what had happened to her: the sound of her father's footsteps in the hallway. Her rising body heat and the sick feeling in the pit of her stomach when he entered her room, the heaviness of his body, his hands, his fingers, his dirty mouth on her bare skin. When Harper had finished, her husband was crying for her and never suggested she let it go again.

Cleo wiped her eyes. "A day doesn't go by that I don't feel an intense hatred. And do you know who I hate more than anyone?"

Harper shook her head, but she did know the answer.

"*Me.* I hate myself more than I hate those boys who patiently waited their turn to stick their dicks inside me. Boys I can still smell. That's fucked up. And now," she continued, "drumroll, please. My husband, the only man I've ever loved, is talking divorce."

"I'm sorry," Harper said.

"Yeah. You and me both. We've been married eight years. We have two great kids, but he says he's not sure how much longer he can live with my anger and sadness."

Harper thought of Nate. She couldn't remember the last time the two of them had gone on a date, let alone sat down and talked about life. She'd been so wrapped up in getting revenge that she never stopped to think about her husband. Nate had saved her after she'd started drinking and doing drugs to make the pain go away. If not for him, she never would have experienced the unconditional love she had for her family. Two beautiful children. Why hadn't that been enough? Would she ever get her life straightened out, or was this as good as it got?

Cleo anchored strands of hair behind her ear.

Not only was she beautiful, Harper thought, Cleo was a good person. And yet, like Harper, she obviously didn't feel whole and couldn't find her way to any kind of normalcy.

"How do you do it?" Cleo asked. "How do you go on, day after day, after everything that's happened to you?"

Harper thought for a moment before she said, "I clean."

Cleo gave her the side-eye. "What?"

"I scrub dishes and sinks and cupboards until they shine. I spend hours every day on the bathrooms alone. Every morning before the sun comes out, I get down on my hands and knees and dust my bedroom floor." She'd never talked to anyone about her obsession with cleaning.

"What does your family think about that?"

"That's a very good question." For the first time ever, Harper tried to imagine what she must look like to Nate and the kids. "They probably think I'm crazy."

Neither of them laughed.

"All that scrubbing and elbow grease, for what?" Cleo questioned.

Harper said nothing because she didn't have a good answer. And it was probably time for her to stop.

"I don't know what I'd do without my family," Cleo said. "But I also know I have to see this thing through. Those rapists are adults now, and I bet you they don't give what happened to me a second thought. Do any of them regret what they did? Does one fucking frat boy relive that time and wish he'd put a stop to it?" She exhaled. "I feel as if I've spent my entire life frozen in time. I just pray I'll find a way to move on when this is over." Cleo rubbed her hands over her face. "What about you? Are you going to spend the rest of your life fighting the fight, one douchebag at a time and all that?"

"When we first got together, if you had asked this same question, I would have told you that I'll never stop going after men like QB and Otto Radley and Brad Vicente." She rubbed her stomach, thinking about the life growing inside her. Her family deserved better. "But after we take care of your frat boys, I think it might be time for me to put it all behind me and concentrate on my family."

# CHAPTER SEVENTEEN

Within an hour of arriving at work on Monday morning, Sawyer was called into Palmer's office. He wanted to see her about the write-up she'd emailed him last night on the Black Wigs.

"Shut the door," Palmer said after she stepped into his office, carrying a couple of files.

She did as he asked, then took her usual seat in front of his desk.

"I read what you emailed me last night, and I noticed you included the recent abduction of Myles Davenport."

"Yes," she said. "I've watched the video clip of the van pulling out of the school parking lot. It does look to me as if the driver is wearing a wig, but I couldn't make out a license plate, and the video is grainy. So I thought you might prefer to leave out the Myles Davenport story until we have more information."

"Which is why you sent over two versions," he stated.

"Correct." She wondered if he was going to lecture her for including information about Myles Davenport's rape trial ten years ago. "I found it interesting that both men have been accused of sexual assault. I didn't name any of Davenport's accusers since they were minors at the time." She cleared her throat. "I did my best to keep an unbiased view."

Palmer nodded but said nothing.

"Originally, I was planning to focus on Brad Vicente, but everything about that man has been told dozens of times, so I decided to concentrate on public opinion instead."

"I see."

"It's been a month since the Brad Vicente incident, and yet social media is still talking about it," Sawyer went on. "Commenters are split down the middle; half are saying the women being assaulted in the videos obviously enjoy rough sex, and the other half are calling for Brad Vicente to be locked up for life."

Sawyer kept her gaze on Palmer. It was difficult to tell whether he was happy with what she'd written or not. The suspense was killing her.

And then he reached across his desk and handed her a USB drive.

"What is this?"

"There might be more to this Black Wigs story than we think," Palmer said. "A source of mine got ahold of security video from outside an apartment building in West Sacramento. The camera faces the park. It looks to me like the Black Wigs have been busy making the rounds."

Sawyer held up the USB. "More footage of Brad Vicente in action?"

Palmer shook his head. "According to my source, the person in the video could be Otto Radley, a man who spent twenty years behind bars for kidnapping and holding a young woman captive for three years."

"Why do they let guys like that out of jail?"

"Beats me. Although it was nighttime when the video was taken and difficult to see, I thought maybe you could find someone to lighten it up."

"What docs this have to do with the vigilante group?" she asked.

"The man in the video appears to be approaching a woman wearing a black wig. If the man is in fact Otto Radley, you might be interested to know that he hasn't been seen since his release from prison."

"So Otto Radley could be getting a taste of his own medicine."

"He could be dead for all we know."

"Why didn't your source take this to Channel 10 News or another local station?"

"He owed me a favor. If you can make sense of what's on the video, we might have a story worth telling."

"I'll do my best." If both videos had indeed captured the Black Wigs in action, that would mean the ladies were keeping busy, Sawyer thought. This story could end up being exactly the sort of break she'd been looking for professionally.

"There's more," Palmer said.

She waited.

"The lab reports have come in. Postmortem data reveal the bones belong to a missing ten-year-old female. Relatives were unable to identify the clothes found at the grave site, but an old-but-healed fracture of her left arm and dental information were a positive match."

Sawyer's insides thrummed. "Name?"

"Cora O'Neal."

"Cause of death?"

"Broken neck."

Goose bumps prickled her skin. "She's on my list of girls who went missing." Sawyer opened one of the files she'd brought with her, pulled out the map that she and Aria had marked up last night, and placed it on his desk in front of him. "Each red *X* reflects the area where a child went missing," she told Palmer. "Although the girls weren't all taken in Sacramento, they all disappeared within a fifteen-mile radius of here."

He looked the map over.

"I talked to Paige Owens, the one who got away," Sawyer went on. "She's sixteen now. She suffers from repressed memories, but guess what?"

Palmer frowned, making it clear he didn't like guessing games.

"Every once in a while, repressed memories that have been blocked are triggered when another girl goes missing. In this case it was the disappearance of Riley Addison that sparked a new memory—an image of the woman's face. From the very beginning—it's all in the police reports—Paige stated that it was a woman who tried to stick a needle in her arm."

Palmer tapped his fingers against the edge of his desk.

"If we could have a composite drawing done," Sawyer went on, "we could put the woman's image on the front page, maybe plaster it all over social media and hope someone recognizes the woman."

"Even if everything Paige Owens told you was the absolute truth, what makes you think the woman who failed to kidnap her is responsible for every missing female on your list?"

"I do not believe that one woman is responsible for all these missing girls. But I do think publishing her image will get attention and hopefully put our readers on alert and maybe bring forth new witnesses concerning old cases and new ones."

Palmer stroked his beard. "White females. All between the ages of ten and twelve. What else have you got to link them together?"

"Bus routes and schools," she said. "Every girl except Riley Addison was walking to or from school. Many of them rode a bus."

His phone rang. He held up a hand to stop Sawyer from saying anything more and picked up the call. "Geezer," he said. "What have you got?"

Geezer wasn't only a photographer for the *Sacramento Independent*. He often worked alongside Palmer since he had a nose for finding interesting tidbits to report and was good at gathering information. Geezer spent most days making the rounds, talking to people, and keeping Palmer apprised of anything new.

Palmer's expression hardened as he listened. "Stay where you are. I'll be there shortly."

Once the call ended, Palmer glanced at Sawyer. "Mark Brennan was arrested."

The news did not compute. "What for?"

"For the murder of Riley Addison. They found blood on his car and near the steps to the house."

*No way,* she thought. "Mind if I tag along?"

He handed her the map she'd given him to look at. She slipped it into the file.

"I've got to make a quick call," he said. "Meet me in the parking lot in five minutes."

Sawyer grabbed her files and headed back to her cubicle. On her way she spotted Derek's assistant, Marilyn, and rushed that way. "Hi, Marilyn. Is Derek in his office?"

Her smile was friendly. "He took a week off. If it's something urgent, I can pass the information to him when he calls in."

"That's not necessary, but thank you."

They parted ways. Sawyer couldn't help but wonder what Derek was doing. He rarely took time off. Thinking about him made her stomach all jittery.

She had called and texted. What else could she do?

She left her files next to her computer inside her cubicle, grabbed her backpack, and headed toward the exit. The moment she stepped outside her thoughts returned to Mark Brennan's arrest.

Her stomach turned.

Had Aria been right about him?

# CHAPTER EIGHTEEN

The minute she heard Bubbles's car pull out of the garage, Riley climbed off the mattress, lay faceup on the floor, and slipped under the bed. She poked two fingers into the hole at the bottom of the mattress and began where she'd left off, twisting and turning one of the coils.

As she worked, she thought of Mom and Dad and her brother. She missed them. Every night she prayed, making promises to God that she would never yell at her brother again. She would help Mom with laundry and put away the dishes without complaint and walk the dog with Dad after dinner.

She wondered if anyone was looking for her. She'd wanted to see if there was anything on the news, but Bubbles refused to let her watch television. Over the weekend she'd heard faint voices coming from the television downstairs, but she'd been unable to figure out what they were saying.

As she made circles with the wire, around and around, she pulled hard, hoping the coil would break free. It had to work. If she didn't find a way out of this place soon, she'd already decided she would make a run for it the next time Bubbles gave her a bath.

Her fingers were already sore. She could feel little indentations from holding the wire tight as she pulled and twisted.

She was about to take a break when the coil suddenly snapped. She let out a whoop of joy, pushed her way out from under the bed, and sat up. She held the coil in front of her face and examined her new tool. It was strong enough that it wouldn't break. There was even a tiny hook at the end where the wire had come loose.

Still sitting on the ground, she tucked the foot with the metal cuff closer so that she could try to unlock it. As she poked and prodded, she felt bits of lead inside from when the tip of the pencil broke.

But nothing was happening. For at least thirty minutes she tried to get the metal cuff free, but it was no use. Frustrated, she pounded a fist against the hardwood floor and groaned.

What now?

She pushed herself to her feet and walked to the cooler. Bubbles had left water and plastic bottles of Tropicana orange juice with screw-top lids inside. The orange juice tasted good. There were also grapes inside and a bag of pretzels.

As she munched on a pretzel stick, her attention went to the closet door. She picked up the piece of wire and dragged the chain attached to her ankle across the room. Very carefully she stuck the hooked end of the wire into the hole in the lock and listened carefully, as she had seen her dad do when he'd accidentally locked them out of the house.

Surprised when she heard a click, she turned the knob.

The door was open—only an inch—and yet she merely stood there. What was inside? She wasn't sure she wanted to know. What does a mentally unstable person like Bubbles keep locked inside a closet?

She was about to find out.

Eyes closed tight, she sucked in a breath of air and opened the door. She counted to three and opened her eyes. It was a small walk-in closet, too dark to see anything. She brushed a hand against the inside wall and flicked on a light switch. The light was bright, and it took her brain a minute to figure out what she was seeing. Plastic containers were stacked high to her right, but that wasn't what held her attention. Every bit of wall space was covered with Polaroid pictures that had been stapled in place.

Swallowing, she walked farther inside to get a closer look. All the girls looked to be Riley's age or younger. Most looked younger. The majority of the pictures had been taken in the same bed she was sleeping in. The wood-slatted headboard and the scarred wooden bedside table looked exactly the same. At one time or another almost every girl wore the same yellow dress and shiny red shoes that Bubbles had dressed her in when she first arrived.

Riley's hand trembled as she brushed her fingers over one particular picture. The girl in the photo had yellow-blonde hair, blue eyes, and a big pink bow clipped to her hair above her right ear. On top of her head was a colorful, cone-shaped birthday hat. The kind with tissue paper pom-poms on top. The girl's mouth was open wide, and tears streamed down both sides of a big red-marker smile that had been drawn on her face.

Chills raced down Riley's spine. Afraid she might be sick, she closed her eyes and drew in a deep breath. Once she was certain she wasn't going to blow chunks, she searched through one of the plastic bins. She found more pictures and shoes and clothes that looked like they would fit a six-year-old. Custom name labels had been sewn into every shirt and dress. Molly Finlay.

Riley dug through to the bottom where she found a baby book. The first two pages were titled BEFORE WE MET YOU and BEFORE YOU WERE BORN. Both pages were blank. Every page after those two were to record memories and milestones. Molly at one month, Molly at two months, and so on. Height and weight and what she liked to eat had been written in great detail.

At the end of the book, when Molly Finlay reached the age of one, there were two pictures of Molly sitting in a high chair. Her hair had started to grow in around the ears. Blonde hair and blue eyes. She looked happy. Her face was covered with chocolate icing. The next page revealed a picture of Bubbles holding Molly. Bubbles looked different.

Much younger and happy. Who had taken the picture? she wondered. And what happened to Molly?

Finished with the book, Riley slipped it back where she'd found it and put the lid of the container on tight before opening the next bin. This one was filled with birthday cards. Many of them unsigned. Bought but never used. There was also a stack of children's books, including a copy of *Goodnight Moon* by Margaret Wise Brown, one of Riley's personal favorites. She plopped down on the floor and began to read, wiping her eyes as she turned the pages.

Somewhere along the way, she fell asleep. In her dreams she heard the doorbell and was so happy that someone had come to visit. Her body felt light, almost as if she were floating as she ran to the front of the house. When she turned the knob and opened the door, it was Bubbles who stood there with those crazy bug eyes and pinched face.

Riley screamed, but nothing came out of her mouth.

Her eyes shot open.

A knock sounded on the door downstairs. Someone was here. She jumped to her feet, rushed as far as the chain would allow, and screamed, "Help me!"

Hearing nothing in return, she clanked the chain against the floor. "Help me! I need help! She locked me up! Please help!"

This time when she stopped to listen, she heard a car engine roar to life.

"Don't leave me!"

But it was too late. If she hadn't fallen asleep she might have been able to save herself. As she wiped tears from her eyes, she inwardly scolded herself for crying and being a baby. She went back to the closet and put everything back the way it was before and then pushed the lock and shut the door.

Only then did she look around for the wire and realize she'd left it on the closet floor.

*Stupid. Stupid. Stupid.*

Dragging the chain along with her as she made her way to the window, she sighed when the chain stopped her from being able to put her face up against the glass. More than anything she wanted to pull the curtains wide, open the window, and take a breath of fresh air.

Movement caught her eye. Leaning forward, straining every muscle, she saw someone in the backyard of the neighbor's house. A little boy was throwing a ball high in the air and catching it—over and over again.

Frantically, she looked around the room, trying to find something to throw at the window to get his attention.

She tried not to think about everything in the closet she could have used. Instead, she glanced over her shoulder at the cooler, then rushed that way, gliding her feet across the floor as if she were wearing snowshoes. It was faster that way.

Unable to lift the cooler, she opened it and grabbed a small plastic bottle of OJ. No schoolbooks today. Of course not. Just paper copies of a math assignment and some lined paper to write an essay about what she did this summer. What a joke. She couldn't remember anything about this summer except the very last day. She'd helped an injured woman with her packages and learned the hard way that it didn't pay to be nice. Mom hated that saying. But whoever came up with it was right.

She grabbed a pencil and eraser from the table by the bed, and her water bottle, then rushed back to the window and tossed the OJ bottle first. It hardly made any noise at all. Next, she threw the pencil and then the eraser. Laughable. With only the water bottle left, she wound her arm up like a pitcher, aimed, and threw the bottle as hard as she could. So hard she thought she might break the glass. It made a good loud bang, but then fell to the ground and rolled out of reach.

When she peered out the window again, her shoulders dipped.

Nobody was there.

# CHAPTER NINETEEN

Yellow barricade tape wound its way around Mark Brennan's brick steps and across the front yard, disappearing around both sides of his house. Sawyer made her way to the front entrance while Palmer went to talk to Geezer.

On the drive over she'd learned that Geezer used a scanner, which allowed him to get to a scene quickly. When the crime scene photographers were finished taking pictures, Geezer would be allowed to take photographs for the *Sacramento Independent*. If there had been a body, or the blood had been located inside the house, more often than not, Geezer would not be given such liberties.

A technician was on bent knees at the steps in front of the house. He used a metal scraper that looked like an instrument a dentist might use to scrape what looked like flecks of blood into a small plastic bag. He placed the sample inside his kit and then straightened and made his way to the front window where the gardenias grew and where Aria and Sawyer had been only yesterday. After putting on a clean pair of gloves, the technician carefully clipped two bloodied blossoms and a number of waxy green leaves, each bagged separately.

Sawyer's heart raced as she pushed the rewind button in her brain. She was 100 percent certain there hadn't been blood on the gardenia bush when she was here yesterday. If less than twenty-four hours ago there was no blood, what did that mean?

It haunted her to think she could have been so wrong about Mark Brennan. Sure, he was clean-cut and personable, but she always made it a point not to judge a book by its cover. It was the way he'd talked about Riley and how he'd expressed himself that had convinced her he was innocent.

But Aria had sensed something else entirely. Had Riley Addison been tucked away inside his house somewhere, maybe in the basement or a bedroom closet, and then taken to his car after she and Aria left?

Her stomach felt queasy.

Directly across the street, she noticed that some of the neighbor's houses had windows with a view of Mark Brennan's front stoop. A group of people stood huddled together in front of one of the houses, so she headed that way. Two people took off before she stepped onto the curb.

"Hello," she said to the remaining people, which included one elderly woman, a young man, and a woman with two children. "I'm Sawyer Brooks with the *Sacramento Independent*. Do any of you live around here?"

"I live in the yellow house," the woman with a cane said. "Did that man do something?"

"Do you know him?" Sawyer asked.

"Not personally. I've seen him around, though, and on occasion I hear music coming from his place."

"Same," the young man said. His hands were shoved deep into his front pants pockets. "I hear music every once in a while, and my wife and I say hello if we run into him on one of his walks, but I don't know him."

"I know Mark Brennan," the woman with the children said. Her hair was twisted into a bun on top of her head. Sawyer guessed her to be in her late thirties. One small child held on to her leg. The other was in a stroller.

"Did you see Mark Brennan yesterday?" Sawyer asked.

"I did. The kids and I waved, and he waved back."

"Do you remember what time that was?"

"Between five and six. He takes a walk around the neighborhood around that same time every day."

"Did you notice anything unusual about him?"

She thought about it, then shook her head. "He's such a friendly man. I usually bring him a plate of holiday cookies at Christmas. He's offered to give my girls free piano lessons since we're neighbors, but I turned him down because that would be taking advantage."

"Do any of you know if the police canvased the area after Riley Addison disappeared?"

The young mother covered her older child's ears. "Nobody came to our house, but I prefer not to talk about what's happened. We better go," she said. "You understand?"

Sawyer lifted a brow, confused by the woman's reaction. "Please call me if you hear anything at all." Sawyer handed the woman her card before she could get away.

"I've got to run off myself," the man said. "But I'll take a card in case we hear anything."

Sawyer thanked him and handed him a card.

"How are those kids going to learn about real life if their mother refuses to let them see what it's all about?" the woman with the cane asked after everyone else was gone.

Sawyer kept her opinion to herself and instead asked, "Did the police talk to you after the little girl disappeared?"

"Not that I'm aware of, and I'm home most every day."

"How did you hear about the missing girl?"

"I get the newspaper, and I listen to the local news. But even if they had come to my door, I wouldn't have been any help since I didn't see anything."

Sawyer thought about returning to the area at another time and going door to door. She knew from everything she'd read that the surest way to solve a crime was to send detectives out to canvas the streets and talk to potential witnesses.

"The couple who ran off when you came this way said blood was found on the man's car. Is that true?" the woman asked.

"It's true," Sawyer said. "They also found blood on his steps and on the gardenias out front. But I just talked to Mark Brennan yesterday. I even took a whiff of his gardenias, and I didn't see any blood."

"How's your eyesight?" the woman asked with obvious skepticism.

Sawyer liked the woman already. She was blunt and unafraid to say whatever came to mind. "I have twenty-twenty vision," Sawyer told her. "And I'm very observant."

"Well then, if you're absolutely certain the blood wasn't there yesterday, he either got rid of the body after the sun went down or someone planted the blood."

"Or maybe he cut himself in the car on his way home," Sawyer said.

"Nah," the woman said. "I recently finished a book called *Framed for Murder* by Allison Krepp, and the blood was planted."

Sawyer smiled. "You read a lot of mysteries?"

"I listen to books on audio nowadays. If it's a murder mystery, I usually solve the case halfway through. My friends tell me I should write my own book." She snorted. "How hard could it be?"

"If you do write that book, I want to read it." Sawyer reached into her bag for another card and handed it to the woman.

She looked it over. "I'll call you if I see anything unusual or when I finish my book. Whichever happens first."

Sawyer thanked her and said goodbye, then headed back to Mark Brennan's house as a string of questions floated around in her head. Who found the blood? Who notified the police? Neighbors? A passerby?

She locked eyes with Palmer as she stepped onto the curb. He came to stand by her side. "Something troubling you?"

"Yes. None of this blood was here yesterday."

"How do you know that?"

"Because I was here. In that house. Talking with Mark Brennan. On our way out, we noticed the gardenia bush."

"We?"

"My sister and I." Sawyer kept talking, didn't want to give him time to be upset that she'd brought her sister along. "When we left, we stopped to admire the sweet smell." Sawyer set her gaze on his. "I swear to you, Palmer. There wasn't a drop of blood on that shrub yesterday. Not one drop. I would have noticed."

"Did you have your camera with you? Take any pictures?"

"No. Why would I have?"

"Maybe you didn't see any blood because that's not what you were looking for."

She wondered if he could be right. The answer ricocheted back at her with a resounding no. She could see it in her mind's eye. There had been no blood on the gardenia bush when she was here.

A loud noise drew their attention to the tow truck being used to put Mark Brennan's car onto a flatbed. Farther down the block, about twenty feet away, reporters and photographers were gathering. "Looks like Detective Perez has agreed to talk to the press," she told Palmer.

They walked that way.

"When was Mark Brennan arrested?" a reporter asked Perez from the back of the crowd.

Perez glanced at his watch. "About an hour ago."

The questions were shot like bullets, one after the other. "Has he confessed to killing Riley Addison?"

"No," Perez said.

"When was the blood found?" asked a reporter from Channel 10 News.

This time Perez referred to his notes. "Approximately 6:35 this morning."

"Has it been determined whose blood was found?"

"Not at this time."

"But the man was arrested."

"Other evidence that I am unable to share was also found."

Sawyer wondered what else they might have found as she wriggled her way into the crowd and asked, "When police questioned Mark Brennan immediately after Riley Addison disappeared, did anyone notice blood at that time?"

"Not at that time."

"How did you know to come take another look?" another reporter asked, exactly the question Sawyer wanted answered.

"We got a call from an anonymous tipster," Perez said before pointing at another reporter.

Sawyer left the huddle to find Palmer again.

He stroked his beard. "What are you thinking?"

"That either Mark Brennan had Riley Addison hidden away until sometime between when I saw him yesterday and now, someone planted the blood to cause confusion and take the case in another direction, or Mark Brennan simply cut himself before or after leaving his house."

"Hmm."

Sawyer crossed her arms. "It's your turn to say what you're thinking."

"I worry that once you get an idea stuck in your head, you can't shake it loose."

"You can rest easy," she said. "Nothing is stuck in my head. I'm simply throwing out ideas and theories while remaining open-minded, just like you."

"Okay," he said. "I'll play. Instead of focusing on one missing girl, you've decided to focus on six missing girls, including the one who escaped."

"Yes."

"You're hoping to find a connection."

"That would be great. But what I really want is to get people, everyday citizens, talking and thinking. Most cold cases are eventually solved because someone decides to talk."

"But Riley Addison's case is not cold."

"Not yet." She didn't like the unsettling feeling creeping up on her. She knew what was bothering her. If Mark Brennan was guilty, then there was a good chance Riley Addison was dead.

"And now," Palmer said, continuing with a thought, "we have Riley's blood—"

"We don't know whose blood it is," she cautioned.

"True."

"Perez said evidence other than the blood was also found. Do you know anything about that?"

"No. That was a surprise."

"When I mentioned the blood possibly being planted," Sawyer went on, "I was merely tossing out ideas. But since we're theorizing . . . If the blood was purposely and conveniently placed in the exact location where Riley Addison was last seen, then my guess is that it was planted by whoever took Riley Addison."

"Why would anyone take such a risk when the authorities have no suspects?"

"Because of the bones," Sawyer said as the thought struck. "She wasn't counting on anyone finding the bones."

# CHAPTER TWENTY

On the drive home from work, Bubbles switched the radio from her favorite station to the local news to see if there were any updates concerning Mark Brennan. After her walk late last night past Mark Brennan's house, she'd tossed and turned until dawn. After showering and dressing and leaving Molly with food and water, she'd used a prepaid throwaway phone to make an anonymous call, letting the police know she'd seen blood on the gardenia bush outside the music teacher's house as she was walking by.

Focusing at work was becoming increasingly difficult. Her darling Molly was finally home, and she wanted to spend time with her. She had only a few sick days left, and she'd used most of her vacation time driving around searching for Molly.

She was nearly home when the story she'd been waiting for blasted over the airwaves: "Authorities say that Mark Brennan, suspected of kidnapping Riley Addison, has been arrested. He is believed to have led the young girl to his dark-gray Prius under the pretense of giving her a ride home. The location of Riley Addison is still unknown."

The garage door clanged shut. Relief floated through her body as she used a key to make her way from the garage to her kitchen. They had a suspect in custody. The music teacher had been the last one to see the girl before she disappeared. Her blood was everywhere. Case closed. "Molly," she practically sang. "I'm home."

Bubbles knew it would take some time for her and Molly to get reacquainted after all this while, but her daughter would come around. She hadn't tried to run off when the cuff was removed, which was a good thing considering the idea of getting rid of the girl did flash through her mind. Not only had authorities found bones belonging to sweet little Cora with the broken neck, but that meddlesome reporter from the *Sacramento Independent* seemed to be a nosy young woman and a Sherlock Holmes wannabe. After seeing Sawyer Brooks with Paige Owens at the coffee shop, Bubbles had done a little prying of her own. Sawyer Brooks had so many issues it had been difficult to pick just one to focus on. She finally settled on Sawyer's best friend, Rebecca. The poor girl had been put in the crawl space in Sawyer's childhood home. They'd found Rebecca's bones during Sawyer's last visit to River Rock. Sweet, sweet Rebecca, according to family and friends, had spent her last days trapped right under Sawyer's feet.

A tiny little cackle slipped between Bubbles's lips as she envisioned the trauma Sawyer must have endured upon discovering that her father was a pedophile and her mother was a cold-blooded killer.

A chuckle escaped. She was getting the giggles.

Her plan was to take Sawyer Brooks's anxiety to the next level by focusing on Rebecca. Bubbles had used the computer at the local library at lunchtime to search for pictures of the town of River Rock and the school Sawyer and Rebecca had attended. She'd struck gold.

Everything was going to be fine. She and Molly were going to be a family, a happy, happy family.

Humming a little tune, she brushed her fingers lovingly over the ladybugs on her favorite cardigan, the one her mom had given her on her eighteenth birthday.

Two of the ladybugs were hanging by a thread. Beneath her cardigan she wore a crew neck T-shirt. She took off her cardigan and went to the kitchen, opened the drawer where she kept a needle, thread, and scissors—everything she needed to reattach the embroidered bugs.

After she was done, as she put the items away, a fly landed on her arm. She swatted at it and missed. The dirty insect then landed on her shoulder. She left her cardigan on the counter and walked slowly toward the pantry, surprised that the fly remained. Very slowly, she reached for the cooking spray, then aimed and fired. She'd made contact, but the insect managed to land on the counter next to the sink. Acting fast, she grabbed a dinner plate still in the sink and slammed it down on top of the fly. Pieces of porcelain flew through the air. But the fly was dead.

She picked it up by its wing and held it in front of her face. "That'll teach you to fuck with Bubbles." Laughter followed as she slid the fly into her pants pocket.

Ignoring the crunch of porcelain beneath her shoe, she examined the red sweater. Happy with her work, she then headed upstairs. The door to Molly's room was open just as she'd left it. Molly was in bed, the homework Bubbles had left for her this morning stacked neatly on her lap.

She sniffed the air as she entered the room.

Something seemed off, but she played it cool as she went to her daughter's side and planted a kiss on Molly's forehead.

*Fear,* she thought. She smelled fear.

"Did you have a good day?" she asked her sweet daughter.

Molly nodded.

"Use your words, darling."

"Yes, Bubbles. I had a good day," she said, her voice like honey.

Bubbles put a hand to Molly's chin and cocked her head so that she had no choice but to look directly at her. "I think it's time for you to call me Mom."

The girl looked different . . . disheveled, even. Bubbles held tight to Molly's chin as she took a look around the room. "What have you been up to today?"

"I did my homework like you asked me to."

Molly tried to pull away, but Bubbles was not ready to let go. "Do you know how to tell when someone is lying?" Bubbles asked.

"No."

"A change in voice is number one. Number two is when the liar tries really hard to stay perfectly still. Just like you're doing now."

"I didn't lie."

Bubbles looked from Molly to the closet. "Have you been inside that closet?"

"No," Molly said in a squeaky voice. "You told me to stay out of there."

The closet was locked, which is why Bubbles knew the answer even before she asked it, but she figured this was a teaching moment and a chance for her to make sure Molly never lied.

Her fingernail cut into Molly's soft skin as Bubbles used her free hand to reach into her pocket and pull out the dead fly. She held the insect in front of Molly's nose and said, "Stick out your tongue."

"No."

Her eyes narrowed. "Do it."

"No," she said, her bottom lip quivering.

"Come on. It's protein and it's delicious." She dug her fingers hard into the area on both sides of Molly's mouth so that she had no choice but to open her mouth so Bubbles could place the fly on her tongue.

As soon as Bubbles released her hold, Molly spit it out and kept spitting.

Bubbles rolled the fingers on her right hand into a fist and slugged Molly in the shoulder. "Don't be such a baby. I'm just having fun with you." A giggling fit hit her again. She couldn't stop herself this time, and she nearly doubled over in laughter. When the fit finally subsided, she said with watery eyes, "Do you want to know what's so funny?"

Molly said nothing. The girl could be a real bore. "That fly was too stupid to live out his twenty-four-hour life span."

"Only mayflies live that long," Molly told her. "Houseflies live for twenty-eight days."

The little shit was definitely going to eat that fly before the night was over.

Downstairs, a knock at the door sent an electrical current through her body. She looked at Molly. "Do I need to chain your hands and tape your mouth shut?"

The girl trembled like a Chihuahua. "No. I'll be quiet."

The doorbell sounded. Somebody was impatient. "Shush," Bubbles said with a finger pressed against her lips. Then she exited the bedroom and shut the door tight behind her.

———

Riley tried to swallow, but her throat was dry; her water bottle was on the floor across the room where she couldn't reach it. Her heart was still beating out of control. She spit again, afraid that parts of the dead fly were stuck to her tongue. She'd been dreading Bubbles's return, afraid she'd discover that Riley had found a way inside the closet and gone through her things. The way Bubbles had looked at her when she first came into the room had freaked her out. She was certain the crazy woman knew what she'd done.

But apparently Bubbles had only wanted to mess with her.

Riley wasn't sure how much longer she could handle this. And yet she knew she didn't have a choice in the matter. Not unless she could find a way to escape. After doing her assignments earlier, she'd spent most of the day staring out the window, too far away to press her face against the glass, but close enough to see if the little boy wandered outside again. But he never did.

As hard as she'd tried, she couldn't get the images of all those girls out of her head. Whenever she nodded off, she prayed that it was all a nightmare. But then she'd wake up, and the cold heaviness of the metal cuff around her ankle reminded her it was real.

Bubbles was real too. She was scary. And yet sometimes her face would soften, and she looked almost normal. Riley didn't like that she never knew what Bubbles was going to do next. She was worse than the villains in her brother's comic books.

The worst part was feeling as if she was losing hope. If that happened, she might not be able to find the courage to make a run for it. That's why it had to be tonight. She had to get away.

Voices sounded below.

Not only Bubbles's voice, but another woman's. A friendly voice. Riley couldn't make out whole sentences, but it sounded as if she was talking to Bubbles about her son. He'd heard a sound, a loud bang.

Riley could hardly breathe. The lady was talking about the boy who had been playing in the backyard, tossing his ball in the air. He'd seen Riley. Or at least he'd heard her.

This was her chance. And yet every muscle in her body felt rigid. Fear held her in place.

*Don't just sit there, stupid! Make some noise!*

Looking around, her heart pumping wildly against her ribs, her gaze fell on the chain around her foot. *Move! Go!*

She jumped off the bed, grasped on to the middle of the chain, and began thumping it against the floor.

Thump. Thump. Thump.

It was loud. This could work. It had to work!

She kept picking up the chain and dropping it against the floor, over and over again until her arms ached.

The door to her room opened wide. Bubbles stood there, her big eyes like shiny marbles, unblinking and filled with rage.

Riley wondered what had happened to the neighbor. Where was the nice lady? The one with the friendly voice? Where did she go? Hadn't she heard her?

Bubbles marched past her. Across the room, she opened the top dresser drawer, pulled out a roll of duct tape, and walked back to her.

Riley dropped to the floor on her butt and pushed herself backward with her legs, trying to avoid whatever the crazy lady had planned for her. But it was no use. Bubbles grabbed hold of Riley's arm, her fingernails digging into her skin as she dragged her across the floor to the bed. She forced Riley to her feet and then made her sit back down on the edge of the mattress.

Bubbles's hands were shaking and her cheeks were a deep shade of red as she rolled duct tape tightly around Riley's legs. Once that was done, she removed the key from her pocket and unlocked the metal cuff around her ankle.

"Stand," Bubbles demanded.

Riley hesitated a second too long. Bubbles grabbed her arm, hoisting her upward, and then told her to turn around and put her arms behind her back.

Riley did as she said, unable to stop the tears as her wrists were bound together. "Please stop. You're hurting me."

"Maybe you should have thought of that earlier when you were making a racket. The neighbor was worried I was being burglarized today. It seems her little boy thought he heard someone upstairs in this very room. But don't worry, she felt much better when I told her there was a plumber upstairs fixing the pipes. When you continued with your game, I had to explain that he was still here and that I needed to go check on him."

Bubbles made a *tsk*ing noise as she went to the closet and unlocked the door. "Your disobedience is such a shame. I was going to take the cuff off you tonight, and we were going to bake cookies. Just you and me in the kitchen all night long. I can almost smell those warm, buttery chocolate chip cookies, crisp on the edges, chewy on the inside, but thanks to you our plans have changed."

Bubbles reached inside the closet and flipped the switch. Her gaze instantly took in the bins that were no longer stacked quite so neatly as before. She stepped inside, bent down, and picked up the piece of wire. She looked at Riley. "You clever girl."

As Bubbles came toward her, Riley squeezed her eyes shut, unsure of what was coming. Suddenly she was in a death grip, Bubbles's arms wrapped tightly around her, hugging her so fiercely her feet came off the floor.

Her perfume was so strong and sweet Riley thought she might be sick as Bubbles waltzed across the floor with Riley in her arms. When Bubbles finally stopped moving, she set her down and took a step back. "Get in the closet."

"Why?" Riley asked. "I'm sorry. I didn't mean to make you angry. I miss my mom and dad, and my brother. I just want to go home."

"Well, that's too bad." She jerked her head, gesturing toward the closet. "Get in there now."

"What about dinner?" Riley wasn't hungry, but she needed to stall.

"You won't be eating for a while, dear. See what happens to little ungrateful brats?"

"Please don't make me go in there."

She smoothed a hand over Riley's head. "It looks like you went to a lot of trouble to get inside the closet today. So now you'll have plenty of time to look around and play and think about what you've done."

"For how long?" Riley asked. It was a dumb question, but the thought of being locked inside scared her.

"Oh, gosh, I don't know. It's not a big deal, silly. My mom kept me in the closet for over a week one time. Two days. Maybe three. Okay?" She pointed toward the closet. "Now get in there, or I'll have to take drastic measures, and I'm really not in the mood, Molly. It's been a rough day. Now!"

Riley couldn't walk normally. She shuffled her way inside. The door slammed shut behind her. The only sound was the turn of the key and the click of the lock. And then she was alone in a closet wallpapered with pictures of all the other girls who had most likely made the mistake of helping a stranger in need.

# CHAPTER TWENTY-ONE

It was nearly midnight. Harper had used makeup and wore a turtleneck to cover the marks on her neck. Nate had arrived home fifteen minutes ago. The kids were asleep. While Harper scrubbed the kitchen counters, Nate took a seat at the table in the nook area and ate the leftovers she'd warmed up.

"How was work?" she asked.

He chewed and swallowed. "Fine. How was your first day of school? Did you like your creative writing instructor?"

"He was okay," she said. "It was sort of a wake-up call for many of us."

"How so?"

She didn't want to lie to him, but she'd been practicing her spiel, and it rolled from her lips without much effort. "Our professor warned the class that we either have talent or we don't, but all writers are not born equal. He said that the 'real deal' is a rarity. He also talked about the class not being a place for therapy and made it clear that he doesn't want to slog through a bunch of memoirs about abuse."

"Sounds harsh."

Nate didn't usually say much, especially after such a long day. She stopped scrubbing long enough to take a good long look at him. His body was tense. He had yet to look over at her. Something wasn't right. "What's going on?" she asked.

He put his fork down and met her gaze straight on. "Shouldn't I be the one asking you that question?"

She tried to slow her breathing. "What do you mean?"

"I called the administrative offices at CSUS. And then, just to be certain, I took time off work and drove there to talk to a staff member face-to-face. You need a degree to get into the creative writing program."

"Yes, but I—"

"Stop," Nate said. "Just stop. You're not even registered at CSUS."

Her stomach quivered. She looked at Nate and wondered when they had grown apart. They made love every so often, but it was robotic and without emotion. For the first time in the years they had been together, she thought he looked like a stranger.

"So are you ready to tell me what's going on?"

"No," she said, unable to keep eye contact.

"I'm not stupid," he said.

She looked at him then. "I know that."

He stood and walked over to her.

She kept her head down, eyes on her sponge, wishing she'd at least told him about the baby. Did he know about the baby? She was still in her first trimester. She'd lost weight, and the baby bump was hardly visible. And talking about the baby would have taken their discussion down a long, slippery slope about their future and goals and plans, and she wasn't ready for that. Before she could think, let alone talk about, the future, she'd wanted to be done with The Crew.

"I checked the outside cameras," he said. "You were gone most of the day. What's with the turtleneck?" Before she could stop him, he pulled down on the fabric around her neck. "Jesus. Who did that to you?"

"Nobody did anything to me. I had to slam on the brakes today, and the seat belt left a mark."

"And why should I believe you?"

She felt a sudden urge to fall to her knees and tell him everything, including shooting and burying Otto Radley. She wanted to be free of all the lies. Nate wasn't a stranger. He was her husband, her hero, the man who had taken her away from her nightmare in River Rock and shown her the healing powers of love. And she'd simply tossed it all out the door.

*Tell him. Tell him everything.*

The shame was too great, and the words didn't come.

"You've always had your quirks, Harper. I get that your childhood was beyond fucked up. It's no secret that cleaning is something you need to do to keep the demons at bay." He raked his fingers over his short, cropped hair. "I gave up a while ago on trying to get you to open up about everything that happened in River Rock. But I can't live with someone who has completely shut me out of their life." He sighed and added, "That's asking way too much."

She looked at him then, her heart racing, confusion swirling. It was as if she were standing on the edge of a cliff, and the rocks beneath her feet were slippery and unstable, but there was nothing to grab hold of. "It wasn't my intention to shut you out," she finally said.

He shrugged. "But that's what you've done. We never talk anymore or go out or make love. Why are we even together?"

She grabbed hold of his forearm. "It will all be over soon. I promise. Please, Nate. I just need a little more time."

"What about the baby?" he blurted.

Her breath hitched.

When she didn't answer right away, he freed his arm from her grasp and shook his head. "I truly don't know who you are any longer. When were you going to tell me about the baby?"

He rubbed his forehead, and she could see the pain in his eyes. She felt like an idiot for thinking he wouldn't notice. A bead of sweat rolled down her back.

T.R. RAGAN

"Or maybe you weren't ever going to tell me," he went on. "Maybe you have other plans that I don't know about."

"Of course I was going to tell you about the baby. I've been waiting for the right time. I swear to you, Nate. I love you, and I don't want to lose you, but I need you to be patient for a little while longer."

"For how long?"

"I don't know. A few weeks. A month at the most."

"God, you must think I'm a complete moron."

"No. You're the best thing that's ever happened to me."

He let out a bark of laughter, then leaned forward, his eyes delving into hers. "Every single day, I go to work to keep a roof over your head. To provide this family with food to eat and a warm bed to sleep in each night. But it's never enough, is it? You're just as fucked up now as you were the day I met you." His face reddened, a vein in his neck bulging. "But the baby . . . that takes the cake. I've been racking my brain over it, and for the life of me I couldn't think of one God damn reason why you would keep that from me. But then it hit me like a truckload of bricks to the head. The only reason you might not tell me about the baby is if it wasn't mine."

Her eyes widened, saddened that he could think such a thing. "It's yours."

"I had a feeling you would say that, which is why I'm going away for a while."

Her stomach lurched. "Please, Nate. I just need more time, and then I'll tell you everything. I want to change, to get better, to be there for you."

"Not good enough," he said. "I'm leaving first thing in the morning. My bags are packed. They have been for days, but I knew you wouldn't notice. Hell, I could have walked out of here tomorrow morning without having this conversation, and you wouldn't have known I was gone."

"That's not true."

"It doesn't matter. I'm going to Montana with Dad to work on Uncle Joe's mountain cabin. He's been begging me to see it, and I can't think of one reason why I shouldn't go."

"How long will you be gone?"

"I'm not sure."

"What about the kids? What am I supposed to say to them?"

"I've already told them. I said it was a surprise for you . . . that we were all going to spend some time at the cabin as a family when it was finished. I guess you're not the only one in the family who's good at lying."

"I'm sorry," she said, reaching for him, wishing she could fall into his arms and tell him everything, but afraid he might leave her for good if she did.

"Yeah, me too." He turned and walked away.

# CHAPTER TWENTY-TWO

As Sawyer drove along the highway, the scenery on both sides of her a blur, she saw a head pop up in the back of the white GMC Acadia directly in front of her. She waved at the little girl, smiling when the child waved back at her. The child's perfect curls reminded Sawyer of the old black-and-white Shirley Temple movies. That kid could do it all—smile, dance, act, and sing—and to top it off, she had perfect ringlets and dimples.

Sawyer's heart pounded as she drew closer and saw that the little girl wasn't waving at all. She was gesturing wildly while mouthing *Help me!* Her eyes were red, her face puffy from crying. Sawyer merged into the left lane and sped up, hoping to motion for the driver to pull to the side of the road.

But the woman driver remained incredibly rigid, her eyes focused straight ahead. She had gray scraggly hair and a long, pale neck. Seconds before speeding away, the woman turned and looked directly at Sawyer with big, round, unblinking eyes and a shit-eating grin.

Sawyer bolted upright, both hands on her chest. The LED clock on the dresser across the room told her it was two in the morning.

*Just a nightmare. Breathe.*

Her bedroom was cool, but sweat dripped down her spine.

She slid off the bed and made her way to the bathroom. As she splashed cold water on her face, her cat, Raccoon, appeared, circling her ankles as Sawyer washed her hands. Raccoon followed her to the kitchen. Sawyer leaned over and scratched the cat's back. "Did I wake you?"

Raccoon was wide awake, ready to start the day.

Movement outside her window caught her attention. As Sawyer straightened, she noticed a car parked at the curb pull away, its headlights off.

Thinking that was strange, she walked to the door, opened it, and stuck her head outside to take a look around.

The car was gone.

An owl hooted. A light breeze made the tops of the trees sway, leaves rustling.

On the welcome mat was an envelope. She picked it up, stepped back into her apartment, and locked the door. She went to the couch and sat down. Raccoon jumped up next to her and settled on her lap as she opened the envelope. Inside was a picture with a note. She pulled out the picture.

Her mouth fell open. Rebecca Johnson. Sawyer's best friend from her childhood stood alone in the middle of the schoolyard, looking lost. The photo was grainy and old, but there was no mistaking who it was or where it was taken.

The picture was like a time machine, taking her back to when her best friend was alive. So much had happened between then and now.

Haunted by old memories, she stared at the photo. Guilt for what happened to her friend swept through her.

Inside the envelope was a note. She pulled it out. It was written in crayon, all squiggly capital letters: *Why didn't you look for me?*

Guilt and sadness were quickly replaced with anger.

It was disturbing to think that someone went to all the trouble of finding a picture of Rebecca and writing such a horrible message.

Who would leave this on her doorstep, and why?

# CHAPTER TWENTY-THREE

First thing the next morning, Sawyer found Palmer in his office. She took a seat and slipped the picture and the note across his desk, under his nose.

He looked at her. "What's this?"

"Someone left an envelope on my doorstep at two o'clock this morning."

"Did you see them?"

"No. Just a car driving away without the headlights turned on. I was half-asleep and couldn't make out what kind of car it was through the window." She pointed at the photo in front of him. "That's a picture of Rebecca Johnson. You remember . . . my best friend from kindergarten until the time she disappeared." Sawyer's stomach turned. "The girl my mother left in the crawl space beneath the house where I grew up."

He stroked his beard as he nodded.

"What do you think it means?" Sawyer asked, doing her best to rein in the thought of her friend being trapped below the floor of the house she lived in. She didn't know for sure if Rebecca had been dead or alive when she was placed inside the crawl space, but all evidence pointed to her being alive. Her mother never would have been able to fit beneath the floorboards. No way could she have dragged Rebecca's deadweight to the far end of the dark space where Rebecca's bones were found. Either way, the answer had died along with her mother.

"It could be a prank," Palmer said about the note and picture.

"A fiery brown paper bag filled with dog shit would be a prank," Sawyer argued. "What sort of person would go out of their way to be so cruel?"

"Why don't you take the day off? Get some rest."

It pissed her off that he wasn't taking her seriously. She put her hands on his desk and leaned forward. "Someone knows."

"Knows what?" Palmer asked.

"That I'm searching for answers. It's possible someone is upset that I'm searching for a link to all those missing girls."

"Does anyone besides me even know you have a list and you're checking it twice?"

"Only you, my sister Aria, and Paige Owens."

"Exactly." Palmer handed her back the note and the picture. "I think you're reading too much into it. You've already written a number of controversial articles that might have set off readers. For instance, you upset a lot of people a month ago when you accused a popular author of being a murderer."

"True," she said.

"Years ago," Palmer said, "an older man came to my house uninvited and launched into a tirade about the columns I had written about racism. When I wrote about abortion, I received a letter smeared with feces. It happens."

"What if whoever left the note is dangerous?"

Palmer appeared to ponder her question. "If you're worried, why don't you take a drive downtown and fill out a report?"

"Thanks," she said, standing. "I think I'll do that."

"Sawyer," he said when she got as far as the door.

She turned and waited.

"I know you want to find Riley Addison, and that's an honorable and worthy goal. I want the same thing."

"But?"

"But I'm concerned about the stress this story might cause you." He sighed. "You've made it clear you carry a lot of guilt for your friend Rebecca's disappearance, and I know for a fact you don't believe anyone looked long and hard enough for her. But I want you to understand that Detective Perez and his team are working around the clock. They want to find Riley as much as you do."

"Maybe so," Sawyer said. "But they don't have the manpower to do what needs to be done."

"That's not your call to make."

He was right. She tried not to judge Detective Perez and his men, but she knew there was more that could be done. "Did you see one missing person poster anywhere near the spot where Riley disappeared?" Before he could respond, she said, "I talked to a handful of people in the neighborhood, and no one had been visited by a detective. Why aren't Perez and his men hitting the pavement, distributing flyers, or even making announcements over a loudspeaker? Sometimes it's not about *wanting* something as much as it is about *doing*."

"Go do what you need to do, and we'll talk later," he said.

Sawyer left Palmer's office feeling defeated and wishing she could do more. She grabbed her backpack from her cubicle on her way out, not bothering to glance down the hallway to see if Derek might have returned from vacation early.

She went straight to her car and drove to the police department. After signing in at the front, she took a seat in an uncomfortable plastic chair and waited patiently to talk to someone. It wasn't until Detective Perez walked by forty-five minutes later, heading toward the exit, that anyone paid her any mind at all.

"Sawyer Brooks," he said with a look of suspicion etched on his face.

She jumped to her feet. "Detective Perez."

He looked over his shoulder at the receptionist who was too busy to notice, then back at Sawyer. "Who are you waiting to see?"

"Anyone. I'm here to fill out a police report."

"What's the problem?"

"I'm being harassed."

He looked at his watch. "I've got five minutes. Come with me."

Without hesitation, he turned back the way he came. She followed him past rows of cubicles to his cubicle in the corner. Her shoes clacked against ugly cement flooring.

"Excuse the mess," he said. "New carpet is going in soon." He gestured toward the extra chair in the corner. "Five minutes," he reminded her. "Go."

Sitting, she reached into her bag for the envelope that had been left at her doorstep and handed it over. She then quickly explained who was in the picture and why it was so disturbing.

"It's not a crime for someone to leave an envelope with a picture and a note at your door. Have you been intimidated, confronted, or threatened with physical force?"

"No."

"Any damage to your property?" he asked, the questions flying at her like darts hitting a bull's-eye.

"No."

"Do you know who left the envelope?"

"Not exactly."

"Are there security cameras outside your door?"

She shook her head.

He cleared his throat. "In that case, you can find a Protection from Harassment form online. But," he said, looking down his nose at her, "if the court finds that you filed a frivolous complaint, they can order you to pay court costs. So before you file a complaint you might want to ask yourself: Do I need this court order to be safe?"

"So there's nothing I can do?"

He gave a noncommittal shrug.

"Do you remember the Paige Owens case?" she asked before he could escape.

He exhaled as he glanced toward the exit. "I do."

"She's sixteen years old now. For five years she's been keeping a list of the names of children who have gone missing. There are five females between the ages of ten and twelve on her list."

He looked at his watch. "You've got thirty seconds."

"Five girls all disappeared within a fifteen-mile radius. Paige's mother believes that the woman who tried to take her daughter still watches them."

His perfectly groomed mustache twitched. "She's welcome to file a report and tell us what she knows."

"What if this woman who tried to kidnap Paige also took one of these missing girls?"

"It would make for quite a story," he said, standing. "Unfortunately I can't operate on feelings and hunches. Only facts."

"The woman is white and about five foot six inches. She has dull, grayish hair and dark eyes. I thought it might be a good idea to have a forensic artist talk to Paige Owens and do a sketch of the woman."

He smiled, but it wasn't friendly. "Paige Owens escaped. She's alive and well. My team's focus must remain on Riley Addison."

"What about the blood spatter at Mark Brennan's house?"

"What about it?"

"Do you know if it's Riley Addison's blood?"

"The results are in, and yes, it's a match."

Sawyer released a long breath. "The day before Mark Brennan's arrest, I was at his house, interviewing him for a story. I took a long look at the gardenia bush, even stuck my nose in the bush to smell the fragrant blooms, and there was no blood." She lifted her hands. "Then suddenly, less than twenty-four hours later, blood appears, which means Mark Brennan either transferred the girl to his car after I saw him or someone is trying to frame an innocent man."

"It's an ongoing investigation, but I'll tell you this. Blood spatter and fingerprints are often missed on the first go-round. Happens all the time, so you shouldn't feel badly about missing it. Or maybe you're right and he removed the girl from the house after you interviewed him."

"Why would the tipster, whoever spotted the blood yesterday, remain anonymous?"

"Too many reasons to list," he said.

"What sort of idiot would carry a missing girl outside without wrapping her up in a blanket or a tarp, anything? And even if he did carry the girl down the stairs, how could he possibly get blood on the gardenias? Instead of making a straight line to his car, he would have had to have made a left at the bottom stair and hold the girl over the shrub. It makes no sense."

"Most criminals are not masterminds." He rubbed his chin. "Before you come to talk to me again, I would appreciate it if you had proof. Proof that the same gray-haired woman who attempted to kidnap Paige Owens is still watching Paige and her mother. Proof the blood wasn't on Mark Brennan's stoop or gardenia bush before yesterday. Whatever it is," he said, "I need proof."

*Proof.* She thought of Geezer. He'd been at Mark Brennan's house the day after Riley Addison disappeared and then again when Mark Brennan was arrested. She needed to talk to him, see if he had "before" and "after" pictures—proof that the blood had suddenly appeared all those days after Riley disappeared. But even then, what good would it do? They had their man.

"Listen," Detective Perez said. "Your heart appears to be in the right place. I have two granddaughters. I understand the urgency to find Riley Addison. But hunches do not solve cases." He shook his head. "I don't know why Palmer has taken you under his wing, but I'll give him the benefit of the doubt and assume there's more to you than feelings and intuition. If you find something I can use, then come on back and we'll have another chat. Until then, I'm going to have to ask you to stick to writing stories and stay out of the way."

# Chapter Twenty-Four

After dropping off Ella at school, Aria returned to her studio apartment and spent more than an hour making a list of the schools the missing girls had attended. She had the name of every elementary and middle school.

Not sure how she might get her hands on a school yearbook, she called the main office of Silver Valley, the school Cora O'Neal had attended in Elk Grove. After explaining what she was looking for, she was told they kept copies in the library, and if she found what she needed, she could check it out for a few days. Aria jumped in the car, and thirty minutes later, she had a yearbook from the same year Cora had attended Silver Valley.

Greenfield Middle School, the school Paige Owens had attended in Carmichael, didn't have any yearbooks left, but she made a note to ask Sawyer to talk to Paige about whether she had a yearbook from five years ago.

Online yearbooks were a thing, but all she could find were digital high school yearbooks. Northstar, the school Danielle Woods had attended, also didn't have any copies available, so Aria decided to look on Craigslist. She jumped up excitedly when she found a copy for sale for twenty dollars. Craigslist never failed to shock and surprise.

Hopefully she would be able to get her hands on the yearbook before the end of the day.

It was noon when Aria decided to take a break from looking for yearbooks and drive to 524 Seacrest Drive in West Sacramento, the Butler family home. She didn't have to be at the SPCA until two thirty. Although investigative work could be tedious, it suited her. And unlike police detectives across the country, she had time to spare. Aria had brought along the file she'd put together with information about all the missing girls, including Carly.

Three years ago, Carly Butler, the oldest of three children, had disappeared on her way home from school. Carly Butler's mother, Gretchen, was a stay-at-home mom.

The air smelled crisp and clean as Aria walked to the front door and knocked. A dog's incessant barking made it difficult to hear if anyone was inside. To Aria's left, the window shade moved. Somebody was home. The door opened, and the woman seemed to take some joy in trying to hold back her barking dog.

Aria wasn't afraid. She could tell he was all bark and no bite. She put her hand out. Sure enough, the animal stopped to take a whiff. The wag of his tail gave him away.

"That's just great," the woman complained. "His name is Bruno. My husband promised me Bruno would make a good watchdog." She snorted.

Aria scratched the dog behind both ears. He had a big head and a thick neck and body. "Bruno is the best-looking Pitador I've ever seen."

"Pita-what?"

"Oh, I assumed he was half Labrador and half pit bull," Aria said. "Highly intelligent and obedient."

"Oh, really?"

Aria laughed. Bruno jumped up on his hind legs, his front paws landing on Aria's chest, forcing her to take a step backward.

"No, Bruno. Sit."

He promptly obeyed.

"Now that you know you're not in any danger whatsoever," the woman said, "I'm Gretchen. And you are?"

They shook hands.

"Aria Brooks, intern at the *Sacramento Independent*. I was hoping you could answer a few questions."

"About Carly?"

Aria nodded as she continued to scratch the dog's head and neck. "I can't imagine what you and your family have been through. But I do want to help."

"Are you a mother?"

"No."

"Then you're right. You could never imagine." She waved her inside. "Come on. Do you drink coffee?"

"I do."

"Great."

Sitting on a comfy couch with the dog's head on her lap and hot coffee in hand, Aria listened to Gretchen Butler tell her all about the day her daughter went missing.

"It was April 15, Wednesday, Carly's eleventh birthday. Her younger sister and brother had gotten out of school an hour earlier. I had made a cake, vanilla with chocolate frosting, and they were dying to cut into it. I told them we'd have to wait until Daddy got home, but still, I remember it all so clearly. It started out like any other day. Scrambled eggs on toast. That's what Carly ate before heading off to Crossroads Elementary."

Crossroads Elementary was Ella's school. "I thought I read that she attended Pleasant Grove, the private school."

"She was at Pleasant Grove from kindergarten until the fourth grade. Once she found out her best friend was transferring to Crossroads Elementary the next year, she spent all summer begging and pleading until we finally caved. The principal at Crossroads Elementary gave us a tour and introduced us to a young and vibrant teacher, Ms. Patti Montoni. She was new and excited about teaching. My husband and I were sold."

Bruno's ears perked up, and he jumped from the couch and disappeared somewhere inside the house.

"For the first few months," Gretchen said, "I walked Carly to school to make sure she waited at the crosswalks, that sort of thing. There were always other kids and parents out and about. I never would have stopped walking with Carly if I didn't think she would be safe."

Aria nodded.

"Since you're here, I'm sure you've done some research."

Aria nodded.

"So you know that nobody is safe in this world."

"It certainly feels that way," Aria said.

"I asked Carly what she wanted for dinner, a tradition around here, you know, since it was her birthday. She said tacos as she ran out the door. That was the last thing I said to my daughter . . . 'What do you want for dinner?'" Her eyes watered, but Aria could tell she had cried all the tears. "When she didn't return home on time, I waited another fifteen minutes before I started to worry. And that's when all the possibilities started to run through my mind: Had she gone home with a friend? Stayed after school to talk to her teacher? Had I forgotten about an after-school activity? Maybe her friends had surprised her with a party.

"It wasn't until after I called every person I knew that I began to wonder if she was in trouble. From there on my imagination ran wild. We did everything we could to keep her name in the headlines: fundraisers, ads, posters, and interviews. But the days and weeks simply drifted by without any news of my daughter's whereabouts.

"A year after she went missing, all the local stations mentioned her in the news: 'Carly Butler has not returned.' The year after that: 'Butler investigation continues' and 'Carly Butler's case is still open,' and finally, 'All efforts to locate Carly Butler have been exhausted.'"

She lifted her arms in defeat. "Life does go on," Gretchen said. "But it never gets easier."

Aria stood and walked over to the fireplace mantel. She pointed to one of many pictures and asked, "Is this Carly?"

Gretchen came to stand by her side. "Yes. That's our Carly. She was such a happy kid. Always smiling."

The photo hardly resembled Carly's school picture that popped up when you googled her name. In this particular photo, Carly reminded her of another girl: Riley Addison. Come to think of it, Carly and Riley both resembled Cora, the girl whose bones were recently found. Petite, blonde, aged ten to twelve. Maybe there was more to these physical similarities than she and Sawyer had thought.

Aria turned to Gretchen. "You wouldn't happen to have a school yearbook from three years ago that I could borrow for a few days?"

"I do," the woman said. "If you promise to take good care of it and return it by the end of the week, I'll share it with you."

# CHAPTER
# TWENTY-FIVE

The slamming of a door downstairs jolted Riley awake. Her neck was sore from being in an awkward position. She sat up and pressed her ear against the wall closest to the front of the house. She recognized the squeaky sound of a garage door being opened before a car engine roared to life and drove away. The garage door clanked shut.

Bubbles had left for work without saying a word. No cooler filled with food and drinks. Riley had thought being chained to the bed was bad. This was worse. *It can always be worse,* her mom liked to tell her and her brother whenever they complained about something stupid. She was right. If she ever saw her mom again, she would tell her how much she loved her and missed her and how she was right about everything. Thinking of her mom caused a lump to form in her throat, making it hard to swallow.

Last night Riley had tried to open the door, but it had a keyhole just like on the other side. Bubbles had thought of everything. Since she couldn't use the bathroom, she'd peed inside one of the plastic bins, ruining pictures and cards and whatever else was inside. But she'd had no choice, since she didn't want to soil the clothes she had on or pee on the floor.

She grunted as she tried to pull her arms apart. Every muscle ached.

The tape had definitely loosened, but she still had a long way to go. Before falling asleep, she'd spent hours rubbing the tape around her wrists on a corner of one of the plastic bins that had cracked enough to give it a sharp edge.

Looking around the space, she instantly regretted doing so as her gaze fixated on the Polaroid picture of the girl wearing the cone-shaped birthday hat. The picture made her heart sink to the bottom of her stomach. She prayed the girl was alive and that someday she would meet her. Riley would make her a present and a cake, and they would spend the day together doing whatever the girl in the picture wanted to do.

Scooting across the floor to the bin with the crack, she had to sit on her knees so that she could saw the sharp edge of the plastic against the tape around her wrist, back and forth, over and over. If she could free her hands, she could work on the tape around her ankles. Just thinking about being free spurred her onward. After that, she would need to find something sharp. Maybe stomp on the plastic bin that was already cracked and hopefully end up with a good sharp piece of plastic that she could use as a weapon to fight Bubbles if she came to check on her tonight.

Her stomach growled. Her lips felt dry. In her mind's eye she saw her mom waving excitedly at her as the bus rolled into the school parking lot after returning from camp. Images of her dad popped into her head. He came into her room, his eyes twinkling, his back hunched over, morphing into the tickle monster. They laughed and said good night. A smile tugged at the corners of her mouth. If only she could see them, talk to them, spend one glorious minute with them.

She stopped what she was doing as a horrible thought overrode all else: If she couldn't even fight off her brother when he wrestled her to the ground, how would she get away from Bubbles—a full-grown woman with fire in her eyes?

She couldn't think about that.

*Stay positive.*

At least she had light. *It could always be worse.*

# CHAPTER
# TWENTY-SIX

After her visit with Detective Perez, Sawyer got back in her car and scrolled through her messages. She had more than one missed call from Aria. She was about to call her sister when her phone vibrated. It was an unknown number. She picked up the call and said hello.

"Is this Sawyer Brooks?"

"It is."

"This is Riley's father, Patrick Addison. You left a message saying you wanted to help."

"I do."

"I can meet you in an hour. You have my address?"

"Yes. I'll be there. Do you mind if I bring my assistant along?"

"That's fine." The call was disconnected.

Sawyer didn't bother calling Aria. Instead she drove straight to Harper's house where Aria lived in an unattached garage that had been fixed up into a one-bedroom apartment.

She went to the door and knocked.

Aria called out for her to come inside. "Shut the door behind you and don't step on Mr. Baguette," Aria said from where she sat on a contemporary two-seater sofa with her laptop and an open file at her side.

Mr. Baguette was a rescue cockatiel Aria had brought home from the shelter where she worked. The bird had come to see Aria as his best friend. He liked to sing and chirp and run around the house. His wings had been clipped, but he didn't weigh much and could still fly.

Sawyer shut the door, then said, "We have an appointment to talk to Riley Addison's father in one hour."

"You're kidding me?"

Sawyer shook her head.

"I can't believe he's going to talk to us."

"He wants to find his daughter. That's all he cares about." Sawyer looked at her watch. "We need to leave in thirty minutes."

"I'm ready to go."

Sawyer pulled the envelope from her bag as she walked over to where Aria sat and handed it to her.

"What is this?" Aria asked.

"A little surprise left on my doormat at two in the morning."

"Rebecca," Aria said when she saw the photo. She read the note. "This is fucked up."

"No kidding." Sawyer took a seat across from Aria. "I was awakened by a noise. When I got up, I saw a car with its headlights turned off drive away. It was gone by the time I stepped outside to take a look. That's when I found the envelope."

"You need to go to the police," Aria said.

"I was just there. Without an inkling of who it might be, no name, and no vehicle make or model, there isn't a whole lot they can do. But I did talk to Detective Perez about Mark Brennan. Did you hear about his arrest?"

"I did," Aria said.

"Palmer and I were at Brennan's house after his arrest yesterday. There was blood spatter on the gardenia bush outside the front window. Did you see any blood when we were there?"

Aria shook her head. "No. If there had been, I'm sure we would have noticed."

"That's what I thought." Sawyer looked around at the stacks of papers and books. "What are those?"

"Yearbooks. I have managed to get my hands on three out of six yearbooks from the year each girl went missing. I was able to find two of them on Craigslist, but I won't be able to pick up Katy Steiner's yearbook until tomorrow. I was hoping you could text Paige Owens and see if she has a yearbook from five years ago."

"What are you using the yearbooks for?"

"Teachers and staff members are usually photographed too. I thought if we gathered all the yearbooks together and then asked Paige to look through pictures of staff and teachers, maybe we'll get a hit."

"It's worth a shot," Sawyer said.

"You said to start with schools and buses, so that's what I'm doing. I'm thinking of this as a process of elimination."

"Smart."

Aria shut her laptop and said, "I had a chance to talk with Carly Butler's mother, Gretchen, today. She was friendly, invited me inside the house, and even let me borrow Carly's yearbook. But I've been dying to tell you that I saw a picture of Carly on the mantel above the fireplace, and I think the girls' resemblance to one another is too striking to discount."

"Other than the fact that they're all white and aged ten to twelve?"

"Also blonde," Aria said, "with the majority of them having light-colored eyes too."

"Riley Addison's hair looks closer to light brown to me. And a couple of the other girls had darker hair."

"It's more than just the hair," Aria said. "It's a particular look. Petite, small-boned girls with light eyes and light hair." Aria put her laptop away, walked over to the dining room table, and brought back a twenty-four-by-thirty-six-inch poster board with pictures of all six missing girls.

Six eight-by-ten pictures set up in two rows of three. Sawyer looked from one girl to the next. There did seem to be something there, and yet it still wasn't even close to being the "proof" that Detective Perez wanted.

"Impressive," Sawyer said. "Talking to Carly Butler's mom, the poster board, and finding all those yearbooks . . . Great work."

"Then why don't you look happy?"

"I guess Detective Perez got to me. I was hoping the police department or the *Sacramento Independent* would hire a forensic artist to do a rendering of the woman who tried to kidnap Paige, but I can't get anyone to bite. Something needs to be done to get the public involved and get the tip lines ringing. If I could afford to have it done and then pay thousands to have her face put on the front page of the newspaper, I would do it, but it's not my decision to make."

"Like you said the other day, we need to keep on trucking. I'll stick with schools, and you work on bus routes."

"Any luck with finding Bob Upperman?"

"Not yet."

Sawyer couldn't pull her gaze away from the pictures. "These two," she said, pointing at Carly and Riley, "could almost pass as twins."

"That's what I thought." Aria gestured at the poster board. "All these girls look like they could be sisters. Do you think there is a chance someone out there could be searching for a particular look?"

"Anything's possible," Sawyer said. "If one person is responsible for all these girls disappearing, then he or she is not a kidnapper, but a killer." Sawyer pointed at the photo of Cora. "She's dead." She then pointed at Paige Owens. "She escaped." Next she pointed to Riley. "And this one, if she's still alive, is running out of time."

Aria nodded her agreement.

Sawyer picked up the envelope with the picture of Rebecca and the note and returned it to her purse. Out of the corner of her eye, Sawyer noticed Mr. Baguette shuffle his tiny feet as he ran from the kitchen to the mirror Aria had set up for him. The bird enjoyed singing to himself.

"Ready to go?" Sawyer asked.

Aria set about putting the bird in his cage, then grabbed her purse, along with her notebook and pen, and followed Sawyer out the door.

---

A couple of reporters stood outside the Addison house. Sawyer ignored their questions as she and Aria walked the path leading to the front entry. The door opened as they approached. Introductions were made as Patrick Addison invited them inside his house. The man was five foot ten, stocky, with short, bristly red hair. His eyes were green like his daughter's. He didn't smile, and he looked like he hadn't slept in months. As he led Sawyer and Aria past the kitchen to a family room with couches and a large flat-screen TV, she noticed floral arrangements and plates of cookies and cakes spread out on every available table.

Music blared from a bedroom down the hall. A boy in his teens poked his head out and then disappeared again and shut his door. He looked a lot like Riley and his dad.

Sawyer took a seat on the couch. Aria sat too.

Patrick Addison sat in a green cotton fabric recliner with deep indentations and stuffing bursting at the seams. "I want to find my daughter," he said flatly.

Sawyer had to stop herself from saying she understood because she didn't. If her niece ever went missing, she wasn't sure she could handle such a thing.

"Riley knew not to talk to strangers," he said, his voice vibrating with anger. "My wife and I have been over it a million times."

"Over what?" Sawyer asked, daring to cut in.

"Over dozens of scenarios of what she should do if she were ever approached. We work with criminals every day."

He was standing now, jabbing the air with his finger for emphasis. His face turned red and blotchy.

"My wife and I both know what people like that are capable of! We know! She knows! Irrational behavior, unpredictable tempers, mental health issues. The list goes on. Riley hears about it every day!"

Patrick Addison's head fell forward, his upper body shaking. He was crying.

Aria looked at Sawyer and gave her a what-do-we-do look. Sawyer shook her head subtly, letting her sister know it was best if they sat quietly and gave him a moment to regroup.

Sawyer also found herself instantly drawn to this man. A father crying for his missing daughter. She simply couldn't relate to the idea of a father caring so damn much. She thought of her brother-in-law. Nate would cry for Ella. She swallowed the lump lodged in her throat.

Patrick Addison looked up, wiped his eyes with his forearm, and sat back down. "The cops aren't looking in the right place."

Sawyer straightened. "Why do you say that?"

"They arrested the wrong man. Mark Brennan is incapable of hurting a fly. I knew that even before I paid him a visit on the day Riley went missing. I was upset. I never would have let her take piano lessons in the man's house if I didn't trust him. My wife and I interviewed him before we ever let her step foot in that place. And you know what? Brennan stayed in his kitchen while I tromped through every room, searching every nook and cranny, rummaging through closets and drawers." He exhaled. "It's just something I had to do."

Sawyer nodded.

"I checked his car too. But I already knew Brennan wasn't responsible."

"I'm assuming you've told Detective Perez all this?"

"I have. After he called to tell me they had arrested Brennan, I screamed at him, told him it was way too easy! I said if you've got your man, then show me my daughter. Where is she? I know monsters, and

Brennan is not one. The police are eager to make this an open-and-shut case. Perez is most likely looking to be appointed chief of police. I will not stand for it. Put that in your damn story!"

After he settled down, Sawyer asked him about Riley, about her favorite things, friends, and what kind of person she was.

"She's one of a kind. She loves people. Smart, like her mother. Loves all subjects at school, including math. Above all else, she's kind."

Sawyer took it all in, noting how determined and strong he was, obviously driven to keep his daughter's story alive despite Mark Brennan's arrest. "Any other extracurricular activities besides piano lessons?" she asked.

He clapped his hands together. "None. Riley plays the piano, reads, and studies. That's her life in a nutshell." He pointed a finger. "And her brother. She likes to tease her brother." He shook his head. "I think maybe she decided to walk home and someone offered her a ride. I can't get the image out of my head. Someone took her. I've talked to friends and family, even neighbors, asking if they saw Riley that day or talked to her on the phone. Riley knew better than to accept a ride from a stranger, but one second of bad judgment was all it took for her to take the bait."

Patrick Addison's son strolled into the room. He was taller than his dad and had a mop of reddish-brown hair. He looked at his dad. "Are we going to go see Mom soon?"

"Yeah," Patrick Addison said. "We're done here." He walked Sawyer and Aria to the door and said, "Help me keep my daughter in the news. Help me find her."

And then he shut the door.

"Wow," Aria said as they walked to Sawyer's car parked on the street. "That was intense. I was speechless."

Once they were in the car, Sawyer said, "Riley was not in Mark Brennan's house, so if he'd taken her somewhere in his car, the blood would have already been on the steps and gardenia bush." Her jaw felt tight. "Perez knew that when I talked to him."

"Maybe Patrick Addison is right about Perez and his team looking for an easy arrest."

"I have no idea," Sawyer said.

Aria's phone buzzed. She picked it up, listened to the caller, and then said, "Someone will be there within the next fifteen minutes." She ended the call. "Shit."

"What is it?"

"That was the nurse from Ella's school. Ella's not feeling well and needs to be picked up." Aria looked at her Fitbit. "I have to be at work in thirty minutes."

"I can get her."

"Thank you," Aria said.

Sawyer drove up to her sister's place five minutes later. Before Aria climbed out of the car, Sawyer asked, "When does Harper get home?"

"I have no idea. Things have changed around here."

"How so?"

"Harper is rarely home. And when she is, she's always in a hurry and never has time to talk. And get this? She was wearing a turtleneck the other day."

Sawyer wrinkled her nose. "What's wrong with that?"

"She's always complaining about the heat, and the temperature was in the mideighties. And then early this morning, I saw Nate toss two travel duffel bags into his truck and take off. Something's going on, but I have no idea what."

Sawyer wondered if her niece and nephew knew what was going on. "How was Ella when you took her to school this morning? Did she seem upset?"

Aria shook her head. "No. Ella was great, as always. Excited about school. Don't you dare tell her I told you, but she likes a boy named George."

"Maybe that's why she's not feeling good," Sawyer said. "I remember having a crush on a boy when I was her age. I couldn't look at him without feeling sick to my stomach."

Aria smiled at her as she opened the door. "You better go before she runs off and elopes with George."

"Thanks again for all your help," Sawyer said, impressed with all she'd done. Aria was a fast learner. She'd interviewed Carly's mom, collected yearbooks, and made a poster board to show the missing girls' resemblance.

"You're welcome. Once I have all the yearbooks gathered, we should set up a meeting with Paige Owens. Do you think her mother would allow her to meet with us?"

"Not in a million years. But I'll talk to Paige and see if she can meet us somewhere."

They said goodbye, and Sawyer drove off, thinking about Riley Addison. Without witnesses or tire tracks or fingerprints, there was little to work with. The blood found at Mark Brennan's house was the only thing telling them that Riley had not vanished without a trace.

So where was she?

# CHAPTER TWENTY-SEVEN

Harper was reading Stephen King's *The Institute* on her Kindle. She didn't know how the author managed to suck her in, but he'd done it again. And she was thankful. It wasn't easy, losing herself in a book when she could hear QB downstairs, pleading for his release.

She hated that she actually felt sorry for him. After nearly choking her to death and then everything he'd done to Bug, he didn't deserve her sympathy. If Cleo hadn't shown up, she could have died.

"Holy shit. Is that smell coming from QB's cell?" Bug asked as she entered the empty house holding a bag from Taco Bell. The clack of her shoes echoed off the walls as she came forward.

Harper shut her Kindle cover and slipped it into her backpack. "The smell is bad, but nothing is more annoying than his constant pleas for help. Come on," Harper said as she got to her feet and reached into her bag for her Taser and pepper spray. "Let's clean out his cell before I leave."

Bug headed for the stairs.

Harper frowned. "What about your wig and mask?"

"No need," Bug said. "He's already figured it out. He knows who I am."

"What the hell?"

Bug turned around and walked back to where Harper stood and grabbed hold of her shoulders. "Once the asshole downstairs understands the frustration of having absolutely no control over what's being done to him, I'm going to blindfold him and release him into the wild," she said, her arms in the air, "where he won't be found for days."

"You're not making any sense," Harper said as an unshakable sense of doom fell over her. "If he knows who you are, he'll come after you. And finding *you* will lead to—"

Bug cut her off midsentence. "By the time he finds his way out of the woods, I'll have a new identity, and I'll be long gone. I swear on my life that you and the rest of The Crew will be safe."

Harper's stomach churned. She wanted to take hold of Bug's shoulders and shake her. "How can you be so sure?"

She sighed. "You'll have to trust me."

"You can't leave until we've finished what we all promised to do."

"Don't worry. I won't leave until Cleo's frat boys have been taken care of."

"What about the other men you were dead set on kidnapping along with QB?"

"I've changed my mind. QB will be enough."

"What if he finds his way out of the woods before you escape?"

"I'm going to drug him. He'll be out for a very long time. You have to trust me."

Harper answered with a robotic nod, but she wasn't sure what to think or what to do. Bug had gone completely rogue. Her insides wobbled like Jell-O as she followed Bug downstairs. Bug was smart, but not street smart. If Bug ever took off before finishing the deal they had made with one another, certain members would make her pay, and it wouldn't be pretty.

"Come on, Myles," Bug said, banging both hands against the bars at the far left of the cell door. "You know the drill. Get over here so I can bind your wrists."

He did as she said. "When are you going to let me go?" he asked. "You've made your point. I'm a shitty guy who has done a lot of bad things, really horrible things."

"Go on," Bug said, obviously enjoying what he had to say.

"Not so tight," he said when she yanked on the zip tie attaching his wrist to the bar.

"Sorry," Bug said with a roll of her eyes.

Harper stood at attention with pepper spray and a Taser, ready to take him down if needed.

"My arm is infected," he complained. "That crazy bitch who bit me passed all her viruses and bacteria on to me. I need to see a doctor."

"Maybe you shouldn't have tried to kill my friend."

"I wasn't going to hurt her. I just want out of here."

Once both wrists were bound, Bug unlocked the cell door and walked inside to collect the dirty buckets while Harper remained frozen in place.

Awkward silence followed. Myles didn't say a word until Bug returned with clean buckets, and then he started jabbering again. "A lot of people are looking for me."

"That's not true," Harper lied, unable to stop herself. "Your disappearance didn't even make the news. People are too busy looking for an innocent young girl who's gone missing. Nobody cares about you."

"I'm sure my brother is rallying the troops as we speak."

Harper laughed. "Your brother is glad you're gone." She had no idea if that were true or not. Although she had spotted QB's brother on the news the other day when he awkwardly admitted to the press that he and Myles weren't close, but he loved him and wanted him back home where he belonged.

Myles looked at Bug. "I've had a lot of time to think," he told Bug as she placed the buckets on the floor in his cell. "I woke up last night, crying. And it wasn't because I was cold and stuck in this shithole. I was crying because of all the suffering I've caused you and others. If you let me out of here, I promise never to touch another woman in my life."

He tried to look over his shoulder so he could fixate his sorry eyes on Bug, but she was directly behind him, and the restraints stopped him from being able to make eye contact.

Bug walked out of the cell and shut the door with a clang. It took her a minute to wrap the heavy chain in place and close the padlock tight. She grabbed a pair of scissors they kept next to a plastic bag filled with zip ties, then walked back to where QB was tied up.

As Bug set about cutting him loose, his eyes met Harper's.

The look on Myles Davenport's face made it clear he wished he'd finished her off when he'd had the chance.

# CHAPTER TWENTY-EIGHT

Sawyer found a parking spot near the front of the school and climbed out. As she reached the front office, she held the door open for a woman carrying a paper bag with the name MASON written on it in big black letters. The last time Sawyer had been to the school was to watch Ella sing in a Christmas concert. Poor Ella had inherited her voice from Harper's side of the family and couldn't carry a tune.

The office was crowded, adults and kids coming and going.

Sawyer stood behind two women waiting in line and thought about her conversation with Patrick Addison and what he'd said about Detective Perez. Although Sawyer didn't know Perez well, she could easily imagine the detective discounting whatever Patrick Addison told him and putting it all down to high emotions.

She then attempted to see it all through Perez's eyes. Patrick Addison was going through an incredibly stressful situation. His wife was in the hospital, and his daughter was missing.

And Detective Perez had his entire team to consider. Overworked and understaffed. For many police departments across the country, morale was low because they worked long hours with little pay. Maybe, she considered next, the most obvious answer was actually the correct answer. Detective Perez was probably under a lot of pressure to close the case, especially since they had evidence.

"I'm sorry. You're going to need a pass," one of two female staff members behind the counter said, stopping a woman who was carrying a large tray of cupcakes from walking through the office and entering the school through a side door.

All thoughts of Perez left Sawyer as she watched the exchange.

"I was told I could go right through," the woman with the cupcakes said. "It's my son's birthday today and—"

"Whoever told you that is sadly misinformed. Please get in line and wait like everyone else." The woman removed her rhinestone cat's-eye glasses, letting them dangle from a gold chain around her neck, then crooked her finger to call the next person in line.

Sawyer felt an urge to tell the woman to chill out, but she was also getting older and wiser and learning to pick her battles. Detective Perez and his men weren't the only ones who were overworked and underpaid. And this wasn't the first time Sawyer was thankful she didn't have any kids yet . . . maybe never. She would be thirty soon. She had plenty of time if the urge struck.

"Can I help you?"

Sawyer stepped forward, thankful she wouldn't have to deal with the older woman. The woman helping her had a name tag pinned to her blouse: Florence. "Hi, Florence. My name is Sawyer Brooks, and I'm here to pick up my niece, Ella Pohler."

Behind Florence, the woman with the rhinestone glasses stopped what she was doing and looked directly at Sawyer. The pinched mouth and cold eyes were a bit unsettling. Sawyer wondered if the woman recognized her name from the news.

The woman looked away, and Sawyer returned her attention to Florence. "My instructions were to pick up my niece at the nurse's station."

Florence grabbed a clipboard with a sheet of paper attached and placed it on the counter in front of Sawyer. "I'll need to see some ID, and sign here." She pointed to the line next to Ella's name. Florence had red, puffy eyes, and Sawyer wondered if she'd been crying.

Once Sawyer's identity had been verified, Florence told her to head down the hallway and knock on the last door to the right. Nurse Amy let her in. In her late forties or early fifties, the nurse had gray hair rolled into a bun, which made her big ears and big eyes appear even larger. She wore sensible shoes and a navy-blue T-shirt tucked into a midlength denim skirt. Like the other ladies out front, her face looked drained of any joy and amusement, leaving Sawyer to wonder if someone had died.

"She doesn't have a fever or a cough," Nurse Amy said as Sawyer swept past her and went to where Ella lay on a cot. "It could be something she ate." Then in a lower voice, "Kids can be dramatic. It's hard to tell what's going on with them sometimes."

"Do you have kids of your own?" Sawyer asked.

"No."

Sawyer put the back of her hand to Ella's forehead and said, "Stick out your tongue and say 'ah.'"

Ella smiled instead.

Sawyer winked at the kid. "Ready to go?"

While Ella put on her shoes, Sawyer's gaze fixated on a syringe inside a glass cabinet, giving her an idea.

It took another ten minutes to get her niece out of what felt like school jail. But they were finally in the car buckling up when Ella asked, "Where's Aria?"

"What? I'm not good enough?"

"You're fine," Ella said unconvincingly. "Are we going to Carl's Jr. for milkshakes?"

"Is that what Aria would do?"

Ella nodded.

"Okay, but first you need to tell me what's going on."

Her niece turned out to be an easy egg to crack. As Sawyer drove, Ella talked.

"I overheard Mom and Dad talking last night. He was mad at her for keeping secrets. He told Lennon and me that he was going to Montana to work on Uncle Joe's cabin so our whole family could go there next summer. But I guess he was lying. He said he didn't know when he would be back. I'm scared. I don't want them to divorce like all my friends' parents."

Sawyer's insides churned. She'd really hoped that Ella's sickness had something to do with her crush on George. Harper and Nate always seemed like the perfect couple. What was going on? "It's going to be okay," she told Ella, hoping that was the case.

Ella reached out a hand. "Pinkie swear?"

"I swear," Sawyer said as she kept her eyes on the road and blindly interlocked pinkie fingers with Ella.

# CHAPTER TWENTY-NINE

Sawyer and Ella were watching television when Harper walked through the front door, her face lined with worry. "What's going on?" she asked. "I waited at the bus stop for Ella, and when she didn't appear, I panicked."

"I called and left you a message," Sawyer said. "Ella wasn't feeling well, so the school contacted Aria at work. Since I was available, I told her I would pick up Ella."

Harper made her way to her daughter.

Sawyer took note of her clothes. Harper wasn't wearing a turtle-neck, but she did have a scarf wrapped around her neck, which was highly unusual for a T-shirt-and-jeans kind of girl.

Sawyer got to her feet and pointed a finger at Ella. "Hope you feel better."

"Thanks, Aunt Sawyer."

"You're welcome."

Harper followed Sawyer out the door, closing it softly behind her. "Wait up," she said.

Sawyer waited.

"What's going on?" Harper asked.

"What do you mean?"

Harper stared at Sawyer, unblinking. "You look like you have something on your mind. Why don't you just say it?"

"I didn't want to say anything in front of Ella. She's worried enough as it is."

"About what?"

"She overheard you and Nate talking last night. She's afraid the two of you might get divorced."

"We're not getting divorced. We just need to work through a few things . . . normal married-people things."

"You don't have to convince me," Sawyer said.

"Then why do I sense that you're upset with me?"

"Come on," Sawyer said. "Let's get real. Aria saw Nate throw a couple of travel bags into his truck and take off this morning. Now Ella is telling me that her dad lied to her and Lennon about his trip. You call that 'normal'? Normal married problems would be arguing about money or getting ridiculously upset about how the other person drives. Not packing up and leaving."

Sawyer felt guilty for learning about all these problems secondhand. If she'd made more of an effort to get to know her older sister, she might not feel so in the dark. But guilt wasn't the only thing troubling her. She didn't like what Aria had said about Harper never being home and suddenly becoming so mysterious. "What's with the turtlenecks and the scarves? It's eighty degrees out here."

Harper crossed her arms. "I had to slam on the brakes the other day, and the seat belt left me with a bruise. I'm covering it so people aren't constantly questioning me about every mark on my body."

The pause and the subtle change in her voice told Sawyer she was lying. "Do you want to tell me what's going on, or not?"

"Nothing is going on," Harper said. "You and Aria and Nate are always making mountains out of molehills. It's ridiculous, and I don't have time for it."

Sawyer raised both hands in frustration. She couldn't force the truth out of her, but she was worried about Ella. "Fine. I'm outta here. But you better talk to your daughter. She deserves the truth."

As Sawyer drove off, she found herself hoping that they were all making a big deal about nothing. Instead of heading home, Sawyer went straight to Walmart and purchased a box of syringes used for insulin, a bottle of corn syrup, chocolate syrup, and red dye. She took everything home and used the ingredients to make fake blood. She'd helped Lennon make blood for Halloween a couple of years ago. It looked and felt like real blood. She filled the syringe and headed off for Mark Brennan's house.

Ten minutes later she was standing in front of the music teacher's house. Arms crossed, she simply stood on the sidewalk and took it all in, including all the neighborhood sounds: birds chirping, a leaf blower, and a UPS truck in the distance. Overall, it was a quiet street.

She then looked at the front door to Mark's house. The crime scene tape had been removed. Everything back to normal. From where she stood, the blood on the stairs was difficult to see. Same story with the blood spattered on the gardenia bush.

Sawyer started walking, imagining she had planted the blood that night. Where would she park her car? She looked around. There were too many two-story homes to risk parking on the same block.

Stopping at an empty lot, she peered across a square of dry grass. Her heart skipped a beat when she noticed a path had been made right down the middle. She used her phone to take video as she made the trek across the empty lot. On the other side, across the street from where the lot ended, was a business. LITTLE STARFISH SWIMMING SCHOOL, the sign read.

There, right where the roof sloped downward, was a camera. Sawyer weaved through the cars in the parking lot and went into the building. The place smelled like chlorine. The young man behind the counter was friendly. Trophies and pictures of swimmers with ribbons around their necks lined the wall behind him.

When she told him why she was there and asked if it might be possible to get video footage from the last forty-eight hours, he took down her name and number and assured her that someone would get back to her.

On her return, Sawyer tried to think like the criminal. She had bought the syringe because where else would he or she have kept the blood before it was placed at Mark Brennan's house? It needed to be kept in something small. Not only easy to carry but also easy to access and sprinkle around quickly. In the nurse's office she'd remembered what Paige Owens had said when she bent over to pick up the package for the woman wearing the sling: *"I saw something in her hand—the one in the sling. It was a syringe with a needle that doctors use to give shots."*

Sawyer guessed a syringe could hold at least twenty drops of blood. She would verify that in a few minutes, she thought as she walked across the empty lot. Back on the sidewalk, Sawyer stopped to extract foxtails from the hem of her pants. Then she pulled out the syringe, removed the rubber cap, walked over to the gardenia bush, and waved her hand over the shrubbery while releasing the fake blood.

She then used her phone to take a picture and proceeded to experiment on the steps. Same results.

Her experiment might not mean anything to Perez or Palmer, but she felt confident she was onto something. If Mark Brennan had carried Riley out of the house bleeding, how would blood spatter end up on the gardenia bush? And the cut on Riley would have had to be fresh to fall in drips from her skin.

It wasn't logical.

Happy with the results, she returned to her car, buckled up, and waited for a yellow school bus to pass by. She merged back onto the road. The bus took the same turn she and Aria had taken a few days ago when they had gone from Mark Brennan's house to Carly Butler's.

On a whim, she decided to follow. Sure enough, the bus stopped three blocks from the house where Carly Butler used to live.

Driving along, waiting patiently at every bus stop, she thought about what Riley's dad had said about his daughter knowing better than to talk to a stranger. Maybe it was someone she knew? Or maybe, just like what happened to Paige Owens, it was an elderly woman in need of assistance?

Proof. She needed proof.

Exactly four stops and thirteen minutes later, she sat up tall as she recognized the street. Her pulse quickened as she realized Paige Owens's house was right around the corner. The bus lurched forward again. Every time it stopped and turned on its flashing lights, she wrote down the name of the street and the crossroad. There were two more stops before the bus was finished for the day.

Nine stops total. With a list of streets and crossroads in her possession, she headed for home, calling Aria on her way and asking her to stop by after work.

# CHAPTER THIRTY

The first thing Sawyer did when she got home was move the futon out of the way so she could use the wall as a giant bulletin board.

Hours later, as Aria cooked up macaroni and cheese in the kitchen, Sawyer stood in front of the wall and stared at her creation. She had used pushpins and string to show where each girl went missing. The string went from Elk Grove to Carmichael to North Highlands to Sacramento.

Sawyer had also made a sketch of the bus route that the kidnapper might have used to keep tabs on certain children in the Sacramento area. For the sake of her experiment, she assumed the kidnapper was either a bus driver or someone who worked at the school, someone who knew which kids rode the bus. The sketch was pinned to the wall along with the poster board Aria had made, and also a sheet of paper with basic information such as a physical description of each girl, where they were from, and when and where they disappeared.

Aria came to her side with a coffeepot and offered to refill her mug.

"No more coffee for me," Sawyer said.

Aria disappeared, then returned with mug in hand and stood facing the wall, taking it all in. "Can I see those pictures you took today of the fake blood?"

Sawyer found her cell and handed it over.

"The blood spatter looks the same. That's crazy."

"I just don't know if it will do any good," Sawyer said.

"We need a suspect other than Mark Brennan to get authorities to pay attention. Tomorrow we'll have all the yearbooks. Did you text Paige Owens yet?"

"I'll do that right now." Sawyer took her phone back and texted Paige, asking her if she could meet again sometime tomorrow.

"We need to catch a break," Sawyer said, slipping her phone into her back pocket.

Aria was back in the kitchen. She returned with two bowls and handed one to Sawyer. They ate as they stared at the wall, both lost in their thoughts for a few minutes.

"Do you really think Riley Addison could still be alive?"

"I do. It's probably more wishing than anything else, but I'm not ready to think any other way."

"Based on what happened to Paige Owens, I wonder how many kidnappers or even serial killers use a fast-acting drug to subdue their victims," Aria said. She took a bite of her dinner, chewed and swallowed, and added, "And why go to all that bother, searching for and abducting a specific type of girl only to kill them in the end?"

"That's what I've been wondering," Sawyer said.

"It could be sexual in nature, or maybe he or she is lonely."

"If it's a woman," Sawyer said, "maybe she's always wanted a child but could never have one."

"Yeah, but again, then why kill them?"

"Cora O'Neal had a broken neck," Sawyer said. "Maybe her death was an accident."

"Or," Aria said, "maybe all these missing girls have something to do with sex trafficking."

Shivers coursed over Sawyer at the thought. If this had something to do with trafficking, then Riley Addison was most likely long gone.

Aria took both their empty bowls to the sink. When she returned, she reached for the piece of paper, unpinned it from the wall, and read the description of the woman who had tried to get Paige Owens into her car. "Pale, big brown eyes, grayish-blonde hair, red Crocs, jean skirt, a white top, a red cardigan sweater with ladybugs, and a sling on her arm. White SUV with two number sevens and the letter *L* in the license plate. Called out 'Molly' or 'Holly' as Paige ran off."

"If you were the woman who had tried to kidnap someone and failed, wouldn't you get a different car?" Sawyer asked.

Aria nodded. "I would. And I would also dye my hair."

Raccoon meowed and circled Aria's leg. She scooped the cat into her arms and smoothed her fingers over his head, scratching him around the ears. "Do we know who called in about the blood found outside Mark Brennan's home?"

"Anonymous caller," Sawyer said.

Aria stepped closer to the wall and repinned the paper in her hand. She then placed her finger in the middle of it all. "Ella's school is right here. Too close, if you ask me."

"Have you ever met Nurse Amy or any of the staff members?"

"No," Aria said. "Why do you ask?"

"I swear they were all intense gray-haired, middle-aged women. If we were looking for someone based on Paige Owens's description of the woman who tried to grab her, they would all be suspect." She chuckled. "I'm being mean and judgmental. The truth is that they all looked tired and overworked, sort of like I feel at the moment."

Aria set Raccoon on the floor. "I better go. We both need to get some sleep." She rinsed the bowls and her mug in the kitchen sink, then picked up her purse from a chair. "Hey, I've been meaning to ask you . . . Whatever happened to that guy from work?" Aria asked. "Are you still seeing him?"

"Derek," Sawyer said. "He didn't think I was that into him, so he set me free."

"He broke up with you?"

Sawyer winced. "Pretty much."

"Why?"

"It's complicated. Bottom line: I blew it. I really like him, but I guess I just don't know *how* to be with someone like him."

"I get it," Aria said. "That's why I stick with animals. After everything that happened back home, I wanted to date, but I quickly realized I didn't trust anyone enough. But you're different from me. If you really like him, and it seems like you do, then you need to find a way to open up to him. We can't let all those assholes from our past fuck with us for the rest of our lives."

"I don't know what to do. I was so afraid of coming across as needy that I closed up even more than usual." Sawyer made a face. "Stupid. I know. Either way, it's over." Saying the words out loud made her heart drop to her stomach.

"But does he still have feelings for you?" Aria asked.

"He said he did, but he also said that we were both adults and that I needed time after my breakup with Chad—"

"If he knew Chad, he'd understand that you were simply passing time." Aria slipped the strap of her purse over her shoulder. "Well, you can't give up on him without a fight."

"I'm not exactly a whole person," Sawyer said. And it was true. How could she be? So many people had betrayed her. Her uncle had drugged her and sold her to the highest bidder, and her parents had let it happen. And now here she was, left to pick up the pieces, doing her best to move onward and upward without looking back.

"Is anyone whole and normal these days? I mean, seriously." Aria anchored a strand of hair behind her ear. "Have you called Derek since this weird little breakup?"

"Many times. He's on vacation, and he isn't returning my texts or calls."

"When he gets back, maybe you should do something special for him."

"Like what?"

"Make him some homemade chocolate chip cookies."

Sawyer chuckled.

"I'm serious," Aria said. "You should see the way Nate's face lights up every time Harper makes cookies."

"I'm not a baker," Sawyer said. "Trying to bake anything would ruin any chance I might have of getting him to hear me out."

"Well, it's worth a shot. If cookies don't work, then he wasn't worth your time anyway." Aria opened her arms for a hug.

Sawyer struggled to take that first step. It was as if she were paralyzed. She was like Raccoon, a stray cat that hadn't gotten any normal human contact growing up. Now when someone wanted to hug or touch, she freaked out. But it was only Aria. Her sister. One of the few people she did trust.

"Come on, sis. You can do it. What did we just talk about?"

"Making cookies," Sawyer said flatly.

"And opening up. That includes learning to trust again, starting with touching." Aria waggled her fingers. "It's time for you to make a few changes. Come on now. I don't bite."

Once Sawyer realized the only way she was going to get rid of her sister was to cave, she stepped into Aria's embrace, surprised by the comfort and support she felt before breaking away.

# CHAPTER THIRTY-ONE

Harper arrived at the construction site at 8:15 a.m. Bug had brought coffee and enough breakfast burritos for a small army. Harper hadn't realized how hungry she was until she scarfed down two of them, one after the other. She also hadn't realized Cleo was there until she came traipsing up the stairs.

"Good morning," Harper said.

"Yeah, morning," Cleo said as she removed her mask. She waved her hand in the air in front of her. "It stinks down there."

"Come over here and eat," Bug said, "then we'll tie him up so I can clean out the buckets."

"That guy is a major dick," Cleo said. "He's never going to apologize to you, Bug."

"I know."

Cleo gave Harper the side-eye before looking back at Bug. "Then why are we keeping him here?"

Bug lifted a shoulder. "I figured it was worth a try. At the very least he's getting a taste of his own medicine: trapped, no control over his situation—you get the picture."

Cleo grabbed a coffee and a burrito and took a seat on the floor so that she was facing Harper and Bug, her back against the wall. She took a bite of her burrito, chewed, and swallowed. "When my turn comes along, I want my frat boys taken care of concisely and swiftly. No questions asked."

"What does that mean exactly?" Bug asked.

"Just like it sounds. I refuse to waste even one minute talking to those scums of the earth. I don't care if they have wives and kids or if they've grown into perfectly respectable adults who have somehow seen the light. I want them to pay."

Harper watched Cleo closely. Exotic, beautiful, thirty-six years old, Cleo had been gang-raped during a weekend party at a fraternity house when she was in college. Her case went to court, and the boys' lawyers painted Cleo as a slut and whore and any name they could think of to call her that would make the jury see that she got what she wanted. Family and friends of the boys, all young, fresh-faced, outstanding citizens, came forward and swore before the judge that Cleo should be the one on the stand because she used her body to get them to do her bidding. Cleo's word against six boys and their allies. She hadn't had a chance.

"So what's your plan?" Bug asked her.

Cleo put her burrito to the side so she could lift the hem of her pants, revealing a black leather sheath on her left ankle. She plucked a knife from the sheath and held it up for them to see. "This is my handy little full-tang survival knife." She put the knife away, then jumped to her feet in one swift move, turned so that her back was to them, and lifted her shirt high enough to reveal another knife attached to the belt around her waist. Then she sank back to the floor and munched on her burrito. "I'm fully loaded," she said with her mouth half-full. "I've got Tasers and pepper spray, all the usual suspects. But in the end, it's my knives that will keep me safe in this crazy little world we live in." She sipped her coffee. "So what's *your* plan?" Cleo asked Bug. "How does this story of yours end? I read that the guy Psycho hit with the van is back home, living the good life. Wasn't he the one who held you down?"

Bug didn't say a word. She just kept eating.

The tension in the room was thick. Harper knew Cleo was having trouble at home. Judging by the dark circles under her eyes and the rigidity of her movements, things had not improved in that regard.

And what about Bug? Was Harper the only one who knew of Bug's plan to drop QB in the woods and then leave the country under an alias? Harper wasn't going to say a word. That one little tidbit might be enough to send Cleo off the edge of the dark abyss she seemed to be clinging to.

Cries from below got them all moving. Wigs already in place, they pushed themselves to their feet and put on their masks. Even Bug wore her wig and mask, which made no sense since Myles Davenport knew who she was. Maybe it was all for show since she didn't want Cleo to know what was going on. They headed downstairs.

Myles Davenport was screaming for help, begging for someone to let him out. All three of them, Cleo, Harper, and Bug, stood silently in a straight row watching him. The place smelled bad.

Bug waited for him to calm down before she said, "You know the drill. Stick your hands through the bars."

He pointed at Cleo. "I want that bitch to do the honors."

"Fine with me," Cleo said as she sashayed that way.

He put a hand through the bars as if he were eager to let Cleo zip-tie his wrist to a bar. His other hand came to rest over his heart. He looked at Bug. "Did you get my heart medicine?"

"You'll be fine," Bug said, watching to make sure QB was secure before she opened the cell door. "You're young."

Harper stepped inside the cell to pick up garbage scattered about while Bug went for the buckets.

Harper thought QB looked pale, but she figured it was from lack of sun and stress. As she bent forward to pick up another used tissue, she saw QB bend down and pull the knife from Cleo's ankle sheath. By the time Harper shouted, "Watch out!" he'd sliced through the zip tie and then pushed Harper out of his way. She lost her footing and staggered backward, hitting the floor, bruising her tailbone.

Bug whipped around, holding the bucket of shit in front of her as a shield. He grabbed it from her and tossed it at Cleo as she tried to come through the door to help.

Before Bug could get hold of her Taser, he plunged the knife into her side. Wincing in pain, she doubled over.

Cleo lunged for him, put a Taser to his neck, and held it there, her eyes wild and unblinking. The knife dropped from QB's hand as he toppled over and hit the ground. Cleo jumped on top of him, straddling his chest. "You fucking useless bastard!" She put the Taser to his chest for another jolt. Some Taser guns lasted only five seconds before shutting off. Cleo's model delivered multiple shock cycles.

As QB stiffened, Cleo dragged him closer to the bars.

Harper pushed herself from the ground and helped her. Once his wrists were zip-tied to the bars, Cleo picked up her knife, returned to her perch on his chest, and put the sharp blade against his throat. "Now do you want to say you're sorry?" she asked him.

Spit bubbles formed at the sides of his mouth, his eyes wide with fear. Harper didn't have to be a doctor to see that something was seriously wrong. "I think he's having a heart attack."

"Is that right?" Cleo sat on his chest as if he were a horse. "Giddyap," she said. "Come on, big man, take me for a ride! Yeehaw!"

Harper bent down next to Bug. There was a lot of blood. She helped her out of the cell, propped her against the wall, then grabbed a roll of paper towels and used a wad of them to try to stop the flow of blood coming from her side.

The paper towels were useless. "I'll be right back." She ran up the stairs, grabbed a cotton towel and a couple of water bottles before returning to Bug's side. "I need one of your knives," she told Cleo. "Now!"

Cleo wasn't ready to give up the one in her hand, but she reached for the knife at her waist and slid it across the floor to her.

Cleo threatened to cut out QB's tongue if he didn't apologize to Bug.

Harper tuned everything out and concentrated on what she was doing. Using the sharp blade, she ripped the towel into strips, then doused the wound with water. It looked as if Bug had moved to one side just as QB lunged at her with the knife. The blade had taken a slice out of her, but hadn't punctured any organs or muscle tissue as far as she could tell. "You need stitches," Harper said as she wrapped the strips of cloth around her waist. "We need to stop the bleeding."

"I can't go to the hospital," Bug said through gritted teeth.

Harper drew her phone from her pocket and called Psycho. She explained the situation and asked her to bring a needle and thread or whatever she had that would stop the bleeding. Harper put her phone away. "Psycho will be here as soon as possible."

"Thanks," Bug said. "I guess we're not exactly the A-Team when it comes to vigilantism."

Harper smiled, but her heart wasn't in it. This whole situation was beyond fucked up. She kept hoping things would get better, but they only got worse.

"I guess you were right about the heart attack," Cleo said. "He's dead."

# CHAPTER THIRTY-TWO

Since Ella was feeling better, Aria drove her niece to school.

Ella climbed into the passenger seat and handed Aria her yearbook. "Don't lose it. All my friends signed it and everything."

Aria merged onto the street. "I'll take good care of it, I promise." If they were focusing on schools, Aria figured she'd gather as many yearbooks within the fifteen-mile radius as possible. Starting with Ella's.

Aria glanced at the rearview mirror.

"Is someone following us?" Ella asked, peering over her shoulder.

"No. I thought I saw a friend, but it's nobody I know." The truth was, ever since Sawyer had been gifted with the old black-and-white photo of Rebecca along with the creepy note, she'd felt as if someone was following her. Even last night after she'd left Sawyer's apartment, she could have sworn someone was watching her. But she'd taken a look around and nobody was there.

Aria wondered if being paranoid was part of the deal when it came to investigative work.

She spared her niece a glance. She looked pale. "Are you sure you're feeling okay?"

"I'm fine."

Ella would be eleven soon, the same age Aria had been when her uncle Theo had started drugging her and selling her body to strange men. Aria still had nightmares of her trauma and saw each rapist's face, blurred like a pixelated square of color used on television to preserve anonymity.

All three of the Brooks sisters had been used and abused. As far as Aria was concerned, Harper had gotten the worst of it. Their own father in her room most nights. Aria couldn't think about it without wanting to puke. As sick as it sounded, she preferred to see blurry faces holding her wrists down instead of Dad. Harper had never called their father "Dad," always referring to their parents as Joyce and Dennis Brooks. Funny how some things never made sense until suddenly they did.

"So you're feeling okay?" Aria asked as they waited in a long line of cars to drop her off in front of the school.

"I'm fine."

"Do you have your lunch?"

"Yes," Ella said. "You can let me off anytime."

Aria began to pull into a parking spot when another car backed up, forcing Aria to slam on her brakes. The driver gave her a look and then took her time cranking the wheel and slowly making adjustments until her car was within the parking lines.

"That's Nurse Slimy," Ella said.

"That's not very nice."

"Well, neither is she. That's why no one will marry her."

"Who said that?"

"Everyone," Ella said with finality. She pointed to a group of kids outside. "There's George," she said. "I gotta go. Thanks for the ride, Aunt Aria."

"Bye, Ella!" She watched her niece run to catch up with George. He had long chocolate-brown hair that swept over both his eyes.

Aria didn't know Ella could smile that big. It made her heart happy.

Once she was back at home, she let Mr. Baguette out of his cage and then brought her laptop to the coffee table in front of the couch and looked up pay databases. Some of the databases were only available to private investigators and required proof of investigating licensing, but there were others that would sell their products to non-PIs. In hopes of saving a few bucks, she started calling pay database companies, telling them that she worked for the Human Resource Department at Intel and was looking for a free trial to see if the database fit their needs when it came to doing background checks on new hires. The third company fell for her story and gave her a username and password that would work only for the next hour.

She logged on as instructed. A drop-down menu appeared. She clicked on "Proprietary Data" and typed in Bob Upperman's name.

# CHAPTER
# THIRTY-THREE

Sawyer sat at her desk inside her cubicle, hoping to catch Palmer on his way in this morning. After Aria left her apartment last night, Sawyer had stayed up to finish writing a couple of stories: the first about a woman and her dog struck by a car and killed in North Natomas, and the second concerning a serial home intruder who liked to wear a bra and panties while he rummaged through people's things. The intruder was a man who had been caught on multiple security cameras, but not by the police. He never took much, although he had a penchant for leftovers in the fridge and loose change.

Sawyer glanced at her phone. Something she'd been doing too much. Still no word from Derek. She couldn't stop thinking about everything he'd said, including the little things he'd first noticed about her—her mouth, the dimple when she smiled, and a freckle she didn't know she had. It had sounded silly at the time, but she realized now that she loved the way he saw her. She loved the way his eyes lit up when he laughed. His dorky sense of humor. And mostly his patience when it came to dealing with her issues with being touched. He always kept his hands to himself, hoping to earn her trust. In return he'd gotten a friend and nothing more. She wanted to be more.

Her gaze fell on something sticking out between her stapler and tape dispenser. She reached for it, surprised to see that it was the USB that Palmer had given her. Too wrapped up in the missing girls' case, she'd completely forgotten about it.

Palmer had told her it had to do with Otto Radley. She knew the name but couldn't remember all the details of what he'd done. He'd held a woman captive. She remembered that much, which was one more reason she wasn't thrilled to have been chosen to work on the Black Wigs story. The men being targeted were rapists. And that hit too close to home.

She inserted the USB drive into her computer. As she waited for the video to load, she did a search on Otto Radley.

Multiple photos of the man popped up on her screen. Row after row of images of Otto Radley, a giant with a bald head and beady eyes. In most of the pictures he wore an orange suit. At some point he'd grown a long, scraggly beard. One picture showed him wrestling, his skin blotchy, his face a maze of angry lines. He looked like an MMA fighter but with more fat than muscle. He'd spent twenty years behind bars for kidnapping a twenty-one-year-old woman by the name of Christina Farro.

Sawyer clicked on the woman's name. There were a few images. Not many, but enough to make Sawyer cringe at the photos taken when authorities found her in a cabin in the woods.

Otto Radley had made an underground room beneath the cabin. For three years he not only sexually assaulted Christina on a regular basis but also made a habit of slicing her open with his hunting knife and then sewing her up with fishing line. Zigzag scars covered 30 percent of her body. There was a cut on her neck and face. She was tall and lean and, in one image taken before her time spent in hell, reminded Sawyer of Charlize Theron. Green eyes, defined cheekbones, and dirty-blonde hair that fell in waves around her shoulders before her abductor cut her shiny locks close to the scalp, using a dull knife.

He was truly a monster.

Sawyer clicked out of that site and used a work database to find out more about Christina Farro. She was forty-two now and lived in Stockton, where she ran a tattoo parlor called The Tattoo Pit.

Sawyer jotted down her name and apartment address.

The men who the Black Wigs had targeted appeared to be specimens scraped from the bottom of the barrel. From what little research she'd done so far, Brad Vicente, Otto Radley, and most recently, Myles Davenport, had all been accused of sexual assault and battery.

Next, she launched the video and played it directly from the flash drive. The image on her screen was a bird's-eye view of a park in West Sacramento. In the distance, a small shadowy figure with dark shoulder-length hair sat on a bench and lit up a cigarette.

It was nighttime, which made everything more difficult to see. Sawyer adjusted the computer screen's brightness, which helped a little, just as a man came into the picture. Sawyer whistled through her teeth. The guy was massive. Leaning closer, she watched the man approach the person sitting on the bench.

Before Sawyer could take another breath, the man grabbed hold of the person, held them close to his chest like a sack of grain, and carried the person off. His victim was hardly moving. Sawyer gasped when another figure stepped out from behind a tree and appeared to karate chop the back of the man's neck. All three figures were on the ground suddenly, rolling out of sight.

*Shit.*

Sawyer's adrenaline was pumping as she watched the video again, this time freezing each frame. It wasn't a karate chop the third person— a tall, slender person with the same dark shoulder-length hair—had used on the man. It was a stun gun. She knew that because she saw a spark of light right before they all tumbled to the ground.

198

Next, Sawyer compared the hair of the person sitting on the bench with the hair of the person who appeared from behind a tree. The hair was identical, the same dark color and blunt cut at the shoulders.

Although she'd much rather spend her time working Riley Addison's case, multitasking and juggling more than one story was part of the deal. She would pay Christina Farro a visit and see if the woman would be willing to talk about Otto Radley's recent release from prison.

If Sawyer intended to give the public the other side of the story, she would need to talk to the victims whose lives had been altered because of these men. She knew firsthand that most victims never forgot an assault. Even nonviolent crimes left victims confused and angry. Survivors like Christina Farro who suffered long term usually went through life triggered by sights, smells, and noises, especially on the anniversary of the crime.

It angered Sawyer that Otto Radley had been released. If the public could understand that rapists knew exactly what they were doing and nothing would stop them, maybe attitudes toward victims would change. As it stood now, many believed it was the victim's fault. There was no easy answer to putting an end to rape, but settling the burden on the shoulders of women who'd been sexually assaulted needed to stop.

After gathering her backpack and files, Sawyer stopped by Palmer's office. It was nine thirty, and he still wasn't in. Odd, she thought, since he was never late. Her next stop was Derek's office. The room was dark. She thought about leaving a note on his desk, but decided there was such a thing as overkill.

Outside, the sun warmed her back as she walked across the parking lot toward her car and noticed a flat tire. *Damn.*

She opened the back door and got rid of her stuff. As she examined the tire, someone called her name. She looked over her shoulder. It was Geezer. A short man with black spiky hair and big ears. A camera was strapped around his neck. He carried the rest of his gear in a bag with a wide strap. "What's going on?" he asked as he drew near.

"I don't know. I have a gash in my tire."

He knelt low and took a look. "Usually if someone was going to slash a tire, they would use a pocketknife, but this looks like it was done with a larger knife that a chef might use."

Sawyer raked a hand through her hair, wondering why someone would purposely ruin her tire. She took out her phone. "I should call someone."

"Does your car insurance cover roadside assistance?"

"No."

"Then let me take care of it." Geezer set his bag on the ground, and she didn't protest when he lifted his camera from around his neck and set it on top of the bag. "I'll need you to open your trunk."

Sawyer did as he said, thanking him profusely for helping, glad he was wearing denim and a T-shirt. Although she didn't know Geezer very well, she found his willingness to jump in and help her heartwarming.

While Geezer loosened the lug nuts and then used the jack to raise her vehicle, she said, "I've been meaning to talk to you about the pictures you took at Mark Brennan's house when he was arrested. Did you take pictures of the front of his house when it was first discovered that Riley was missing?"

He unscrewed the lug nuts and removed the flat tire. "Yes. I took pictures the day after she went missing and again when the Music Man was arrested."

The Music Man was what the press had been calling Mark Brennan. "Any chance I could take a look at the pictures?"

He grabbed the spare tire from her trunk, slid it in place, and tightened the lug nuts. "I've got a couple of deadlines to meet, but I should be able to pull those up for you at the end of the day. Does that work?"

"That would be great. Thanks."

Once he lowered the vehicle, Sawyer put the equipment and flat tire back in her trunk. "I owe you a drink," she said.

He brushed himself off. "No need. Just put in a good word for me next time you talk to Palmer."

"I'll do that. Palmer wasn't in his office earlier," she said. "Any idea where he's at?"

"Doctor appointment. The old man is having difficulties with his heart."

Sawyer's heart sank. "How bad is it?"

"High cholesterol," he said. "He's getting a screening or something to see if his arteries are clogged."

Sawyer didn't like the sound of that. Palmer could be a pain in the ass, but she looked up to him, respected him, and didn't like the thought of him being sick.

"You're good to go," Geezer told her as he gathered his camera and bag.

"Thanks."

"Any idea who might have sliced your tire?"

"No," Sawyer said, wondering if the same person who had left her the envelope on her doorstep was responsible.

"Stay safe," Geezer told her before walking off.

# CHAPTER THIRTY-FOUR

Harper was out of breath by the time they got Bug upstairs.

Psycho, Cleo, Lily, and Harper had carried Bug upstairs and set her on top of a sleeping bag on the floor, her back against the wall. Psycho not only brought a needle and thread to the construction site where The Crew was hiding out, she also brought a couple of Xanax pills for Bug to take and a good ole leather belt for her to bite down on, just like they did in the movies when someone needed surgery without anesthesia.

They all found a seat and waited for the drugs to take effect.

"Looks like another one bit the dust," Psycho said, referring to the dead man downstairs.

"What are we going to do with the body?" Lily asked.

"Leave him in the woods," Bug said in a weak voice.

"We could bury him," Cleo offered.

Psycho gave an adamant shake of her head. "No. None of us are prepared for that. It took us half a day to dig a hole big enough for Otto Radley. This place isn't isolated enough . . . Too risky."

"What do you propose?" Harper asked.

"I know of a place an hour away in Pollock Pines. After I finish sewing Bug up, I have to run home for a flashlight and a tarp. When it's dark enough, we'll roll the body in the tarp and place him in the trunk of Bug's car. We'll take two cars. Harper will drive with me in my car, and we'll lead the way."

"Why do we all need to go?" Lily asked.

Psycho fixed her gaze on Lily. "Because Bug is injured and we'll need all the help we can get, carrying deadweight."

"Wouldn't it be easier to dump him on the side of the road somewhere?" Cleo asked.

"We need to do this right," Psycho said, unable to hide her frustration. "If the animals don't get to him before he's found, investigators won't know what to make of finding him naked in the woods. We need to keep them confused. Once Bug sends the information regarding QB's embezzlement via email or whatever method she decides to use, the public, not to mention his family, will go berserk. If all goes well, his deeds will become the focus, sending authorities on a wild ride as they search for clues in all the wrong places."

"Shouldn't you sew her up now?" Lily asked. "She's bleeding through the cloth again."

"In a few minutes," Psycho said. "I want to give the drugs time to take effect."

"Why does it feel like we're the bad guys?" Bug asked, wincing when she tried to adjust her hip to one side.

"That fucker downstairs ruined multiple lives," Cleo said. "Fuck feeling bad. I'm glad he's dead."

Harper didn't say anything, but it seemed as if Cleo had hardened since they joined forces.

"Is all this bullshit worth it?" Psycho asked. "Yeah," she said, answering her own question. "Otto Radley and QB won't be hurting anyone else. End of story."

"What about Brad Vicente?" Lily asked.

Psycho rolled her eyes. "Big deal, he lost his penis. I've never seen an inmate give so many interviews. He's still a thorn in my side."

"You wanted to teach QB a lesson," Cleo reminded Bug. "And you did. You taught him the ultimate lesson—don't fuck with me."

"It could have turned out different if the system had worked," Harper said.

Lily snorted. "In your dreams."

Cleo looked at Harper and asked, "You're pregnant, aren't you?"

Harper tried not to show her surprise. She didn't want to discuss her pregnancy with The Crew, but now that the cat was out of the bag, fuck it. "I am pregnant. Why do you ask?"

Cleo had taken a bite of her unfinished burrito. She swallowed, then said, "Hormones are kicking in and making you soft."

"Maybe so," Harper said. "Now is probably a good time to let you all know that after we finish taking care of Cleo's frat boys, I'm done. It's time for me to put my bitterness and anger to rest."

"What about you?" Cleo asked Psycho. "Any plans for the future?"

"Whatever happens with The Crew, I'm good. I'll just keep doing what I always do . . . taking things one day at a time." Psycho's fingers brushed over the scar on her neck. "It's worked for me so far."

# Chapter Thirty-Five

On her way to Stockton to talk with Christina Farro, Sawyer got a call from Aria.

"I've been trying to call you for the past hour. Where have you been?"

"I've been busy. Somebody sliced my tire."

"That's fucked up," Aria said. "You need to arm yourself."

"I'll be fine."

"If you say so, but I don't like it one bit. Did you get my message about Bob Upperman?"

"No. You found him?"

"I did. His name is Alexander Robert Upperman, and he lives in Midtown. I left him a message. Hopefully he'll return my call. Otherwise we might have to go to his house unannounced."

"Sounds like a plan."

"Have you heard from Paige Owens?" Aria asked.

"Not yet."

"I have one more yearbook I want to collect and then I'm going to the hospital to see if I can find a way into Mrs. Addison's room. Wish me luck."

"Good luck. And Aria, thanks for everything. I don't know what I would do without you."

"You're the most badass Brooks sister of the three of us. You would be fine."

---

The apartment building where Christina Farro resided looked like any other severely neglected apartment building in the area. The puke-pink paint was chipping away, and the stairs were littered with garbage, including drug paraphernalia. Sections of chain-link fencing, rusted and warped by time, encircled the property and served no purpose.

Sawyer walked up three flights of stairs and knocked on the door to apartment 313. Nobody appeared. Listening carefully, she heard no sign of life inside. She turned toward the railing to take in the view of the parking lot. What she thought was a public park across the street turned out to be a cemetery. A man was walking around and removing dead flowers from markers. The wrought iron fence was still intact. The gate was shut. She was too far away to make out whether the man was a groundskeeper or a visitor who liked things neat and tidy.

Sawyer turned back to apartment 313 and was about to knock again when footsteps sounded behind her. She looked over her shoulder and recognized the woman immediately. "Christina Farro?"

The woman sort of nudged Sawyer out of her way and slipped her key into the lock. "Who wants to know?"

"I'm Sawyer Brooks. I work for the *Sacramento Independent*. I'm doing a story on the Black Wigs."

Christina stepped into her apartment and disappeared into another room, leaving the door open behind her.

Sawyer poked her head inside, but didn't go in. "The Black Wigs are what the media are calling the women who wear disguises and appear to be cleaning up the streets, so to speak."

"Yeah, I know who you're talking about," Christina said as she returned wearing a fresh T-shirt. "It's all old news, isn't it?"

"Well, yes, but I've been asked to update the public."

Christina made a face. "Lucky you."

"Yeah," Sawyer said with a half-hearted chuckle. She continued to stand at the door after Christina Farro had once again wandered to the back of her apartment. It had taken Sawyer forty-six minutes to get here. She wasn't going to give up that easily.

"You can come in if you want," Christina said when she reappeared. "I needed a quick change. I'm good now."

Sawyer stepped inside and shut the door behind her.

Christina gestured toward the couch. "You thirsty?"

"No, but thanks," Sawyer said, taking a seat.

Christina filled a plastic cup with water from the faucet, then joined her, taking a seat in a recliner. "So why are you here? What does your story have to do with me?"

Sawyer sat up tall, notepad and pen in hand. "I've decided to take a different approach from what's been all over the media. I plan to focus on the survivors. I want my readers to know what these men have done and how they're getting away with ruining people's lives."

"Okay," she said.

"What do you think about Otto Radley getting out of prison?" Sawyer asked, pleased the woman was willing to talk.

"I don't give a shit. Whatever. I've moved on."

Sawyer was writing that down when Christina added, "I probably feel the same way you felt when your uncle got out of jail."

Sawyer looked up and met Christina's gaze straight on.

"Journalists aren't the only people who know things," Christina said. "I read the paper. I also know how to google shit. I knew who you were the minute I saw you. I know your story and you know mine. If your readers want to know something about me or you, it's all out there. They just need to do a little work."

"But no matter how many hours they spend on their computers and reading Wikipedia, they still won't know how you felt when you found out Otto Radley had been released from jail."

Christina smiled as she raised her glass as if to say "Cheers." "I felt nothing. You can tell your audience that."

"It didn't piss you off?"

She shrugged. "If the FBI and the police don't care, why should I?"

*Because he didn't deserve to be released,* Sawyer thought but didn't say.

"If he harms someone else," Christina went on, "they're the ones who will have blood on their hands. Not me." She chugged the rest of her water. "If anything, I'm surprised they kept him locked up as long as they did."

"He hasn't been seen since his release."

The sarcasm in Christina's tone rang clear when she said, "That's too bad."

"I have video footage of a man who could be Otto Radley approaching a woman in a park. She appears to be wearing a black wig. The images are grainy, but still interesting."

"So what happened—you know—to the woman?"

"The man grabbed her and carried her off, but another woman appears with an identical wig and used a stun gun on him. The rest happened off-screen, and I couldn't find any reports of a mugging in the area for that time and place."

"I agree. That *is* interesting," Christina said. "Maybe there's more to the Black Wigs than I thought."

"How so?"

"If they're responsible for cutting off a man's dick, that's cute and everything, but making a hulk like Otto Radley disappear . . . Well, that's something else altogether, isn't it?"

Sawyer was a bit surprised by her nonchalance. "He kept you hidden in a secret underground room without electricity. How did you cope?"

OUT OF HER MIND

"At first I sang to myself and made up stories. As the days became weeks and then months, I exercised to keep my blood flowing. What was interesting to me was how quickly I stopped dreading his weekly visits."

Sawyer lifted a brow and waited for her to continue.

"I was always hungry and thirsty," she explained. "His visits usually meant I would get something to eat and drink."

"Did you ever give up hope of getting away?"

"Oh, yeah. Right away. There was no way out of the place. I tried pulling away a floorboard and digging my way out, but the dirt beneath was like granite, and I didn't have any tools. There were no windows, and the door was made of steel or something. If you've seen pictures of Otto Radley, you know he's a big man. Without a gun or a knife or any sort of weapon, my single-mindedness became all about staying alive. Period."

Christina went on answering Sawyer's questions for twenty minutes before she pushed herself to her feet, a signal that it was time to go. She wore skinny jeans and a V-neck T-shirt, and it was difficult not to fixate on all the scars covering her arms. Christina caught her looking and stepped closer to give her a better look. "I used to hide all my mutilations. Not anymore. Every mark is a part of me. It's who I am."

Sawyer liked her gumption. By the time she left, she felt a tremendous amount of respect for the woman. Christina Farro had survived three years in hell, and yet she wasn't going to let Otto Radley ruin one more day than he already had.

# Chapter
# Thirty-Six

Hours later, Sawyer sat inside the tire store lobby with her laptop and wrote a first draft of her interview with Christina Farro as she waited for her car to be ready. The total cost with labor was $212. Highway robbery. But they were the only tire store that could get her in without an appointment and take care of it while she waited.

When that was done, she remembered she was out of cat food. It was getting dark by the time she drove into the Walmart parking lot. She needed cat food, sourdough bread, avocados, and fruit.

The fluorescent lighting inside the store was incredibly bright. Sawyer rubbed her eyes and made the mistake of heading down the candy aisle. Her stomach growled. She grabbed a box of Good & Plenty and tossed it into her cart, proud of herself for passing up the red licorice and Snickers. When it came to candy, she had no willpower.

She walked by the floral department and found the bread she was looking for in the deli area. On her way through produce, she grabbed a bunch of not-too-ripe bananas, two avocados, and a basket of strawberries.

The cat food was at the other end of the store. Halfway there, she heard a crash and looked up. A child had dropped a jar of pickles and was crying as his mom did her best to take control of the situation.

Beyond the pickle incident, Sawyer recognized a woman at the back of the store, looking through racks of clothes. It was the nurse from Ella's school. Sawyer headed that way, intent on thanking the woman for taking care of Ella and spreading a little cheer.

As she drew closer, she saw that Nurse Amy was looking through a rack of little-girl dresses and rompers.

Sawyer came to a stop when she saw what Nurse Amy was wearing. A denim skirt and red Crocs with holes in them—the same outfit the woman who had attempted to take Paige had been wearing.

The woman fit the description to a T.

No children. So why would she need a new dress for a little girl on a Wednesday night?

Nurse Amy selected a dress and left the little girls' department. Once she was gone, Sawyer made a beeline for the rack where the nurse had finally selected a turquoise pleated skirt dress with a tie at the waist. She'd chosen the one with a blue marker on the hanger, which fit girls aged ten to twelve, according to the tag.

Goose bumps prickled Sawyer's skin. She pushed her cart back to the front of the store and watched from a middle aisle as Nurse Amy checked out with only the dress. Nothing else.

Leaving her cart, Sawyer exited the store and walked straight to her car, keeping an eye on Nurse Amy the entire time, frowning when Nurse Amy climbed into a white SUV.

Sawyer climbed into her car, turned on the engine, and followed the SUV out of the parking lot and back onto the main street. That's when she saw the license plate number: 6 VKL 277.

She called Aria, who picked up on the first ring.

"I'm glad you called," Aria said. "I stopped by your apartment, but you weren't home, so I started to worry."

"I'm following Nurse Amy."

"What? Following her where? Why?"

"Looks like we're headed to East Sacramento. She drives a white SUV and the license plate has an *L* and two sevens, just as Paige described."

"This is so weird because Ella was just talking about the woman. They call her Nurse Slimy, and apparently she's single."

"She has no children," Sawyer added. "But I just saw her purchase a dress for a ten-to-twelve-year-old in Walmart."

"Maybe she has a niece."

"That's true. I'll feel better, though, once I see where she lives and take a quick look around."

"Are you planning on knocking on her door?"

Up ahead Sawyer saw the SUV turn onto H Street. "I want to, but she met me the other day when I picked up Ella."

"I could do it," Aria said. "What should I say if she comes to the door?"

Sawyer thought for a moment. "You could pretend like you're looking for an old friend. Make up a name of someone who used to live in the neighborhood. Tell her your cell phone died and ask if you can use her phone."

"Knocking on the door is one thing, but you want me to go inside?"

Aria was right. Nurse Amy could be dangerous. "Never mind. It was a stupid idea."

"No. We need to do this."

Sawyer watched the garage door open. Neat and clean, plenty of room for her SUV. "Looks like she's home." Sawyer gave Aria the address.

"Don't go anywhere. I'll be there soon."

---

Sawyer was sitting back at an angle across the street from Nurse Amy's house, a two-story Tudor with leaded-glass windows in the front, when Aria pulled up to the curb directly in front of the house.

Aria climbed out of the car, shut the door, then looked around until she spotted Sawyer across the way. She dipped her chin in acknowledgment and then turned and walked up the pathway to the front of the house.

The tree-lined street where Sawyer had been parked for thirty minutes was fairly busy. She'd seen bikers, mothers pushing strollers, and a man and woman out on a walk, holding hands.

Nurse Amy's porch light flicked on right before the door opened. Sawyer had no idea what Aria was telling the woman, but she had her attention. She even handed her a clipboard as she talked.

As Sawyer watched, a light upstairs came on. Curtains covering the window moved just enough for her to see a shadowy figure peeking out. Someone else was in the house? Sawyer's gaze returned to Aria just as someone knocked on the passenger window and made her jump. A short man with disorderly straw-colored hair was peering through the window. Glad the doors were locked, she turned on the engine so she could roll the window down halfway.

"Can I help you?" he asked. "My wife noticed you've been parked out here for some time, so I thought I would come out here and investigate to ease her mind."

Sawyer smiled and held up her phone for him to see. "I came to visit a friend, Stacy Anderson, but she's not answering her phone, and I didn't write down the address."

"Well, hmm. I don't know of any Anderson family living on the street, but I could go ask my wife for you. She knows everyone on our block."

"I thought she gave me the address to the house right across from you," Sawyer said, gesturing toward Nurse Amy's house.

"Oh, no. That's Amy Lennox. She was living in that house when we moved in. Sorry I'm not more help."

Sawyer looked back at the house. Not only was Aria gone, the curtain upstairs was closed tight and the light was off. "I wonder if she rents out the upstairs room and that's where my friend lives? Because right before you tapped on my window, I saw someone peer through the upstairs window."

He frowned. "She definitely lives alone."

Sawyer's phone buzzed, and she quickly picked up the call.

Aria said, "I know you're talking to someone, but I wanted you to know that I'm at a small market on McKinley Boulevard right around the corner. I'll wait for you here."

The call ended, but Sawyer didn't want the man still looking at her to know that. "Hi, Stacy. Yes, I've been sitting in my car for a while now, but I didn't have your address, and you weren't answering your phone. I know. I'm so sorry. Hold on for a second." Sawyer looked at the man. "Looks like I had the wrong street entirely. Sorry to bother you and thanks for the help."

Sawyer merged onto the street, turned onto McKinley Boulevard, spotted the market Aria had mentioned, and parked next to her sister. Sawyer got out of her car and slid into Aria's passenger seat. "What happened?"

"That was crazy," Aria said. "I don't know why I got myself so worked up, but my heart is still racing. Who was that man talking to you?"

"Just a neighbor checking on me since I had been parked there for a while. He said her name is Amy Lennox. Said she lived alone, and yet while you were talking to her, I saw an upstairs light go on before someone peered through the curtains."

"I knew I heard a noise upstairs," Aria said. "I brought a clipboard with lined paper and pretended I needed her to sign my petition to have more trees planted."

"She fell for that?"

"I guess so since she signed her name. After the noise sounded from upstairs, she seemed distracted. I asked her if someone else was there at the house and if maybe they could sign the petition too, but she was adamant about it being the television that I heard. In fact, that's when she signed the paper and shut the door in my face. She looked a little freaked out to me. What should we do now?"

"I need to talk to Palmer."

"Do you think it could be Riley inside her house?"

"I don't know, but we need to find out."

# CHAPTER
# THIRTY-SEVEN

Sawyer and Palmer sat in his Jeep across from Nurse Amy's house, waiting for Detective Perez. Although Detective Perez had been unable to obtain a search warrant since the judge determined there was not probable cause that a crime had been committed, the detective did agree to knock on the door and question the woman who lived there.

"I wish the judge had signed off on the warrant," Sawyer said. "It would have made the process so much easier. Amy Lennox fits the description given by Paige Owens. She drives a white SUV with the numbers and letters Paige mentioned, she has access to syringes and needles, and she bought a dress for a little girl even though she has no children."

"For starters," Palmer said, "everything you've got is circumstantial. We're lucky Perez agreed to knock on the woman's door. If she's innocent, she'll open the door and agree to let Perez into her house for a look," Palmer said, his voice weary, reminding Sawyer of what Geezer said about Palmer's health.

"I heard you were at the doctor's today. Everything okay?"

"I'm fine." He straightened in his seat. "Looks like they're here."

An unmarked car and a police cruiser double-parked in front of Nurse Amy's house. Palmer had taken the soft top off his Jeep, making it easy for Sawyer to see what was going on. A neighborhood dog had been barking since Palmer arrived ten minutes ago. Aria had left before that.

It was go time.

Detective Perez stood on the sidewalk, waiting for the uniformed officer to join him. It was dark out, and the two men looked like tall silhouettes as they approached the front door.

The warm air hinted of jasmine.

Palmer was about to tell her something when the door to Nurse Amy's house opened. Beneath the porch light, Sawyer could see that it was Amy Lennox. Perez was talking to her. She could hear his voice, but she couldn't make out the exact words being said.

Perez took a step back, giving the uniformed officer a chance to speak. He had a booming voice that carried. He pointed inside and asked her if anyone was there.

"She's shaking her head," Palmer said.

A crash sounded. Loud enough for both Sawyer and Palmer to hear.

Gun drawn, the officer disappeared inside. Nurse Amy's voice became shrill as she told the officer he didn't have permission to enter her home and must leave.

Detective Perez asked her to step outside, but she wasn't having it.

Sawyer saw the upstairs light go on in the same room where she'd seen someone peek through the curtains earlier.

"It's got to be Riley," Sawyer said. "They found Riley."

"Leave him alone," a woman shouted.

Moments later, the officer ushered a shirtless man with his hands cuffed behind him toward his cruiser. He opened the back door and pushed the man's head low enough that he could slide in before he shut the door. Perez joined the officer outside. The door to the house closed.

"What's going on?" she asked Palmer. "Where's Amy Lennox?"

"Wait here." Palmer climbed out, jogged across the road, and before he could get a word out, Perez let him have it, his voice explosive, every word tumbling over the next.

Sawyer's stomach hardened into a tight ball. What happened in there? Where was Riley Addison? She wanted to jump out of Palmer's Jeep, run across the road, and march through the front door. Neither Perez nor the officer had been inside the home long enough to do a thorough check. There could be a basement or shed out back. What about the garage?

It all happened way too fast.

Nothing she had witnessed made any sense. Her gaze fixated on the man in the back of the cruiser. *Who the hell was the shirtless man? A lover? Had she gotten it all wrong?*

Palmer was on his way back to the Jeep. He climbed in and said, "You're off the case."

It was worse than she thought. "Why? I don't understand. What happened?"

"Amy Lennox insisted no one was in the house, but the noise coming from upstairs alarmed the officer, and he took off only to find a man hiding under the bed in the master bedroom. He's married and worried about being found out. He was arrested after he made the mistake of throwing a couple of punches at the officer."

"But what about the dress Amy Lennox bought—"

"It was a gift for her coworker's daughter, Molly. She showed Perez the box she'd wrapped in colorful paper and tied with a ribbon."

"Molly was one of the names the woman called out when Paige Owens escaped. And what about the SUV she's driving? Did anyone question her about that?"

"Enough," he said, rubbing his temple.

Sawyer exhaled. The woman needed to be questioned, but nobody wanted to listen. "Don't take me off this one, Palmer."

"I don't have a choice. Perez wants you fired. He threatened to press charges against the *Sacramento Independent* for what he called 'the excessive stream of false information being reported.'"

"Can he do that?"

Palmer shrugged. "I don't know. But I do know that my department can't afford to get into any sort of feud with Perez. It's best if you take the next couple of weeks off and stay off the grid."

She could see that Palmer was struggling with what he felt he had to do. "I understand," she finally said. "You took a chance on me, and I messed up. I'm sorry I've made things difficult for you—"

"Stop," he said. "We all make mistakes. Even Perez. You might only be a decent journalist, *but* you're a top-notch investigative reporter."

"I wanted to find her so bad. I wasn't trying to impress you or Perez. I just wanted to find her."

Palmer rested a hand on her shoulder. "I know you did."

She'd blown it. Her rapid appraisal of the situation had gotten the best of her. She shouldered her bag. As she climbed out of the Jeep, Palmer said, "Don't stop listening to your instincts, Sawyer. It's not your instincts that get you into trouble. It's your impatience and overconfidence that get in your way."

She nodded. He was right. Her knees wobbled when her feet touched the ground. It took everything she had to keep her head high as she walked to her car. Palmer waited until she started the engine before he drove off.

And just like that, the longest day of her life was over. And so was her career if she wasn't careful.

# CHAPTER THIRTY-EIGHT

Riley's stomach wouldn't stop gurgling. Her every thought was of a juicy hamburger with french fries dripping with ketchup. And water. She could drink a gallon of water right now.

The days and nights had gotten away from Riley. Time was a blur inside the closet. It smelled so bad. She'd spent hours working to remove the tape from her hands and legs. Once that was done, she began to prepare for Bubbles's return, but the woman never came back.

There were no longer any pictures on the wall. Tired of looking at so much misery and pain, she'd torn them down. She was going to die. Riley knew that much. And eventually she figured her photo would go up on the wall of shame with the others.

By the door, Riley could see the pencil she'd found in one of the bins. Next to the pencil was the jagged piece of plastic. She planned to use both weapons to fight Bubbles if she ever opened the door. But it better be soon because Riley was growing weaker by the moment.

Bored and hungry and frightened, she turned off the light, then got down on all fours and looked under the sliver of space beneath the door. It was nighttime. During the day, she could see sunlight hitting the floor. As she pushed herself to a sitting position, she heard someone walk into the room. A light flicked on.

Her heart raced.

Padded feet crossed the floor. It sounded as if Bubbles was opening and closing drawers. Next came clinking and clanking sounds as she moved the chains from under the bed. Shivers rolled over Riley as she quietly picked up the pencil and the piece of plastic, stood tall, and readied herself in case Bubbles opened the closet door.

No sooner had the thought passed through her mind than a key was inserted into the lock. The light filtering in under the door allowed her to see the knob turning. The moment her eyes connected with Bubbles she screamed as loud as she could and pummeled her arms, stabbing the woman with both the pencil and the hard, pointy plastic.

The pencil took root in Bubbles's arm!

That would have been a good thing except for the look on Bubbles's face. Her teeth were clenched tight, her skin bright red, and her eyes bulged as she looked from the pencil to Riley.

An unnatural silence fell around them. Riley could hear her heart thumping against her ribs as Bubbles yanked the pencil from her arm and tossed it to the side. Her wild-eyed gaze pinned Riley where she stood. She grabbed both of Riley's wrists, shaking hard until Riley thought her arm might break off. The jagged piece of plastic dropped to the ground.

Bubbles dragged her to the bed. Riley could see the metal cuffs, wide open and waiting. She needed to get away. This was it. Her chance. Half starved and weaker than she'd ever been, she yanked her arm out of Bubbles's grasp and ran, slamming the bedroom door shut behind her before scrambling for the stairs.

She missed a step and went spiraling downward, thump, thump, thump. Her side bumped the railing, her hip banged against the wood step, but she couldn't stop the momentum. She rolled all the way down and landed on her face, knocking her mouth on the tile landing.

She was sprawled out across the tiles. Blood trickled from the sides of her mouth. Through a heavy-lidded eye, she saw the front door.

Freedom was only a few feet away.

When she tried to push herself that way, a sharp stab of pain sliced through her right leg. She used her arms, dragging herself forward an inch at a time. *Almost there. Just a little bit farther.*

Footsteps sounded on the stairs.

*Faster,* Riley thought. *You've got to move faster.*

She grimaced. She could hardly move.

Bubbles stepped in front of her, hands on her hips, looking at her like a mom might do if you got caught eating cookies before dinner. Calmly, without a word spoken, Bubbles grabbed hold of both of Riley's arms and dragged her across the tiles and back up the stairs, one step at a time. Riley's screams were high-pitched and raw.

By the time Bubbles had hauled Riley up the stairs and into the bedroom, she could hear the crazy lady's raspy breath, in and out, like an angry bull. She quickly put a cuff around Riley's ankle and clamped it shut, making sure it was secure before she scooped Riley into her arms and plopped her on top of the mattress.

Riley screamed again. Her leg was broken, the pain unbearable. She was going to be sick. The bone wasn't sticking out of her skin, but her leg was bent in a weird position.

Bubbles grabbed hold of Riley's upper body and yanked her toward the headboard, prompting another cry of agony. Riley's arms hung limp at her sides as Bubbles clamped metal cuffs over one wrist and then the other.

The blood coming out of her mouth, Riley realized as she used her tongue to feel around, was from missing and broken teeth. One of her front teeth had shattered, leaving only a sharp fragment. Two of her bottom teeth were cracked, and one was gone.

Intense rage seemed to have given Bubbles increased strength as she worked on cleaning up the room. Moving to the closet where Riley had spent the past few days, Bubbles grabbed the smelly bin and carried it into the bathroom.

Riley heard the toilet flush and then the sound of the bathtub faucet turned on full blast. As Bubbles marched back and forth from the bathroom to the closet carrying a rag and a large plastic bag, she cursed and muttered under her breath. "You blew it," she told Riley, her eyes wild. "We could have had a wonderful life together."

"Why me?" Riley asked. Nothing made any sense.

Bubbles had been about to disappear inside the closet when she looked at Riley and said, "Because you were special and I chose you. The moment I saw you, I knew."

Riley swallowed. Even that hurt. "I have a mom and a dad and a brother," Riley said. "Why can't you understand that?"

Bubbles shook her head, looking sad and weary instead of angry. "You're *my* daughter. But look what you've done."

Riley wasn't sure exactly what Bubbles was referring to: the scratches and the hole in her arm where blood ran down from her elbow where the pencil had pierced her skin, or the mess Riley had made in the closet. Either way, for the first time in her short life, she was pretty sure she was witnessing the type of people her mom counseled in prison on a daily basis. Somewhere along the way, people like Bubbles simply lost their minds.

But Bubbles had a job. She ate, dressed, and did what millions of other people did every single day. She'd heard the term "functioning alcoholic," so maybe Bubbles would be considered a functioning lunatic? "What happened to you?" Riley asked her.

Bubbles pushed her hair out of her face and looked at Riley as if she were talking in another language. She had no idea what Riley meant, so Riley asked a different question. "What happened to the real Molly?"

Bubbles dropped the bag on the floor and disappeared back inside the bathroom. She returned to the side of the bed with a towel and bucket of soapy water, and washed the blood from Riley's face, neck, and arms with a washrag. "My first Molly was an angel," Bubbles said. "Perfect in every way. All the nurses in the hospital where she was born said she was the most beautiful baby they had ever seen."

Bubbles looked toward the ceiling.

"What happened to her?"

"My husband was away on business. I was on a leave of absence from work, and I was tired . . . *so* tired. Babies are a lot of work."

She looked at Riley then, and she reminded her of an actor onstage, every expression animated. "Diapers and feedings and baths, over and over again. Never sleeping." Touching her temple, Bubbles let out a long sigh. "That night my darling Molly was crying all night, up every hour on the hour. It was three in the morning when I slid off the bed and made my way down the hallway and into Molly's room." Her eyes grew twice their size as she said, "I remember it still. I scooped up my precious bundle and brought her to bed. She was ravenous, and she latched on to my breast as if she'd never eaten before. She ate and ate, tugging and pulling on my nipple."

Riley inwardly cringed.

Bubbles had grown quiet, her gaze fixated on the ceiling again when she said, "The next morning, I woke up feeling refreshed and better than ever. I looked at the clock, surprised that it was already seven and Molly hadn't awoken. I nearly wept with joy until I got up and saw her lying there on the bed. Her lips were blue. She was gone. I killed my sweet Molly."

Silence stretched out before them.

Riley didn't know what to say, especially when Bubbles looked at her again, her eyes rounder than she'd ever seen them. "For all those years I'd wanted nothing more than to have a baby to call my own." A wistful sigh escaped her. "And now she's gone." Bubbles tossed the washrag into the bucket, then took a seat on the edge of the bed, making the mattress sink lower.

Riley gritted her teeth as pain clawed into her. "I think my leg is broken."

"That's too bad. If you'd been a good girl, none of this would have happened."

"I'll never be a good girl," Riley said, and she meant it. She could never live here with Bubbles and pretend everything was okay.

"I know that," Bubbles said. "You're a smart girl, though, and you know what happens next, don't you?"

"You're going to kill me. Maybe with a gun or a knife. I'm not sure which one."

A giggle escaped Bubbles. Her big marble eyes sparkled. "You're a clever one, all right. Despite all the pain and grief you've caused me, I'm going to make sure you don't suffer overly much." She rested a hand on Riley's bad leg and squeezed. "Just kidding."

Fiery hot pain made Riley scream again.

Bubbles reached up and clamped a hand tight over Riley's mouth. Dizziness made the room spin. Riley thought she might pass out. She was looking forward to it. Instead, she desperately sucked in air through the cracks between Bubbles's fingers, again and again, her eyes open just enough to see Bubbles's mouth move as she said, "When the time comes, I'm going to give you enough pills to put you to sleep and then carry you into the bathroom for a good long soak in the tub. Doesn't that sound nice?"

Riley tried to shake her head, but she was pretty sure nothing happened.

Bubbles finally dropped her hand from Riley's mouth and said, "I'm going to finish cleaning up here and then get you something to

eat." Her smile reminded Riley of the Cheshire cat's grin. "Think of it as your last supper."

Riley wanted to ask her when she would be dying—tonight? Tomorrow? But she couldn't form the words, let alone push them out of her mouth.

Her lips trembled as she watched Bubbles pick up the garbage bag and head into the closet. She thought of the girl in the birthday hat and prayed for someone to save her.

The tears came flooding out of her. She couldn't stop crying. She wanted her mom, needed to feel the comfort of being held in her arms.

# CHAPTER THIRTY-NINE

Harper wasn't sure how long she'd been scouring the cement floor where QB had stayed. Her fingers were red and raw, her mind numb. No matter how much or how hard she scrubbed, she still saw blood in her mind's eye.

Lots of blood.

Bug's blood.

Trying to keep Bug quiet while Psycho had sewn her up with a needle and thread had not only fried Harper's nerves, it had been heartbreaking to watch. The Xanax had hardly seemed to take the edge off. The second Psycho had finished, Bug had passed out from exhaustion. The rest of them used that time to scour the place, getting rid of all traces of evidence.

Hours later, Psycho returned with the tarp, and together they rolled QB inside and placed him in the trunk of Bug's Volkswagen Passat. Psycho had gotten rid of the van used to take QB captive days before, dumping it in a canal where she said hundreds of other vehicles had been laid to rest. They had no choice but to take her word for it and hope it was never found.

Under the cover of darkness, The Crew set out for Pollock Pines, a heavily wooded area with a population of six or seven thousand. It would take an hour to get there.

As Psycho had suggested, Harper drove with her in her electric-blue Mini Cooper, while the others followed behind in Bug's car. Since Bug was injured, Lily drove while Bug slept in the back seat. All cell phones had been turned off. Nobody was allowed to text or make calls. The closer they got, the lower the temperature dropped.

They took Exit 57 off US-50 East to Gilmore Road, then to Barrett Pass Road. Looming on both sides were tall gray pines and blue oaks. It wasn't long before Psycho made a left onto what might have once been a road but was now overgrown with forest debris that cracked and popped beneath the tires. They drove at a snail's pace less than a half mile from the road when Psycho brought the car to a stop and killed the engine.

The car following behind did the same.

Doors opened and closed as they all climbed out, everyone zipping and buttoning jackets tight to protect themselves against the cold wind.

Bug was wide awake now, making apologies as she insisted on helping.

"You can come with us," Psycho told her as she strapped a band with a light around her head, "but you can't help carry the body. I'm not in the mood to sew you up again, understand?"

Bug nodded.

"Okay," Cleo said, opening the trunk of Bug's car. "Let's get this done."

From the beginning it had been clear that Psycho was The Crew's leader. Once they made plans, she never wavered. And tonight was no different as she grabbed a section of the tarp and led the group through the forest with only the light on her headband to guide her.

It might have been an easy walk had there been daylight and they weren't carrying a dead body, but as it was, they lost the trail more than once.

The gusty wind caught them all by surprise. If they happened by anyone, the plan was to make it appear as if they were setting up camp. But that didn't happen. Psycho knew the area so well it prompted Harper to wonder if they were anywhere near the cabin where she'd been held captive in an underground room.

Harper kept her thoughts to herself.

"This is good," Psycho said. "Let's set him on the ground and roll him out."

The body did indeed roll out from the tarp that Cleo clung to so the wind wouldn't take it from her grasp. Thick brush stopped his body from rolling out of sight. They would have preferred to leave him fully dressed, but his pants and shirt and socks and shoes were covered in Bug's blood, and his clothes would need to be burned. If they'd done their jobs right, investigators would have a difficult time figuring out how he got from point A to point B. And an autopsy would reveal that he'd died of a heart attack.

They arrived back at their cars without any mishap.

Harper looked up at the night sky, refusing to feel guilty. Those men—QB, Otto Radley, Brad Vicente, and even her father—had all gotten what they deserved. Her only regret was what her involvement with The Crew had done to her marriage. She might not be able to change the past, but she would do everything in her power to win back her husband's trust.

On the way home, Psycho told her that a reporter named Sawyer Brooks had paid her a visit. It was clear by Psycho's tone that she knew Sawyer Brooks was her sister. Apparently Sawyer was doing a follow-up story on the Black Wigs, a.k.a. The Crew. They had gained a lot of notoriety after chopping off Brad Vicente's penis.

It wasn't a big surprise that Psycho knew her real name. Most of The Crew had been involved in court proceedings and trials. Their stories were sensational and easy to find on the internet. But The Crew had decided early on to use aliases to try to protect themselves when sending electronic messages. Their nicknames caught on quickly, and there had been no reason to call one another by any other name.

Although Psycho said she wasn't concerned about Sawyer's visit, she thought it best not to mention it to the rest of the group.

Harper was thankful for that. She was also thankful that Psycho didn't know her sister. Sawyer might look harmless, but when it came to solving a case or finding answers to a puzzle, Sawyer was a bloodhound, following trails for days on end until she was satisfied.

It made sense that Sawyer would be doing a write-up about the Black Wigs since the media exposure had already gotten out of hand. It didn't mean Harper liked it, but her hands were tied.

———

At three in the morning, Harper arrived home where she'd lived with her husband, Nate, for half her life. It shamed her to think she'd simply let him walk away when all he wanted to do was make things better. He'd been her rock since the day she'd met him. She'd lived in this house all these years, surrounded by love and enveloped by warm arms, and yet the wounds from her childhood continued to hang on like a drowning man clinging to a life raft.

Quietly, she made her way into the house. She'd texted her son early in the day, asking him to fix Ella dinner and make sure she did her homework and went to bed on time. He'd answered with the thumbs-up emoji. Good kids. Great kids. And yet her quest for revenge had taken her down a very dangerous and slippery slope. Her husband was already onto her. He knew she'd lied to him. If she got caught, her kids would find out what she'd done.

As soon as she walked into her bedroom she locked the door, then made her way into the bathroom and turned on the water in the shower. Standing in front of the mirror, she stripped out of dirty clothes. There were bloodstains on her pants that she hadn't been able to scrub off at the construction site. She rolled the jeans up and stuffed them into the cabinet beneath the sink. Tomorrow she would wash them in bleach and then decide how best to discard them.

Hot water sprayed and rolled down her body. She opened the shampoo bottle and poured it on top of her head, scrubbing the dirt and blood from her hair and body and watching the stream of brownish water disappear down the drain at her feet.

Everything that had happened with The Crew already seemed like a lifetime ago. She didn't know who she was any longer. No. That wasn't right. She'd never known who she was. That's why she was so obsessed with cleaning, always trying to scrub away her feelings and emotions.

For the first time in a long while, Harper smiled.

Instead of feeling remorse for the part she'd played in ridding the world of those awful men, an unexpected release of tension lifted from her shoulders. She was a survivor. And now the world was a safer place.

# CHAPTER FORTY

Early the next morning Sawyer's phone rang.

It was Aria.

Unable to sleep, she'd been lying in bed for hours thinking about what happened last night, chastising herself for acting so hastily. She picked up the call and said hello.

"I know you've been suspended or fired," Aria said, "but you'll never believe who just called."

Sawyer rolled her eyes. "I wasn't suspended or fired. Palmer told me to take a few weeks off and let it blow over." She sat up and adjusted the blankets. "So who called?"

"Bob Fucking Upperman. He *did* have a piano lesson immediately after Riley Addison on the day she went missing. He said he'd been taking lessons for six months to surprise his fiancée since she's been playing the piano for most of her life—"

"And?" Sawyer asked, cutting her off.

"And he never saw Riley Addison, but he did see a woman shutting her trunk. He said it was odd because she was wearing a sling."

"Why would he think that was odd?"

"Because she used the arm in the sling to reach up and shut the back compartment."

"Why didn't he tell the police what he saw?"

"He said he thought about it, but the idea of calling to report seeing a woman in a sling seemed silly. Once he learned of Mark Brennan's arrest, he was doubly glad he hadn't called it in."

"Did he remember the make or model of the car the woman was driving?"

"He said it was silver and was the size and shape of a Highlander. He never looked at the license plate, so he had nothing helpful to offer in that regard. He did say he was having a difficult time believing Mark Brennan had anything to do with the girl's disappearance."

"Because Mark Brennan is a nice guy?" Sawyer asked.

"Pretty much. Don't you think you should at least tell Palmer about Bob Upperman?"

"Not yet. He's not happy with me, and it's just another piece of circumstantial evidence. If he had seen Riley in the car, that would be something else entirely."

As Sawyer talked to her sister, texts flashed across her screen. Most from her coworkers offering sympathy and asking her to call. What they really wanted was the scoop—details of what happened last night.

"Harper is taking Ella to school today," Aria said, "so I thought I'd grab coffee and doughnuts and come over for a bit before work. Sound good?"

A part of Sawyer wanted to be left alone to soak in her misery, but she knew it wouldn't do her any good. "Sure. I'll be here." Her phone buzzed. "Hang on for a minute," she told Aria. "Paige Owens is calling."

Sawyer put Aria on hold and picked up the call. "Hi. What's going on?"

"You left me a text saying that you and your sister wanted to meet. If you give me your address, I'll come to you since I have an hour before school. Is now a good time?"

"Now is perfect," Sawyer said, trying to sound like she meant it. Sawyer rattled off her address and said goodbye before reconnecting with Aria. "Are you still there?" she asked Aria.

"I'm here. What did Paige want?"

"She's coming over right now, but she only has an hour. Do we have all the yearbooks?"

"Most of them are in your living room, and I have one in my car. I'll skip the coffee and doughnuts and be there soon."

Sawyer got out of bed, slipped on a robe, and made her way into the main room where she picked up the remote and turned on the TV. The kitchen was her next stop. She needed coffee. Once she spruced up the place a bit and had a mug of hot brew in hand, there was a knock on the door. Sawyer peeked out the window, saw Paige, and invited her in.

"Have a seat," Sawyer said. "Do you drink coffee?"

"I do, but I'm good."

Sawyer took a swallow before placing her mug on a side table, then grabbed the pile of yearbooks and set them on the table in front of Paige.

"What are these?"

"My sister Aria and I—she's on her way—decided we needed to focus our search and concentrate on schools and bus stops. So we've been gathering yearbooks from schools that the missing girls attended in hopes that you might recognize a teacher or a staff member."

"It's worth a shot," Paige said.

"Exactly. And it shouldn't take long since these aren't high schools with two thousand students." She picked up one of the yearbooks, opened it, and counted the number of administration and staff members. "Let's start with the elementary school yearbooks first. This one has forty-five staff members, which includes the principal, librarian, office staff, and teachers."

Aria arrived two minutes later with another yearbook. She introduced herself to Paige and then took a seat next to the girl, watching closely as Paige examined each picture.

Sawyer inwardly groaned when she saw Nurse Amy on the news as she arrived at Crossroads Elementary School.

Aria looked at the TV. "Yeah, they've been running a video clip of that same scene all morning."

Sawyer watched Nurse Amy step out of her SUV. She was immediately swarmed by a mob of reporters with microphones. She didn't try to run from the press. Instead, she waited for everyone to gather around before saying, "I'm going to sue the Sacramento Police Department for misconduct and emotional distress. I will not allow authorities to barge into my house and attempt to ruin my exemplary reputation."

Behind Nurse Amy, a car pulled into the parking lot. Sawyer recognized the woman who climbed out as the lady who worked the front office. Sawyer watched the woman walk at a good clipped pace across the parking lot. As she passed by the chaos surrounding Nurse Amy, she glanced at the camera. Sawyer hit the "Pause" button on the remote so she could go to the bathroom.

"Take your time," she heard Aria tell Paige as she walked away.

"I see the woman every night in my mind," Paige told Aria. "If her picture is here somewhere, I'll know her when I see her."

Sawyer admired her confidence. When she returned to the living room a few minutes later, Sawyer recognized the cover of the yearbook in Aria's lap. "Is that Ella's yearbook?"

"Yes. I got it from her the other day. I figured we might as well collect as many as possible from within our fifteen-mile radius."

When Sawyer glanced at Paige, she noticed a terrified expression on her face. Sawyer followed her gaze to the image frozen on the TV screen.

"That's the sweater I told you about," Paige said.

Sawyer looked closer. The woman's button-down sweater was red with little black polka dots. "Are those ladybugs?"

"What are you two talking about?" Aria asked.

"She's dyed her hair," Paige said. "But that's her."

Sawyer's adrenaline spiked. She looked at Paige. "You're absolutely certain?"

"Two hundred percent."

Aria was catching on, and she opened Ella's yearbook and flipped through the pictures of staff members. "The woman on the TV screen is right here," Aria said.

Paige glanced at the picture and nodded. She pushed off the couch to her feet, every part of her trembling. "I need to go home and be with my mom."

"Go," Sawyer said. "I'll talk to the police, but they might need to talk to you."

"I understand. Mom will understand too." Paige looked at Sawyer, her eyes watery. "She needs to be stopped."

"I know," Sawyer said. "I know." She couldn't believe what was happening. Excitement swooshed through her. This could be the person she'd been looking for. Turning toward the wall with all the pushpins and notes and string outlining the bus routes, she recalled the strange vibe the woman had given off the day Sawyer had picked Ella up from school. The look the woman had shot her way had been strange and intense. Sawyer thought about the envelope left on her doorstep and the slashed tire.

"Her name is Melony Pershing," Aria said, jabbing her finger at the picture in the yearbook.

"We need to do this right," Sawyer said. "We need to find out who Melony Pershing is. I'm going to grab my laptop."

Five minutes later they were both clacking away on their keyboards.

"She's not on social media," Aria said. "Don't you have access to a bunch of database providers through your work?"

"Give me a minute." Sawyer logged in, relieved that her account hadn't been blocked. If she had been suspended, she wouldn't have been able to log on. It didn't take long to find what she was looking for.

"Melony Pershing is in her forties, single, and she lives on 1624 Brace Way off Higgins Road in West Sacramento."

"I think we should go to her house and at least knock on the door," Aria said.

"No," Sawyer said. "If I can't give Perez probable cause, there's no way he or anyone else will be able to set foot in Melony Pershing's house, especially with Amy Lennox all over the news threatening to sue."

"Paige Owens just identified Melony Pershing as the woman who tried to abduct her five years ago. I don't understand why that's not enough."

"It might be enough to get a uniformed police officer to go to her house and talk to her, but it won't be enough to get a warrant." She kept typing, logging in to another database. "Bingo."

"What did you find?"

Sawyer read aloud. "Melony Pershing changed her name after she moved to Sacramento. Her birth name is Deena Thatcher, and she was born in 1972. Her father died when she was three, and her mother passed away after falling down a flight of stairs. Deena attended North Central University, married Frank Finlay in 1995, and gave birth to Molly Finlay in 1998." Sawyer looked at Aria. "Molly. Nurse Amy bought a dress for a child named Molly, and Paige said the woman who tried to grab her called out Molly or Holly."

"What else does it say?"

"That Frank and Molly Finlay currently live in Minnesota, where Frank works as a Billing Representative at UnitedHealth Group in Hopkins, Minnesota." There were addresses and phone numbers. Sawyer set her laptop aside and grabbed her phone. "I'm going to call him."

Aria looked at the time. "I can't believe I have to go to work."

"You should go. I'll keep you updated."

"Call me if you need me. I'll try to get someone to cover for me."

After Aria left, Sawyer called Frank Finlay's work number. She was feeling impatient, exactly what Palmer had said was one of her flaws.

He might be happy to know that her confidence had taken a beating. She needed to be thorough. But she also needed to work quickly. Even if this was the same woman who had attempted to kidnap Paige, that didn't mean she had abducted Riley Addison.

"Frank Finlay speaking. How can I help you?"

"Hello," she said, trying to calm her nerves. "My name is Sawyer Brooks. I'm an investigative reporter with the *Sacramento Independent*, and I need to talk to you about Deena Finlay."

A long bout of silence was followed by, "What do you need to know?"

"I'd like to send you a picture via text to see if you can identify a person by the name of Melony Pershing."

"Okay," he said.

Sawyer used her phone to take a snapshot of Melony Pershing's picture from Ella's yearbook, then emailed it to him.

"That's Deena, my ex-wife. Looks like she dyed her hair. What has she done now?"

"She's been connected to the attempted kidnapping of a young girl."

She heard a deep intake of breath and then silence before he asked, "What else do you need to know?"

"Everything you can tell me about your ex-wife."

"We met at North Central University in Minneapolis. Deena worked at the bookstore. She was the smartest and the sweetest girl I'd ever met," Frank said. "I'm going to give you the condensed version. Does that work?"

"That would be perfect."

"After we married it was as if a light switch had been turned on because suddenly all Deena talked about was having a baby." He paused. "Unfortunately for us it wasn't that easy. Fertility treatments are expensive. It cost us our savings and our sanity, but three years later, Deena was pregnant. In 1998, our daughter, Molly, was born."

Sawyer had put him on speakerphone and took notes as he talked.

"We tried to have more children," Frank said, "but the years passed quickly and we couldn't afford to do the same procedure as before. Molly was about three or four when Deena became paranoid and possessive of Molly and me."

"How so?" Sawyer asked.

"She thought I was having an affair. I couldn't talk to family or friends without Deena accusing me of talking to a mistress who didn't exist. She didn't like Molly being away from her, so she began to home-school our daughter. The poor girl was with her mom 24-7."

"Did Molly have friends her age?"

"No. By the time Molly was ten, Deena wouldn't let her out of her sight. If Molly talked back or didn't keep her room pristine, she wasn't allowed to talk to her friends on the phone. Deena wanted full control of both our lives. Tired of Deena's paranoia, I began working long hours. Everything changed, though, when Deena accused me of having an affair with a woman at work. I called her insane, and she slapped me across the face. That was the first time I can remember her becoming violent. She started hitting Molly too, so I divorced her and went to court to get full custody of Molly."

He stopped when someone, possibly a coworker, opened the door and said a few words.

"I have to go in a few minutes, so I'll talk fast."

"Okay," Sawyer said. "I'm listening."

"Molly has always been an exceptionally smart child. She knew there was a chance the judge wouldn't believe me, so she used my cell phone to record her mother in action: locking Molly in closets, hitting Molly with a hairbrush, and purposely burning her with a curling iron. All that and the judge still gave Deena a chance to have visiting rights if she agreed to go to counseling."

"Did she agree?"

"No. She was angry. She began to leave dead animals in my car and in the mailbox. I noticed her following me and my daughter to and from school. I didn't know for sure, but I sensed that if I didn't do something, Deena might try to kidnap Molly, and that scared me more than anything."

"Did you get a restraining order?"

"Yes. The papers were served. I filed the proof of service and waited. On the date of the court hearing, Deena didn't show up."

"So that's when Deena moved to Sacramento," Sawyer stated.

"Is that where she is?"

"Yes. As far as I can tell, she changed her name to Melony Pershing and moved to Sacramento in 2009."

"Sounds about right," he said. "I have to go, but if there's anything else, feel free to text me, and I'll get back to you when I can."

After the call ended Sawyer logged in to the database where she'd found the most information on Melony and began piecing it all together. Melony's first job after moving from Minnesota was a secretarial position at Silver Valley School in Elk Grove where she worked from 2010 to 2015. That was the school Cora O'Neal had attended.

Breathless, trying not to get ahead of herself, Sawyer got up to look through the yearbooks. The Silver Valley School yearbook was dated 2014, one year before Cora disappeared. The staff members' pictures were close to the front. Melony Pershing's name was listed in the margin to the left of the page, but there was no picture.

In 2015 she got her California Substitute Teaching License and began working as a substitute teacher. Deena got a full-time job in the front office of Crossroads Elementary in Sacramento, Ella's school, less than a year ago.

Another interesting tidbit was that Molly Finlay was ten years old when her parents divorced and eleven when her mother left.

It was time to talk to Palmer.

# CHAPTER FORTY-ONE

Sawyer drove to work, relieved when she was able to walk into the building without being questioned by security. She kept her head down as she made her way to Palmer's office. His Jeep was parked out front, so she knew he was here. She also knew he wouldn't be pleased to see her.

His door was shut. She knocked, then walked in without waiting to be invited inside.

The look on his face said it all—hard, flinty eyes and a vein in his forehead that became engorged when he was upset. He dropped the pen in his grasp, clasped his hands together, and said in a controlled and steady voice, "I thought I told you to take some time off."

She held up the manila file in her hand. "It couldn't wait."

"Of course it couldn't."

She slid the file across the desk next to a stack of papers in front of him.

He didn't make a move to open the file. "You look like shit."

"I didn't sleep well last night."

"That makes two of us."

She sat down in her usual seat in front of his desk and said, "I believe I know who took Riley Addison."

"Jesus, Sawyer." He rubbed his fingers across his forehead. "You've got to stop this. It ends now. Don't make me say or do something I'll regret later."

Her phone vibrated for the second time since she'd walked into Palmer's office. She ignored it. "Go ahead and fire me," she told Palmer. "I don't care. If you don't want to come with me, that's fine. Because it won't stop me." She breathed in through her nose, trying to collect herself. "What if I'm right this time, and Riley Addison is alive, hidden away inside a lunatic's house? I don't think you want to go through the rest of your life knowing you could have done something but chose not to."

His face reddened. "I'm going to have to ask you to leave. I have work to do."

"These are the moments that define us, Palmer. It's not about winning some stupid award," she said. "It's not about sitting at a desk and finding ways to inform the public. It's about moments like this . . . right here, right now. We might be able to help one little girl." She squeezed her eyes shut, trying to get rid of the image in her head of her friend Rebecca pounding on the cement walls in the crawl space under her feet. She opened her eyes and sucked in a breath of air. "What if it's not too late?"

Palmer picked up his pen and looked at a stack of papers piled in front of him as if he were going to go back to working on whatever he was doing when she'd interrupted him.

She sat there and watched him to see what his next move might be. Palmer was the kind of person who needed to let things settle before he made a decision.

"What proof do you have this time?" he asked. "Or is this another one of your hunches?"

"It's both. It's always both, Palmer. You know that. That dress Nurse Amy bought—"

Palmer groaned. "The dress again? Really?"

"Hear me out," she said. "Nurse Amy bought the dress for a *friend's* daughter named Molly."

He sighed.

"The *friend* works at Crossroads Elementary school and goes by the name Melony Pershing," Sawyer went on. "Paige Owens said that the woman who nearly abducted her called out the name Holly or Molly when she ran."

"It's not enough," Palmer said. "Not even by a long shot."

"I'm not finished. Melony Pershing isn't even her real name. Her ex-husband was afraid she was going to take their daughter, so he got a restraining order. That's when she changed her name and moved to Sacramento. She was working at Silver Valley in Elk Grove, the school Cora O'Neal attended. She then got her substitute teaching license and worked at many of the same schools that the missing girls on my list attended."

"What's her real name?" Palmer asked.

"She was born Deena Thatcher and then became Deena Finlay after she married. I talked to her ex-husband this morning. He said she's dangerous." She gestured with her chin to the file on his desk. "It's all in the file. You'll also see my notes about Bob Upperman, a man who was at Mark Brennan's house the day Riley went missing."

Her phone vibrated. This time she glanced at the screen. It was a text from Harper: Ella is missing.

Her heart plummeted. "I've got to go."

"Sawyer, wait," Palmer said, but she didn't dare turn back. Instead, she swept through the door to his office and ran, her mind filled with images of Ella being tricked into climbing into Melony Pershing's car. Ella knew the woman, probably even trusted her. Her niece was ten years old with light-colored hair and blue eyes.

Why hadn't she warned Ella the last time she'd seen her?

Rebecca's image flashed in her mind. She thought about the envelope left on her doorstep, the slashed tire, the look Melony Pershing gave her when she went to pick up Ella from school.

The stabbing pain in her gut told her it might be too late to save anyone at all.

# CHAPTER
# FORTY-TWO

Palmer sat at his desk, pondering everything Sawyer had told him. She never slowed down, and he was beginning to realize she never would. Her compassion was matched only by her boundless energy. He glanced at the pile of papers that needed to be looked over and signed, then swept them to the side and opened the file Sawyer had left behind.

As he read her neatly compiled notes that included a summary of Deena Finlay's history, Paige Owens's report of what she saw, and an account from a man named Bob Upperman, who had seen a woman fitting the description of Melony Pershing wearing a sling and getting into a car in front of Mark Brennan's house the day Riley Addison went missing, a fire stirred within. Sawyer was onto something.

He shut down his computer and sent Cindy, his editorial assistant, a message letting her know he was following a lead and would be out of the office for the next hour.

Palmer slid behind the wheel of his Jeep, cursing under his breath as his gaze fixated on his granddaughter. He opened Sawyer's file, found Melony Pershing's address, and logged it in to his car's navigation system. His plan was to simply take a look around the residence and knock on the door. If no one answered, he would take the file to Perez and let him take over from there if he saw fit to do so.

The woman lived in West Sacramento. Because of traffic, it took him fifteen minutes to get to the cozy yellow house with regular square windows and a covered porch on both sides of the bottom level. He continued on to the end of the block where he found a parking spot and climbed out.

As he walked toward the house he enjoyed the warm sun against his back. A woman and her son exited the house next door. The kid was probably nine. He wore a blue-and-yellow soccer uniform with the number ten.

"You're not the plumber, are you?" the woman asked.

It took Palmer a half second to realize she was talking to him. He rested both hands on his chest, looked around, and said, "No. I'm not a plumber."

"Oh, that's too bad. Melony told me she'd hired a plumber to fix her pipes in the upstairs bathroom, but as soon as she drove away this morning, I heard some clinking and clanging coming from up there again."

She glanced up at the side window visible from the woman's driveway.

The window was tinted, probably to keep the heat out and the cool air in. "So you never saw the plumber coming or going?" Palmer asked.

"No. I never saw a truck either. But my son swears he saw someone through the upstairs window that looks into our backyard."

"Mom," her son called, "we're going to be late."

"I better go," she said. "If you see Melony, will you tell her that her pipes are still making noises?"

"I'll do that," Palmer said as he headed for the front door.

———

Bubbles drew the curtain shut.

With all the hoopla happening at the school between stupid Amy Lennox and the media, she'd realized this morning that the walls could very well be closing in on her. Timing was everything. If she'd known Cora's bones had been discovered, she would have waited before she went searching for Molly.

She never should have left the envelope or slashed the idiot reporter's tire. Completely unnecessary, but oh, so fun. A giggle erupted at the thought. She slapped her hand over her mouth. The second time she giggled, she grabbed a fistful of her hair and yanked hard until the pain made her eyes water.

"You dumb bitch!" That's what her mother would have called her if she were here now. "You stupid, stupid girl."

Bubbles looked over her shoulder at Molly. It saddened her to think she had to get rid of her so quickly. Molly could have been the perfect daughter.

She sighed and tried to cheer up by telling herself that if she and Molly had spent another year or two together, the child would only grow older, and maybe she would even leave her. She couldn't let that happen.

She had to take care of the problem now so that Molly could be remembered as the perfect child for eternity.

The first thing she'd done upon returning home was dissolve a pill in Molly's water. That's when she'd heard voices outside. A peek through the window revealed her nosy neighbor talking to a man Bubbles didn't recognize.

She walked back to the bed. Molly looked so peaceful. Her eyes were shut, her breathing even.

*But all good things must come to an end,* she thought when she heard the dreaded knock on her front door. Scooping up the syringe and pills on the bedside table, she shoved it all into the top drawer of the high dresser and then exited the room.

Before shutting the bedroom door, she looked back at Molly and felt her chest tighten.

This was Molly's fault. She had made a racket and managed to get the attention of her nosy neighbor. As she fought the urge to march back inside and strangle the girl with her bare hands, there was another knock.

Quietly she shut the door, hurried down the stairs, and then came to a lurching stop. What if the man was here about something that had nothing to do with Molly? He could be a neighbor from across the way for all she knew.

Another knock got her moving. Straightening her spine, she opened the door.

———

Palmer hadn't expected the door to open, but it did, and the woman staring out at him reminded him of his third-grade teacher. The one who'd thrown an eraser clear across the room, hitting him squarely between the eyes. There was something overly authoritative about the woman. Maybe it was the way she held her head painfully high, as if she were straining to do so. Her big round eyes looked even bigger set beneath overly plucked brows. High cheekbones and a straight nose made him think she might have been a looker in her heyday.

"I'm with the *Sacramento Independent*," he said, "and I was wondering if I could talk to you about your friend, Amy Lennox." The lie came easily enough.

"Now is not a good time. Amy is at the school. If you hurry, you might catch her before she leaves."

"Help!"

The cry for help came from the second floor.

"I've got to go," she said. "My daughter isn't feeling well."

Before she could shut the door, he lodged his foot next to the frame, preventing her from doing so.

"Leave now," she said in a rumbling voice, "or I'll call the police."

There was no mistaking the call for help. His insides tingled in a way he hadn't felt in a long while. He didn't need that good old intuition Sawyer used at full throttle every day of her life to know that something was horribly wrong. "Your daughter is in Minnesota," he said flatly. "Who is upstairs?"

"Don't leave me!" came another weak cry for help.

Wild elephants couldn't pull him away. There was no turning back now. He'd never barged into a person's house uninvited in his life, but to hell with it. He was going in.

# CHAPTER FORTY-THREE

Sawyer left her sisters at Harper's house and drove to Ella's school. Harper had called the school office and was told that Ella got on the bus with everyone else, but Sawyer wanted to personally check the school property. Aria would drive to Ella's friend's house while Sawyer headed for the school. Harper would stay home in case Ella showed up.

Sawyer had a call coming in from a number she didn't recognize. She picked up.

"This is Bernie at Little Starfish Swimming School. I finally got a minute, and I think I found the video footage you were interested in seeing."

Sawyer had visited the swimming school when she'd trekked across the field next to Mark Brennan's house. "Was there anyone on the video the night before I talked to you?"

"Yes. There sure was. A woman parked her car across the street at two in the morning, then got out and made her way across the field. Less than ten minutes later, she returned to her car and drove off. The car is silver. I'm guessing if you know someone with the right equipment they might be able to make out the license plate or maybe even zoom in on the woman's face."

"Thank you, Bernie. If you could hold on to that until I can get there, I would appreciate it."

"I'll do that."

Sawyer ended the call before arriving at Ella's school. On any other day and in any other moment in time, she would have been racing to Little Starfish Swimming School. But her niece was missing and nothing else mattered.

She felt sick to her stomach at the thought of Ella being taken. She drove through the parking lot. There were a couple of kids sitting on benches, waiting to be picked up, but for the most part, the school grounds were empty.

Sawyer parked, climbed out, and hurried to the front office where two women were closing shop for the day. One of them was Nurse Amy. She looked up and scowled. "Your sister called here already. Ella took the bus."

"How do you know for sure?" Sawyer asked.

"Mrs. Kerry, Ella's math teacher, was here when your sister called. Mrs. Kerry saw Ella get on the bus."

"I'd like to talk to Mrs. Kerry."

"She's gone for the day. Perhaps your niece got off the bus and walked home with a friend."

Sawyer looked around the office. On the coat hook at the far end of the room was a red cardigan with ladybugs. Her stomach tumbled and turned. "Where is Melony Pershing?"

"She went home early," the other woman said. "She wasn't feeling well."

Sawyer left the office and ran back to her car, her heart racing. *This couldn't be happening. Ella, where are you?* Tires screeched as she pulled out of the parking lot.

She called Palmer in hopes he'd taken time to look at the file and call Detective Perez. His editorial assistant answered the phone and told her he'd left the building thirty minutes ago to follow a lead.

Where would Palmer have run off to? There had been a stack of work in front of him, which told her he had no plans to leave the office early.

Sawyer drove another two blocks, then pulled to the side of the road to send Palmer a text: Where are you?

About to drive away, on the sidewalk up ahead she saw a young boy and girl sitting on a retaining wall. From where Sawyer sat it looked like Ella and her friend George. She merged onto the street. As she drew closer she saw that it was definitely Ella, smiling and laughing. Not a care in the world.

Relief flooded through her, and the tears came fast. There was no stopping them. Again, she pulled to the side of the road. Leaving the engine running, she jumped out of the car and ran toward her niece, shouting, "Ella!"

Both Ella and her friend froze when they spotted Sawyer.

Ella jumped off the wall to her feet. She looked especially worried, maybe even slightly terrified when Sawyer wrapped her arms around her and held tight.

"What's wrong?" Ella asked.

Sawyer stepped away. "You weren't at the bus stop. Your mother has been looking everywhere for you. What were you thinking?"

"It's my fault," the boy said. "I talked her into walking home with me."

"You're grounded," she told Ella. "And you too," she told the boy. She stared Ella down. "Get in the car. Now!"

The two kids exchanged worried glances.

"Do you need a ride home?" Sawyer asked.

He pointed to a brick house nearby and shook his head. "I live right there."

"Come on," Sawyer said to Ella, ushering her niece to the car. Once she was buckled in, Sawyer called Harper. The line was busy. She called Aria next.

"I'm back home with Harper. We still haven't found her," Aria said. "None of her friends know where she is."

"Ella is here with me," Sawyer told her. "I'm bringing her home."

"Oh, my God! Harper! Sawyer has Ella! Where was she?"

"I found her walking home with her boyfriend."

Ella moaned. "He's not my boyfriend. And what is wrong with you? You hugged me. You never hug anyone."

Sawyer ignored her.

"Ella, are you really there?" Harper asked.

Harper was on the line now so Sawyer handed her niece the phone.

"I'm here, Mom. Geez. Why is everyone making such a big deal out of my walking home?"

"Don't ever do that to me again," Harper said in a tearful voice. "Do you hear me?"

"Yes," Ella said. And then she began to cry too.

Sawyer dropped Ella off at home. While Harper simultaneously lectured her daughter while holding her close, Sawyer thought about Melony Pershing. Why had she gone home early? Had the swarm of media at the school scared her? Her stomach quivered as she called Palmer's office again. He still hadn't returned. *Fuck it.* She was going to Melony Pershing's house. She'd found one girl, and now it was time to find another.

Aria stopped her as she made her way back to her car.

"What is it?" Sawyer asked.

"You're going to that woman's house, aren't you?"

Sawyer shook her head, not wanting to drag her sister down with her if she decided to break and enter.

Aria reached into the front pocket of her sweater. "You're a horrible liar. Take this." Aria slipped her gun into Sawyer's hand, careful to keep it pointed downward. "It's loaded and ready to go. That woman is out of her mind. If things get out of hand, hold firm and then just aim and shoot."

Sawyer nodded and then took off again, this time for Melony Pershing's house.

# CHAPTER FORTY-FOUR

Palmer pushed his way into Melony Pershing's house and went straight for the stairs. By the time he reached the top, he was winded and wishing he was in better shape. He looked down at the landing. The woman was gone, probably in her car ready to take off. The police would have to catch up to her later.

The bedroom door to his left was closed. He turned the knob and entered the room. The smell hit him hard, making him gag.

His heart sank when his gaze fell on a little girl lying on a bed in the middle of the room, her head propped awkwardly on stained pillows. Her wrists and ankles were shackled within metal cuffs. Her hair had been cut off at various lengths and at odd angles. He'd seen Riley Addison's picture enough times to know it was her.

As he drew closer, he couldn't tell if she was breathing. Not until he felt for a pulse and watched her fingers curl around his hand, too weak to lift the heavy chains. The bruises and scratches covering her arms made him sick to his stomach.

She opened her eyes. Her face was gaunt, her eyes hollow.

Sawyer had been right; Riley Addison was alive, just waiting for someone to save her.

He squeezed her hand and forced a smile, afraid she wouldn't make it if he didn't get help soon.

The key.

He needed to find the key to unlock the cuffs. The drawer to the bedside table was empty. He reached for his cell to call 9-1-1. Before he could press the side button, he saw a look of horror cross over the girl's face at the same moment someone punched him in the back.

*What the hell?* The pain ripped through him.

He whirled around. The woman hadn't run off, after all. She held a sharp blade, blood dripping from its tip. She had stabbed him. Her big round eyes gleamed with excitement as she lifted the knife and thrust the blade into his side.

There was a sickening swoosh as she pulled the blade out. He raised an arm to stop her, but she thrust the knife into his arm.

The searing pain was white hot. He felt as if he were on fire, being burned alive. Shades of purple and white, red and brown clouded his vision as he stumbled backward away from her, his back against the wall when she came for him again.

Aided by a single moment of clarity and rage, his adrenaline soared, giving him the strength he needed to lift his leg and jab the hard sole of his shoe into her stomach.

Melony Pershing grunted as she fought to find balance and instead fell and landed on top of the bed.

Riley came alive, screaming. She sat up like something in a horror movie, her face stained with food or blood, he couldn't tell. It wasn't only her arms that were covered with cuts and scratches, her neck and face were too. Her eyes looked momentarily clear and bright as she wrapped the chains attached to her wrists around the woman's throat, grimacing as she pulled, every muscle straining. It was as if she'd been waiting for this moment her entire life.

Melony Pershing's arms flailed like a human windmill, the blade narrowly missing the girl and slicing through the mattress instead. The woman's face turned crimson with shades of blue and then her body fell limp. The knife slid from her hand to the ground and skittered across the floor.

Weak from loss of blood, Palmer sank to the ground, wishing he could help Riley escape.

His eyes closed in a long blink.

When he opened them again, his vision was blurred, but there was no mistaking the horror unfolding before him as Melony Pershing pushed herself off the bed, found her footing, and went in search of her knife.

His failure to help the girl cut deeper than Melony Pershing's knife.

Riley's eyes were closed. She'd given it her all, and yet it hadn't been enough.

———

Sawyer's heart thumped against her ribs when she saw Palmer's Jeep parked at the end of the block from Melony Pershing's house. She found a place to park, grabbed the gun Aria had given her, jumped out of the car, and ran.

Once she reached the front door, she stood quietly on the welcome mat and listened.

A couple of kids rode by on their bikes. A squirrel rustled the leaves in the high branches of a tree. She grasped the handle, surprised to find the door unlocked. Pushing the door wide open, she stepped inside.

The front entry was empty. The house was quiet.

Leaving the door open, she took slow, careful steps into the main room.

Empty.

Same with the kitchen.

Shoulders tight, elbows close to her sides, gun aimed straight ahead, she made her way quietly up the stairs. The temptation to shout Palmer's name weighed heavily, but calling attention to herself made zero sense until she knew what she was dealing with.

She held her breath as she reached the landing. After taking two steps to the right, she turned back the other way when she heard a voice coming from the room to the left.

"Leave her alone. She's done nothing to you."

She recognized Palmer's voice. He was here.

The moment she stepped into the room the stench hit her in waves: urine, feces, the smell of rotten eggs.

Palmer was on the floor, his back against the wall, blood pooling around him. In the center of the room was a young girl chained to a bed. Riley Addison. One arm hung over the side of the mattress, dragged down by the weight of the metal cuff and chain. Her finger twitched.

She was alive!

Melony Pershing stood at the girl's side and raised her arm high, a sharp blade glinting in a ray of sunlight coming through the window.

There was no time to think.

"*Aim and shoot,*" Aria had said. "*Aim and shoot.*"

Arms straight, gun gripped tight, instead of pressing the trigger, she said, "Put the knife down."

Melony whipped around, a look of surprise on her face when she saw Sawyer standing there with a gun aimed at her chest.

"You just couldn't leave it alone," Melony said through gritted teeth.

Sawyer held her ground. "Put the knife down. It's over. The police know everything. They're on their way." She hoped the woman fell for her bluff because she didn't want to shoot.

"*The police know everything?*" Melony Pershing laughed. "So dramatic."

"Your real name is Deena Thatcher, and you moved to Sacramento after your husband got a restraining order to keep you from harming your daughter, Molly. It's over."

Her face twisted. "I never hurt Molly. I loved Molly. She loved me too, but that man put thoughts in her head, told her falsehoods. You've never been a mother. You wouldn't know what it feels like to have a child taken from you."

"Put the knife down."

"I did nothing wrong."

"You killed Cora O'Neal," Sawyer said.

"That was an accident."

Sawyer hadn't known for certain if Melony had taken Cora until now. "You'll be spending the rest of your days behind bars."

"Are you going to read me my Miranda rights?"

Sawyer glanced at Palmer. His face held a lingering grimace, but he was holding on.

"You can't help him. And you can't help Molly either. Just like you couldn't help Rebecca. It must be tough living with yourself, knowing your very best friend spent her last days trapped in the crawl space beneath your feet as you plodded around on top of her, coming and going as you pleased."

*Aim and shoot.*

"Put the knife down," Sawyer said. "I'm not going to ask again."

The woman's marble-size bloodshot eyes, just as Paige Owens had described, were wide open and unblinking. The tip of her tongue poked out between thin grayish lips.

Was she sticking her tongue out at her like a five-year-old?

Melony waggled her tongue at Sawyer and then released a bark of laughter right before she rushed toward Sawyer with the sharp blade held straight out.

Melony had been trying to distract her, and it had worked. Sawyer fumbled with the gun slightly before finding her footing and pressing the trigger. A shot rang out just as the woman slammed into her, taking them both to the floor.

Sawyer's head hit the ground. A jolt of pain tore through her. The woman's deadweight was heavy on top of her. Panicked, Sawyer kicked and pushed her way out from under Melony Pershing, then jumped to her feet. Her breathing was ragged as she steadied the gun and aimed it at the woman.

Lying facedown, Melony Pershing wasn't moving.

Sawyer ran her free hand over her stomach and side, surprised she hadn't been struck with the blade. The knife had skittered across the floor. She picked it up, then returned to the woman and used the tip of her shoe to nudge Melony Pershing's body.

Still no movement, but that didn't stop Sawyer from wanting to put a bullet through her head just to be sure. Kneeling down, she checked the woman's pulse. There was none. She took in a breath as she moved to the girl's side, watched her chest rise and fall, then set both weapons on the end of the bed and used her phone to call 9-1-1.

She made her way to Palmer and put a hand to his neck to feel for a pulse. He stirred, opened his eyes, and winced when he tried to move. "The girl needs help," he said.

The girl was alive. Her first priority was to stop Palmer from bleeding out. She ripped off the button-down shirt she wore over a white tank top and used it to make a tourniquet around his waist. She placed his good hand on the cloth and told him to keep pressure on it. The deepest wound appeared to be on his arm. She had on a sports bra so she stripped off the tank top next and wrapped it around the wound on his arm. It was the best she could do for now other than pray the medics hurried.

"I'm good," he said. "Help the girl."

The girl's face was pale, and her head had fallen to one side, making Sawyer wonder if she'd imagined the slight movement she'd seen moments ago.

They had come too far. She couldn't die.

Again, Sawyer felt for a pulse, then sucked in a breath as she tried not to lose it. Riley and Palmer were both alive. And they both needed medical assistance immediately.

She was examining the metal cuff, trying to figure out how to remove it, when the girl's eyes parted halfway. "Mom?"

Sawyer's heart twisted. "No. My name is Sawyer Brooks. You don't know me, Riley, but I've been looking for you since the day you went missing."

The chains rattled as the girl reached for Sawyer. She leaned low and took the girl in her arms and held her close, didn't want to let her go. She had done it. She'd found Riley. In her mind's eye she saw Rebecca smiling at her. Sawyer pulled away so that she could look at Riley. "I need you to stay strong until I get you out of here, okay?"

"I'm not dreaming?" Riley asked.

"No," Sawyer said, trying to keep it together as tears rolled down her cheeks. "You're not dreaming." Exhaustion and all the emotions she'd felt when she'd thought Ella had been abducted still flowed through her bloodstream. "You're going to be okay. The ambulance is on its way, but I need to get these chains off you."

Riley let her head fall back onto the pillows. Her arms dropped to her sides. "The key is around Bubbles's neck."

The girl's voice was groggy. Clearly she'd been drugged, but who the hell was Bubbles?

It could be only one person.

Sawyer didn't want to go anywhere near Melony Pershing, but she didn't have a choice. She walked that way, knelt down beside the woman, her hands trembling as she reached around the woman's neck and undid the chain. Back on her feet, she walked to the bed.

Riley winced when Sawyer fiddled with the locks. Her wrists and ankles were red and raw. Her clothes and the bed were soiled. The stench made it difficult to breathe, and yet the girl hadn't broken down and cried. She was tough.

Once the chains were off, Riley told her she had a broken leg, then asked in a shaky voice if Sawyer could help her change her clothes. She didn't like the scratchy, ugly dress and the shiny shoes.

Sawyer tried not to cause the girl any more pain as she removed the shoes, then walked to the dresser across the room. In the top drawer were syringes and pills, a sling, and a Polaroid picture of Riley, her head strapped to the headboard and a gruesome smile on her face that had been drawn with a red marker. A thing of nightmares.

She shut the drawer, opened another, and found an oversize T-shirt. "Is this good?"

Riley nodded, her eyes watering.

It was such a simple thing—a big tee—but Sawyer could see that for Riley it was more about taking off the outfit that Melony Pershing had dressed her in than it was about being dirty and soiled.

Sawyer helped her change. Her body and soul had been bruised and beaten. It was clear Riley struggled not to cry out in pain.

"Will you take me out of here?"

Sawyer looked at Palmer. He nodded and said, "Get her out of here."

Sirens sounded in the distance as Sawyer scooped the girl into her arms, surprised how light she was.

"She was going to kill me," Riley said as they walked past Melony Pershing's body. "That man saved me."

"He's a good guy," Sawyer said.

"Do you think he'll be okay?"

Sawyer wasn't so sure, but she smiled and said, "I think he will be. He's tough like you." The sirens grew louder. *Thank God. Please hurry.*

Riley frowned. "Bubbles was going to drug me and then drown me in the bathtub."

"She told you that?"

Riley nodded. "She killed other girls. Lots of them. There are pictures of them in the closet."

Chills swept over Sawyer as she thought of Aria's poster board with all those young faces. "She'll never hurt anyone else."

"Bubbles killed her daughter, Molly, when she was a baby. She told me it was an accident."

"She lied."

Riley's eyes grew round. "Are you sure?"

"I am. Molly is alive and well and living with her father," Sawyer said as she carried Riley out of the stench-filled room and down the stairs. The front door was open, the sun shining bright as she stepped outside.

A string of police cruisers with lights flashing and two ambulances pulled up in front of the house, one after another.

Three uniformed officers and an emergency technician rushed past them and disappeared inside the house.

Perez climbed out of an unmarked car and looked at Sawyer.

"She's going to be okay," Sawyer told him.

He didn't say anything. He didn't need to. The gleam in his eye said it all. He was glad she'd followed her instincts. Apologies might come later, but she wouldn't hold her breath, and she didn't care about any of that.

"Palmer is upstairs," Sawyer said. "He's hurt bad. He needs help. And you might want to look in the bedroom closet."

Perez tipped his head and continued on toward the house.

The doors at the back of the ambulance were open and Sawyer walked that way. "Don't leave me," Riley said when a paramedic approached.

"I won't. I promise." Sawyer explained to the paramedic that Riley had a broken leg and that she was going to ride in the back of the ambulance with her to the hospital.

"What about you?" he asked, taking note of the blood smeared across Sawyer's arms and chest. "Are you hurt?"

"No. I'm fine. Let's get out of here."

# CHAPTER FORTY-FIVE

*Three Days Later*

Sawyer stepped out of the hospital elevator and then got out of everyone else's way. Her phone was vibrating. She set the vase filled with flowers on the floor and picked up the call.

"Is this Sawyer Brooks?"

She could see the door to Palmer's hospital room from where she stood. "Yes, this is Sawyer."

"This is Mark Brennan. I just wanted—" His voice wobbled, emotion getting the best of him.

He'd been released the same day Riley had been found. She'd seen it all on the news. She said nothing as she waited for him to pull himself together.

"I needed to call you," he said, "and tell you thank you. I owe you my life."

She scoffed at that. "You don't owe me anything. I was just doing my job." It sounded cliché, but it was the truth.

There was another pause before he said, "If you ever need anything, anything at all, I'm your guy."

"Thank you for calling," she said. "Take care."

"You too."

Sawyer put her phone away, picked up the flowers, and made her way to Palmer's room.

"You look like hell," Palmer said when Sawyer walked into his hospital room with a vase full of flowers she'd bought at the farmers' market downtown.

"Ditto," she told him, glad to see him awake. For days now, she'd been in and out of his room. He'd been stabbed once in the back, once in his right side, and had taken a muscle-severing jab to his left arm. Bubbles had missed his artery. Not only was he alive, doctors were optimistic about a full recovery.

He used his good hand to gesture weakly toward his mouth. "Can a guy get a drink around here?"

She filled his pink plastic cup on the tray with water. "Here you go. Small sips."

He gulped it down.

She put the cup back on the tray and said, "You're lucky to be alive."

He grunted. "That woman scared the shit out of me."

Sawyer moved a chair close to the bed. She gave him a good long look, happy to see him awake and talking. She was going to say something, but the words got stuck in her throat, and she simply let her forehead fall to the side of his mattress. Palmer was her mentor, her friend, one of the few people who believed in her ability as an investigative journalist.

After a few seconds, she felt his hand on the top of her head, petting her as if she were a small child or a beloved dog. She sat up, grabbed a tissue from the table, and blew her nose. "I'm sorry. I'm just glad you're okay. When I brought the file to you, it never dawned on me that you might get hurt."

"I'm okay, Sawyer. And even if I wasn't, it's not your fault. You're the hero in all of this."

She said nothing.

"What? You don't like being a hero?"

She shrugged. "If doing the right thing makes me a hero, then sure, whatever."

"Well, I don't like it either." He coughed. "But all the nurses around here keep making a big deal over what happened, heralding me as a saint this morning when I woke up for the first time since being carried out of that house on a stretcher."

He coughed, took a sip of water after she refilled his cup and handed it to him. "It was all you," he went on. "Perez took you down a notch when you went to see him. I tried to do the same. But you wouldn't quit," he said. "It was your dogged determination that saved the little girl."

More coughing. More water. He lifted a brow. "How's the kid doing? Do you know?"

"Riley was dehydrated when they brought her in. Her leg is broken in two places, but she never cried out in pain, even when I picked her up and carried her out of that house of horrors." Sawyer shook her head in awe. "She'll be going back home today to be with her family." She smiled, but Palmer wasn't buying it.

"What is it?" Palmer asked.

Sawyer scoffed. "Nothing. I'm fine."

"Tell me," he said, his voice groggy from the drugs. "Get it out."

She anchored her hair behind her ear. "It's nothing and everything all at the same time. Riley Addison has been traumatized, and she'll never be able to forget it. All of the horrors have been imprinted in Riley's mind, and for the rest of her life, even with therapy, she'll remember every detail of her time spent with that woman."

"So saving Riley wasn't enough? You have to carry her pain too?"

She met Palmer's gaze. "Did you ever consider becoming a therapist instead of a journalist?"

"Not until this very moment."

OUT OF HER MIND

She smiled then and changed the subject. "Detective Perez called me an hour ago. His team has found two bodies buried in Melony Pershing's backyard. They're still digging, but they also found Polaroid pictures of every girl on my list."

Palmer groaned, the color draining from his face as he clutched his middle.

"I'll get the nurse," she said.

He waved her off, but she could tell he was hurting. "First thing tomorrow morning," he said, his voice strained, "I want you to get hopping on the Black Wigs story."

"I thought I was supposed to take a couple of weeks off."

"Don't be a smart-ass."

"Are you sure about the Black Wigs story? I had gotten the feeling you didn't like the angle I was taking—"

"I changed my mind." He sipped his water. "If the Black Wigs are going after specific men for a reason, I want to know why. The public will be interested too. I'm not saying it's right to take the law into their own hands, but I think it's important to know all the details."

"I'll get right on it," she said with a smile.

His brow furrowed. "First get that nurse for me, will you?"

# CHAPTER FORTY-SIX

Sawyer tossed and turned for most of the night. A thumping noise sounded, then the creak of a door. When she opened her eyes, she saw Melony Pershing standing over her, a bullet hole in her chest, her hands tucked behind her back. Her hair was back to its natural gray, and she was wearing the red cardigan with the ladybugs, most of the insects hanging on by a thread.

"I found Rebecca," the woman told her. "Your friend looked thin as a rail, ghastly. She kept banging on the floorboards and wouldn't stop asking for you. I told her you were never coming." Melony drew out a hand hidden behind her back and held it high in the air, where Sawyer could see the ax in her grasp, ready to strike. A freaky, wide grin had been drawn on her face with a red marker.

Sawyer bolted upward as she let out an ear-piercing scream.

Breathless, Sawyer sat still.

Nobody was there. Just a nightmare.

But the banging coming from the other room was real, and it grew louder. She heard the doorknob rattle. Someone was trying to get in.

She jumped off the bed, her heart racing as she rushed to the kitchen and grabbed the first metal object she felt inside one of the drawers.

A shadowy silhouette stood outside her door. She should have kept Aria's gun.

"It's Derek. Are you in there?"

*Derek?* She opened the door, the weapon still in her hand, her body trembling.

"Are you okay?" he asked.

She jumped into his arms, almost knocking him over, the object she was holding clunking him in the back. For a long moment they simply held one another. Finally he stepped away, took the meat tenderizer from her hand, and brought it to the kitchen.

Sawyer shut the door and locked it. Shivering, she looked at the time. It wasn't yet five in the morning. "You never returned my calls."

He was staring at the wall with the stickers and string and notes plastered everywhere when he said, "I lost my phone somewhere in British Columbia."

Dumbest excuse she'd ever heard in her life.

Raccoon meowed from his hiding place beneath the couch, most likely traumatized by her screams. Her heart still raced, thumping hard against her ribs.

Derek was here, standing in her living room. She quietly pinched herself. This wasn't a dream.

Their gazes locked.

He looked as if he might be searching for the right words before he said, "I had no idea you had called me. I didn't get your texts until an hour ago when I got home and restored messages on a new phone. I just finished listening and reading all thirteen of them before coming straight here."

"Thirteen. No way. It couldn't have been that many."

"Thirteen," he repeated. "I counted."

She crossed her arms. "You should have given me a chance to explain before running away."

"You're right. I should have. I handled the whole thing like a jerk."

Satisfied with his answer, she asked, "You were in British Columbia?"

He nodded.

"Alone?"

"No."

Her chest tightened.

"You were there with me every step of the way."

She walked toward him and circled her arms around his waist, her head resting against his chest. She could tell by the stiffness of his body that he didn't know what to make of her wrapping her arms around him. Not once, but twice.

When he sighed, his warm breath moved the hair on top of her head.

"I heard you scream," he said.

"A nightmare," she said, her voice muffled within his chest.

He held her tighter.

She could hear the beat of his heart. "Maybe an outspoken girl with anxiety and a seminormal guy with a few issues of his own could make it work," she said.

"I've had a lot of time to think out there in the wilderness, and I think it's worth a shot."

# CHAPTER FORTY-SEVEN

While Harper waited for the computer to boot up, she recognized the wooded area on the television where the reporter was standing, picked up the remote, and turned up the volume.

"This is Rachel Denning with Channel 10 News, reporting from Pollock Pines. Placerville Police have identified the body found in the woods near Barrett Pass Road as Myles Davenport, the man abducted in the parking lot of Green Meadows High School, where he was attending his ten-year high school reunion. An investigation is underway."

Harper turned the TV off and made her way to the computer. The Crew had agreed to check in at noon.

*Three men in six weeks,* she thought. All connected to the Black Wigs.

Brad Vicente.

Otto Radley.

Myles Davenport.

One without a penis. One missing. And one dead.

With the kids at school and Nate still in Montana, nothing felt right, her world shadowy and gray. Sending Ella off to school after everything that had happened seemed wrong. But she'd thought it best to play it cool, didn't want her daughter going through life fearful of strangers.

More than anything, she wished Nate was home. He'd been gone for over a week. She missed him. As soon as The Crew finished dealing with Cleo's frat boys, they could destroy any evidence that their group ever existed. And then, if it wasn't too late, she would find a way to make things right between her and Nate. He was a good man, and he deserved to know the truth. If she was lucky, he would stand by her.

She logged on to their private group.

CLEO: Everyone is accounted for except Bug.

Harper cringed at the thought that Bug might have left the country.

LILY: Let's give her another five minutes.

HARPER: They found and identified QB's body.

CLEO: Bummer. I was hoping all the forest critters would have made a meal out of him.

PSYCHO: I don't have a lot of time. What's the plan, Cleo?

CLEO: The plan is to wait for Bug.

PSYCHO: Jesus. Just tell me the plan, or I'm out of here. Bug can read about it later.

CLEO: You're not the leader of the pack, Psycho, so quit acting like you're the one in charge.

LILY: No arguing. We're all busy and tired. Let's get on with this.

CLEO: Who votes that we wait for Bug?

MALICE: I think Bug may have left the country.

For the next thirty seconds, Harper stared at the blinking cursor.

CLEO: I seriously hope that isn't true.

PSYCHO: Agree. Malice, who told you this?

MALICE: Bug told me she planned to get a new identity and leave the country after we finished. Don't shoot the messenger.

CLEO: The messenger should have told us before now!

Harper typed an answer and then deleted it. She would give everyone time to calm down.

CLEO: My life has been turned upside down. I was bait for Lily and then again for Psycho when it was time to lure Otto Radley to the park. And now you bastards want to quit.

PSYCHO: I'm not quitting.

MALICE: I'm here until the end.

LILY: Take a breath. There are four of us left. We don't need Bug. We're here for you, Cleo.

After agreeing to talk again in a few days, Harper signed off.

She reflected on the past year when she'd first joined with these women because of one common denominator—rape.

They were survivors and victims, their lives plagued by PTSD, thoughts of suicide, distrust, and always looking over their shoulders. She was proud of The Crew for taking control and setting out to remind these rapists that their actions had consequences.

Harper took a breath.

She had killed a man.

Her father was dead.

She was not sorry. No regrets.

For a blink of an eye, she'd lost herself. But she was back, and she was stronger than ever.

# CHAPTER FORTY-EIGHT

Sawyer's first stop of the day was Paige Owens's house.

She knocked and waited.

Last time she was here, she'd been greeted with disdain. This time when the door opened, Mrs. Owens invited her inside, ushered Sawyer into the living room, and asked her to have a seat while they waited for her daughter.

"Paige told me that you two met and have been sharing information on the missing girls."

Sawyer nodded, hoping she wasn't getting Paige into trouble. The changes in Mrs. Owens's appearance were mind-boggling. Her hair was combed back tight and rolled into a bun. The fear and anger etched into her face and the dark circles under her eyes were gone. The look on her face appeared to be a joyful one. "Stay right here," the woman said. "I have something for you."

The interior of the house had a very calming vibe. There were candles and succulents on the tables and windowsills. A diffuser dispensed a rosemary scent into the air, and a large rubber tree plant reached for the sun coming through the windows.

Mrs. Owens returned, carrying a small black box tied with a gold ribbon. "This is for you," she said.

Sawyer blushed as she took the box.

"Go ahead and open it," Paige told her as she entered the room.

Sawyer untied the ribbon and lifted the lid. Inside was a pretty purple rock.

"It's an amethyst," Paige told her.

"Place it high on a bookcase or shelf," Mrs. Owens said. "The amethyst will emit a spiritually protective light into the space."

"It's beautiful. Thank you."

Mrs. Owens rested both hands over her heart and said, "I can't explain it and I don't want to embarrass Paige, but I knew the exact moment you found that girl. I felt it right here." She patted her chest. "She's not the only one you saved." Mrs. Owens struggled to contain her emotions.

Paige put an arm around her mom's shoulders. "Everything is going to be okay now."

Mrs. Owens nodded as she used a tissue to wipe her eyes.

"We're going to go visit Riley Addison," Paige told her mom. "I'll be back within the hour."

Paige sat in the passenger seat of Sawyer's car as they drove to Riley Addison's house.

Yesterday, Sawyer had gotten a call from Riley's mom, asking her to visit despite the media circus outside their home. Sawyer had asked her if it was okay if she brought Paige Owens, explaining that without Paige's help she never would have found Riley. Sawyer thought it would be good for Riley to have someone closer to her age to confide in when she was having a bad day or feeling scared or confused. Riley's mom had agreed wholeheartedly.

On their way, Sawyer asked Paige how things were going.

"Great. For the first time in years, I saw my mom smile."

"She looked happy," Sawyer said.

"Mind if I ask you a question about the woman who took Riley?"

"Go ahead."

"She had to be fairly clever to get away with everything she did, but why do you think she wore that sweater after all these years?"

Sawyer had wondered the same thing and even asked Melony Pershing's ex-husband about it. "Apparently her mother gave the sweater to her when she was about the age you are now."

"I read that she was abused by her mother, so why would she care?"

"That's a good question, but I don't have the answer."

"I've decided to go into police work after I graduate from college," Paige said. "I haven't told Mom yet."

"You'll make a fine police officer." Paige Owens was smart and resourceful, and she'd played a big part in helping find Riley Addison. It was a miracle that they'd found her alive.

For fifteen minutes they talked about what it would take to be a great police officer.

By the time they arrived at their destination and Sawyer parked the car, they had agreed that communication, compassion, and integrity were at the top of the list.

The white-and-gray house was one story with an oversize garage.

Patrick Addison opened the door before Sawyer could knock. He looked different. Happy.

He ushered them inside. The last time Sawyer had visited, the house had been quiet, weighed down by grief. Not any longer. The house was filled with balloons and flowers. A colorful "Welcome Home" sign hung from the ceiling in the front entry. The dining room table was covered with baked goods.

Mr. Addison's eyes sparkled, and his smile was wide as he introduced them to his wife, a petite woman with wavy brown hair and green eyes who was still recovering from her accident. She wore a neck brace and her eyes and nose were black and blue. The cast on her arm was covered with colorful drawings and signatures. But she was standing, and she happily led them to another room.

"We've set Riley up on the couch in the living room," Mrs. Addison said in a quiet voice. "She doesn't want to be anywhere near a bed or enclosed in a room. All the lights were left on last night, and her brother slept in a cot next to her."

Riley looked away from the television when they entered the room. She smiled and sat up taller. "Thanks for coming," she said.

"It's good to see you," Sawyer told her. "I brought a friend with me—Paige Owens."

Riley looked at Paige and said, "Mom told me all about you."

"I've heard a lot about you too," Paige said.

Sawyer left the two girls alone and made her way back to the kitchen to talk with Mr. and Mrs. Addison. They all took a seat at a small round table.

Sawyer reached into her bag and handed Mrs. Addison the file. Inside was all the information Sawyer had gathered on the woman who had taken Riley.

As Mrs. Addison read through Sawyer's notes, Mr. Addison clasped his hands on the table and said, "I wish I knew what to say to you. I've written you two letters before tearing them up. I can't seem to find a way to express my gratitude for what you've done for us. We've been through hell, but because of you we can now begin to dig our way out. You brought light to our world . . . a world that had grown dark very quickly."

"We were lucky," Sawyer said.

Mrs. Addison closed the file and joined the conversation. "We know a little about what you've been through, and we wanted you to know that we're here for you if you ever need anything at all." She handed Sawyer her business card. "It takes tremendous courage to reach out for help," Mrs. Addison told her. "But if there is ever anything you need, anything at all, please call."

Sawyer didn't know what to say other than, "Thank you." Everything they had said warmed her heart, and yet she still resisted opening up to people. Even when she met with therapists in the past, she'd held back because deep down she saw opening up to a stranger as a weakness. Therapy meant digging deep into the psyche and bringing forth painful memories. Emotional honesty was difficult. Maybe someday, though, she could find a way to speak her truths and continue to rebuild herself, one day at a time.

Although she and her sisters had a ways to go as far as healing, Sawyer had begun to realize that it had never been Harper's responsibility to take care of her and Aria. Not then and not now.

*Little steps,* Sawyer thought.

She was making progress.

She would continue to work on her fear of being touched. Physical closeness had always been uncomfortable for Sawyer, but recently she'd found herself relishing in the joy of holding someone close. She'd experienced it with Aria, Ella, Riley, and then with Derek when he showed up unexpectedly.

Things were definitely improving.

She could feel it.

She was getting better.

# ACKNOWLEDGMENTS

*Out of Her Mind* is my fifteenth thriller. What a fun and wild ride! Many thanks to the amazing team at Thomas & Mercer, Liz Pearsons, Charlotte Herscher, Amy Tannenbaum, Sarah Shaw, The Jane Rotrosen Agency, Brittany Ragan, Brian McDougle, Morgan Ragan, and Cathy Katz.

For those curious readers out there, Mr. Baguette, the cockatiel mentioned in the Sawyer Brooks series, takes after my daughter's real-life cockatiel by the same name, and he is adorable.

Lastly, a big shout-out and thank-you to Lisa Gardner, one of my absolute favorite writers of all time, the author whose work inspired me to start writing thrillers, for giving me a fabulous quote for *Don't Make a Sound*! A pinch-me moment I will not forget.

# ABOUT THE AUTHOR

*Photo © 2014 Morgan Ragan*

T.R. Ragan is the *New York Times, Wall Street Journal,* and *USA Today* bestselling author of the first book in the Sawyer Brooks series, *Don't Make a Sound*; the Faith McMann trilogy (*Furious, Outrage,* and *Wrath*); the Lizzy Gardner series (*Abducted, Dead Weight, A Dark Mind, Obsessed, Almost Dead,* and *Evil Never Dies*); and the Jessie Cole novels (*Her Last Day, Deadly Recall, Deranged,* and *Buried Deep*). In addition to thrillers, she writes medieval time-travel tales, contemporary romance, and romantic suspense as Theresa Ragan. She has sold more than three million books since her debut novel appeared in 2011. An avid traveler, her wanderings have led her to China, Thailand, and Nepal. Theresa and her husband, Joe, have four children and live in Sacramento, California. To learn more, visit her website at www.theresaragan.com.